She saw Beau   rm smile creasing his face, his beautiful blue eyes probing deeply into hers. They were in a lovely quiet room with low-burning candles, and beautiful flowers filling the air with their perfumed fragrance. . . .

Charity could feel herself growing warm, her strength slowly ebbing as the illusion wove its way in and out of her snow-numbed consciousness.

She could feel Beau's mouth searching for hers as his hands slid down her back, pulling her against him, letting her feel his need. He was whispering his love for her. Her body ached.

The desire in his face made her tremble as he drew her across the bed, his gaze telling her more clearly than spoken words that he adored her. She came to him raining kisses over his eyes, his cheekbones, the thick column of his neck.

And then the terrible waiting was over.

She felt his power encompassing her, drawing her into him, boldly claiming her as his wife . . . flesh of his flesh. . . .

P9-ASY-510

Lori Copeland

A DELL BOOK

Published by
Dell Publishing
a division of
The Bantam Doubleday Dell Publishing Group, Inc.
666 Fifth Avenue
New York, New York 10103

ISBN: 0-440-20134-9

Printed in the United States of America

Published simultaneously in Canada

August 1988

10 9 8 7 6 5 4 3 2 1

KRI

To Janet and Tom Colliatie:
cherished friends

Chapter 1

The day had started like any ordinary one.

The pungent aroma of earth mixed pleasantly with the tangy smell of sweat rolling in rivulets down the back of the tall, powerfully built man who gently urged the team of oxen to pull their heavy load. Overhead, the bright sun hammered down on man and animals as they steadfastly went about furrowing the ground for fall planting.

Nature's elements rarely bothered Beau Claxton. Truth be, nothing much bothered him because he was an inordinately happy man. The good Lord had provided a roof over his head, food on his table, close family ties, and the prettiest, sweetest woman in all of Missouri for his wife.

As far as Beau was concerned, he had everything a man could ever want.

Oh, he had to admit that times were still hard. The country was trying to put itself back together since the War Between the States, and many people still went to bed hungry each night, but Beau knew he and his family had fared better than most.

Beau's mother, Lilly, still lived on the old homestead a couple of miles down the road. His father, Samuel Claxton, had moved his wife and their two sons from Georgia to Missouri when Beau and his older brother had been small.

Cass, Beau's youngest brother, had been born shortly before Samuel had died. Beau's eldest brother, Cole, and his wife, Wynne, lived two miles on the other side of Beau's land. Fifteen months ago they'd produced a baby boy named Jeremy who was growing like a weed and cute as a bug's ear.

Beau had to grin when he thought about how downright silly Cole was about his wife. They both acted like lovestruck youngsters whenever they were together. Beau would've bet his spring crop that no woman could have worked Cole Claxton into such a lather, but two years ago the feisty little woman from Savannah had waltzed in and stolen Cole's heart, and the man hadn't been the same since.

But Beau understood how Cole felt. As he gave a sharp whistle for Sally to yaw right, Beau's grin broadened. Hadn't Betsy Collins done the same thing to him? He recalled how they'd no sooner decided to marry than war had broken out. Beau had left to join the fight, and when he returned, Betsy was still waiting for him. Though they'd married two years ago, Betsy could still make his insides go soft when she smiled up at him with those big blue eyes.

Just the thought of holding her in his arms and making love to her caused a familiar ache to tighten his loins. Any day now, they'd be having their own child—a son, he hoped, though a little girl wouldn't upset him any. It had seemed to take forever for Betsy to get in the family way, but the Doc had said she was healthy as a horse and should be able to have all the babies they wanted. And Beau wanted a large family.

"Easy, girls, easy." Beau turned the oxen and leaned over to wipe his dusty face on the sleeve of his sweat-dampened shirt. The days were still hot, even though they were nearing the end of September. Beau would welcome the cooler days and crisp nights of October. There was still a lot of work to be done before winter. He had to butcher the old sow, lay in a good supply of firewood, and stock the root cellar. . . .

The sound of Betsy's voice made him glance up and slow the team's pace. He grinned at her and waved. Must be close to noon, he thought, and she's bringin' my dinner. His mouth watered at the thought of the fatback and cornbread she'd have in his dinner pail. She'd been making fried apple pies when he'd left the house. No doubt she'd packed a couple of those too.

He heard her call to him again, and Beau whistled for Kate and Sally to halt. Strange, he thought, Betsy wasn't walkin' toward him like she usually did. He enjoyed watching her move. The enticing swing of her hips always managed to get his juices flowing, even when they shouldn't be. After their meal, they'd often lie under the old cottonwood tree and kiss. Like as not, they'd end up making love, and it'd be well past his allotted rest hour when he'd finally go back to work.

Betsy called his name a third time, and Beau's smile began to fade. He dropped the reins and shaded his eyes against the hot sun to see her more clearly.

Her slender frame, swollen with child, was silhouetted against a broad expanse of blue sky. For a moment he hesitated, expecting Betsy to start toward him again. But she lifted her hand feebly in the air, and then dropped to her knees.

A cold wave of fear shot through him, and

his feet began to move. Something was wrong. The baby. Yes, that's it, he reasoned, as he began to pick up speed. The baby was coming, and Betsy was scared. How many times had he told her not to be afraid; he'd be there with her when their child was born. He'd be there to share her pain, to hold her hand, to tell her how proud he was that she was the mother of his child. Together they'd share an incredible joy when their son or daughter came into the world.

Beau was running fast now, taking long deep breaths as he watched Betsy slump down on the ground. His feet covered the hard-packed dirt with lightning speed. "I'm comin', Bets!" he called to her.

She raised her head once as if she were trying to answer him, but with growing horror Beau saw her fall back limply to the ground.

God . . . oh, God . . . Beau's lungs felt as though they'd explode as he raced to her. Something deep inside told him that this was more than their baby coming, but Beau refused to listen. On he went, over rough tufts of ground, his boots gouging the dry, crusty earth, his eyes never once leaving the silent form crumpled close to the woodpile.

It couldn't be anything serious . . . she was teasing him . . . no, Betsy never tried to scare him . . . it had to be the baby . . .

maybe she was going to have a harder time than most . . . the pains were sharp, and she'd dropped to the ground to wait for him . . . that must be it. . . .

Gut-wrenching fear clutched his windpipe as Beau pushed himself faster. Betsy wasn't moving. She lay on the ground in deathlike stillness.

When Beau finally reached Betsy, he fell to the ground and gathered her in his strong arms. His heart was pounding, and his breath was coming in painful gasps as he cradled her head and called her name.

At the sound of his voice, her eyes opened slowly, and she smiled at him. With trembling fingers she reached up to touch his cheek and felt his tears drip gently on her hand.

"What is it, sweetheart? The baby . . . is it the baby?" he prompted in a voice husky with emotion.

"My baby . . ." she whispered softly, so softly that he could scarcely make out her words. "Dear God, Beau . . . our baby. . . ."

"Bets, what's wrong? Tell me, sweetheart. Should I get Ma or Wynne?"

She lifted her hand to cover his lips. "Snake . . . over by the woodpile . . . rattler . . . don't worry . . . it's dead now. . . ."

Rattler! The word hit him with the force of

a bullet, and suddenly he felt his heart drop to his stomach.

He whirled around, his distraught gaze searching the woodpile by the house until he saw the sickening evidence. A large timber rattlesnake, almost seven feet in length, was stretched out on the ground. Its head, severed by a hoe, lay in the dust some five feet away. The small pile of wood Betsy had been gathering was scattered about the ground, mute testimony of what had happened. Betsy had encountered the snake unexpectedly while gathering wood to prepare dinner.

Immediately, Beau began searching for the bite. If she'd been bitten by a rattler, there wasn't much time.

"Where's the bite, Betsy?" Beau's voice trembled, but he fought to remain calm. He didn't want to scare her more. She moaned softly, and he remembered that she should be still. The more she moved, the faster the poison would spread through her body. "Don't move, sweetheart, I'll find it . . . I'll find it!" His eyes and hands searched her body. It didn't take long to locate the two small puncture marks on her right arm. He bit back a shout of despair as he saw the angry swelling. My God, it had hit the vein squarely.

Beau swallowed the knot in his throat. He knew without being told that the poison would go straight to her heart; there was nothing, *nothing* he could do to save her.

But he'd try. Swiftly, he pulled his knife from his pocket and cut two small slits across the vein. He brought her arm to his mouth and sucked the venom, then spat it on the ground, while he stemmed the tears brimming in his eyes.

When he'd done all he knew to do, he talked to her in soft, reassuring tones, telling her how much he loved her, reminding her of the good life they'd share with their baby. He whispered to Betsy not to be afraid. He'd protect her and never let anything hurt her again. He apologized for being neglectful, and promised her that from now on he'd make certain there was sufficient wood in the box before he left the house every day. He should have done that anyway, he agonized, though Betsy had insisted on carrying the wood herself.

"Don't leave me, Bets," he pleaded as he heard her moans growing weaker. "God, I have to go for help," he murmured a few moments later when he saw her face turn a ghastly shade of white. "I have to get the Doc out here—"

"No . . . no . . . don't leave me, Beau." Her hands clasped him anxiously, and he rested his head on the swollen mound of her stomach as both began to sob softly. They knew what was happening, and Betsy needed him with her now.

Beau began to pray. Lifting his face to the sky, he begged and pleaded and promised until he became outraged. Then he threatened. Tears streamed down his cheeks as he railed against the unfairness. He'd been taught that there was a God who cared, a God who watched over him, a kind, benevolent God. Surely such a God wouldn't take his wife and child from him in such a cruel and senseless way.

Paralyzed with terror, Beau clutched Betsy and crooned to her, rocking her back and forth, gently back and forth, back and forth, until the sun began to dip low on the western horizon. The golden rays spread across the parched earth, enveloping the young couple in an ethereal glow. Still Beau wouldn't let go.

He didn't know the exact moment she left him. His arms had grown numb from holding her, yet he could not release her. If he put Betsy down, she'd be gone from him forever, and he couldn't accept that.

It was his brother, Cole, who found them. Cole had known something was wrong when he rode through the newly furrowed field and saw the oxen, Kate and Sally, still hitched to the plow. His tall frame swung out of the saddle slowly as he dismounted and walked to where Beau sat cradling Betsy in his arms.

"Beau?" Stunned and puzzled by the pitiful sight before him, Cole hesitantly knelt beside his brother.

Beau was crying openly, deep, heart-rending sobs that shook his entire frame as he clasped his young wife tightly to him, murmuring her name over and over.

Cole glanced around him, then he saw it. The object responsible for such overwhelming grief lay lifeless on the ground beside the woodpile.

It took a moment for it to register, but when Cole understood what had happened he swore softly under his breath and dropped his head helplessly. "Oh, Beau, hell."

Cole struggled to regain his composure, but when he had he reached to remove Betsy gently from his brother's arms.

"No . . . no . . . don't take her, Cole." Beau spoke for the first time, his voice steady —almost serene.

"Beau, I have to take her."

Beau's grip tightened possessively around his wife's body, and he shook his head.

"Beau, give her to me," Cole commanded softly. Since the day Sam Claxton had died of a heart attack, Cole had been both father and brother to Beau and Cass. He'd been there for them through the good and bad times, and they still looked upon him as head of the household. It was no wonder that after years of strict obedience, Beau reluctantly began to relinquish his hold.

"Don't hurt her," he whispered hoarsely.

"I'll take good care of her."

Carefully lifting her in his arms, Cole stood and carried Betsy into the house that Beau had built for her two years before.

The Claxtons were a prominent family in River Run, so everyone turned out for Betsy's funeral. Such a lovely young thing, the townspeople whispered among themselves. Why had tragedy struck such a fine couple when they'd only begun to live? What would poor Beau do now? She was so young . . . and the innocent baby she was carrying . . . why, it would have been born soon . . . it's horrible . . . just   terrible . . . simply   unthinkable. . . .

Beau hadn't shed a tear since the afternoon Cole had found him holding Betsy. Standing straight and tall between his two brothers, Beau kept his face an empty mask as the preacher droned on.

At the graveside, Lilly Claxton wrapped her arms around Betsy's mother and suffered with her. To Lilly, Betsy had been more than a daughter-in-law; she had been like one of her own.

Beau showed no emotion until the first spade of dirt fell atop the simple pine coffin. As the sound reached his ears, he flinched as if he'd been burned, but his eyes stayed dry and his face stoic. After the burial he turned and walked away without a backward glance.

Wynne Claxton, flanked on either side by Cole and Cass, approached Beau. Such strong men, the Claxton brothers, she thought fleetingly. It hurt her to see one of them brought to his knees by tragedy.

She loved all three men, each in a different way.

Her husband, Cole, was the love of her life, with his solid ways and curly dark hair and incredibly blue eyes. He'd made her the happiest woman on earth for the past two years.

And Beau. He was exceptionally handsome with his golden hair and eyes the color of a bright summer sky. He was the sunshine in the Claxton family. Before Betsy's death, Beau had always looked at the good side of life. Happiness had bubbled over in his eyes, eyes that always caught her attention, laughing eyes, eyes that twinkled devilishly and flirted outrageously. Dear, sweet Beau. He'd been so kind to her at a time when she'd needed kindness the most.

And then there was young, lovable Cass. Every bit as handsome as his older brothers, Cass seemed destined to give some girl a run for her money before she got him to the altar. He was the lover in the family, and at one time he'd nearly broken Wynne's heart, but that had been long ago, and since then she'd forgiven him.

The Claxton brothers were strong but gentle men, incredibly tender in the way they loved their women. Wynne had seen the love Beau had shared with Betsy, and she knew how deeply he was grieving.

Handing baby Jeremy to his father, Wynne enfolded Beau in her arms and hugged him tightly. "I want you to know we share your pain and that we love you very much," she whispered.

"I don't know how I can go on. . . ." Beau's brave façade shattered, and his voice filled with raw emotion.

"But you will. You will, Beau." He was young and strong, and with time his wounds would heal. Wynne had to believe it, even if Beau couldn't yet.

For a fraction of an instant Beau's arm tightened around Wynne to show his appreciation, then it dropped back to his side and he walked on.

Cole matched stride with his brothers as Beau marched to his horse. "Why don't you come over and spend a few days with Wynne and me?" Cole invited. It was unthinkable to him that his brother would return to an empty house.

"Thanks, but I think I'll be leavin' for a while." Beau paused and turned to face his brothers.

"Leavin'? Where you goin'?" Cass demanded.

Beau's gaze rested upon the small mound of newly turned dirt as he spoke. "I don't know. Just away somewhere."

"Aw, Beau, I can understand you feelin' that way, but don't you think this is a bad time to be runnin' off?" Cass protested gently, looking to Cole for support when he spotted a bedroll and pack behind Beau's saddle. "Tell him, Cole. He shouldn't be wanderin' around by himself . . . at least not right now."

Cole's clear blue gaze met Beau's with silent understanding. "I think he should do what he feels he has to, Cass."

Beau nodded gratefully. "Thanks, Cole. Bets . . . well, she'd have appreciated all you've done. . . ."

Cole reached out and clasped Beau's shoulder reassuringly. "Let us know when you're ready to come home."

"I will. I want you to take Kate and Sally and the rest of my stock."

"I'll see to them for you."

Beau reached out and touched Jeremy's nose, drawing a happy gurgle from the baby.

"Take good care of this little fella." Bright tears stood in Beau's eyes as he thought about his own baby and what might have been.

"I will," said Cole. "You take care of yourself."

Beau nodded. "Tell Ma not to worry." Slowly, Beau mounted his horse and pulled his hat low on his forehead.

"She'll worry anyway—you know Ma," said Cass, still not sold on the idea of Beau's leaving. The way Cass figured it, a man should stay with his family at a time like this. "Listen, let us know where you are, you hear?" Cass commanded anxiously.

Beau's eyes returned to Betsy's grave and lingered as he said a final good-bye in his heart. "I hear."

Chapter 2

"Shoo! Shooeeee! Get out of here you—you miserable . . . ungrateful . . . ham hock!" Charity Burkhouser was determined to show no pity as she swatted the old sow across its fat rump and herded it right back out the front door. It was a sad day when a woman couldn't step out to hang the wash without being invaded by pigs!

She slammed the heavy wooden door and leaned against it to catch her breath. She *had* to do something about getting the fence back up.

A woman alone in the world just doesn't have a chance, she muttered to herself. Her husband had died in the war three years ago, and since Ferrand's death Charity had been on her own. Not that she wanted to be—far from it. She wasn't equipped to homestead a piece of land in this godforsaken place they called Kansas, nor had she *ever* had the least desire to do so.

Shortly after they'd married, Ferrand had decided to take advantage of the federal government's Homestead Act, signed into law in May of 1862.

Charity could still remember how excited Ferrand had been the day he'd come home, swung her into his arms, and announced they were moving to Kansas. "A hundred and sixty acres, Charity. Just think of it! They'll *give* us a hundred and sixty acres of whatever land we stake out."

"But, Ferrand, *Kansas*?" For a girl who'd spent all of her life in Virginia, Kansas sounded like the end of the earth. Charity fanned herself as she paced the parlor of her ancestral home. "I don't know why you want to run off to some foreign land when we have a perfectly good home right here with my parents."

"Charity," he reminded her patiently, "Kansas is not a foreign land."

"Well, it would surely seem so to me, Ferrand." Charity was accustomed to nannies and servants who attended to her every whim without a moment's hesitation. Somehow, she had a strong feeling Kansas wouldn't have those essentials.

"But that's my point. It would be *our* land, darling, not your parents'," Ferrand pointed out tactfully. He'd gotten along well enough with Sherman and Lareina Pendergrass, but he wanted a home and land of his own now that he was married. "Under the Homestead Act, all a person has to do is begin improvements on the land within six months of the time he files for application, remain a permanent resident there for five years, and the land becomes his, free and clear." Ferrand pulled Charity against his chest to kiss her soundly. When their lips parted a long moment later, he winked at her and gave her bottom a reassuring pat. "Come on, Charity, where's your spirit of adventure? We'll raise a family of pioneers. You'll love it."

"But, darling," Charity protested, "why do we have to go to Kansas to have our own land?" Ferrand Burkhouser came from an old, aristocratic line in Virginia. His father could well afford to buy any amount of land his son desired. Why, even her own papa had offered to purchase a plantation for Ferrand on their wedding day three months ago. Her husband didn't need to travel hundreds of miles to acquire just a hundred and sixty acres.

Charity didn't understand her man sometimes.

"Well . . . this is all so sudden, Ferrand."

Charity bit her lower lip pensively. She felt obligated to at least consider her husband's dream. She did love Ferrand, and her papa always said a man was the undisputed head of his own household, but still . . . "Would I be able to hire my own help? I wouldn't want to take up . . . housekeeping and . . . and farming myself."

Charity couldn't imagine worse punishment. Why, she didn't know the first thing about farming!

Ferrand threw back his head and laughed at his young bride. She was a pure delight. Her beauty was unsurpassed, with those clear, snapping green eyes and black, shining curls that cascaded down her back. And her disposition, though at times a bit trying, gave him his greatest joy. He'd give her the moon if he could. "Of course you will, my darling! Your life won't change that much. I'm sure there'll be plenty of people looking for work in Kansas."

"But I'll miss Mama and Papa and Faith and Hope. And what about the war, Ferrand?" So far, he'd miraculously escaped the fighting, but Charity feared he might have to leave any day.

"After we're settled, your parents and sisters can come and visit us," Ferrand promised. "And as for the war, we'll worry about that when the time comes."

As it turned out, there'd been virtually no one looking for work in Kansas. Lordy, everyone had had enough to do just trying to survive on the rugged frontier, Charity recalled. She and Ferrand hadn't lived on their new settlement for more than a few months when Ferrand decided it was his duty to join the fight for the Confederacy. Then she'd been left to face the bewildered looks of her neighbors when they found out Ferrand had decided his loyalties still belonged to the South.

And since Kansas was so far away, her family had never once been able to make the long trip to visit their eldest child.

After they'd learned of Ferrand's death, Charity's parents had written, urging her to come home. When Charity informed them she was staying on to claim the land, her family had begged her to reconsider such a rash decision.

But Charity was a stubborn woman. She was determined to remain in Kansas, though at times she hated every waking hour in this wild, uncivilized land, where the winds were fierce and the winters long and unbearably cold. The heat could be suffocating and the droughts endless. There were tornadoes and grasshoppers and Indians. And wolves. She hated the wolves. They prowled around her little soddy at night, snapping at her dogs, Gabriel and Job, while Charity huddled in a corner, grasping Ferrand's old rifle tightly, praying they wouldn't come through the door.

Still, Charity couldn't bring herself to relinquish her right to the homestead because, in a strange, inexplicable way, she felt a certain pride to think she owned the land, or would, if she could hold on just one more year.

Then maybe she'd go home and visit her parents. The thought was mighty tempting. There hadn't been any servants or nannies out here to take care of her. In truth, she'd barely been able to manage.

She felt herself smiling, something she rarely did anymore, as she thought of how poor Ferrand had struggled to mold her into a pioneer woman.

Lordy, he'd been good to her. He'd seen her through her crying spells and days of loneliness. Sometimes weeks would pass before they'd see another human being, and at times Charity thought she couldn't bear the solitude.

But she'd survived. And when the news of Ferrand's death had reached her, Charity had had a good long cry, but by then she'd begun to adjust to the harsh realities of the world.

Oh, she'd been furious at Ferrand for getting himself killed in that foolish war and leaving her all alone to care for a miserable chunk of worthless land. But that feeling had passed, and she'd started remembering what a really good man Ferrand was, and then Kansas didn't seem all that bad.

It was home now, her home, so she guessed she'd best make do and quit feeling sorry for herself.

What she and Ferrand had shared had been special. Despite all her domestic failings, Charity knew she had to do this one last thing for him. Ferrand had worked too hard in the brief time they'd been granted together for her to be fainthearted now. She'd see this thing through. Though she had to admit, she couldn't see how she was going to do it.

She needed a man. Not for the same reason a woman usually wanted a man, but Charity needed a man from a purely practical standpoint. She had to make improvements on the land just to keep her claim, but she simply didn't have the knowledge, the strength, or the skill necessary.

Thanks to Grandmother Pendergrass's personal tutelage, Charity knew how to piece a pretty quilt and bake a tasty blackberry pie, but she didn't know how to build a barn or plow a field. Oh, she'd tried. Her hands, once lily-white and soft as rose petals, were now calloused and beet-red.

When it had come to setting posts and planting wheat, she'd done an atrocious job. Ashamed for anyone to see the way her fence

posts leaned westward when they were supposed to stand straight, Charity had ripped
them out and cried herself to sleep one night.

No, a man was her only answer.

But a man was a rare commodity around
these parts. It was unlikely that anyone would
walk up and knock on her door and say, "Well,
hello! I hear you're looking for a husband,
Mrs. Burkhouser. Take me."

Though the town of Cherry Grove wasn't
far from her land, Charity rarely socialized.
Once a month she made the trek into town to
purchase staples and yard goods from Miller's
Mercantile, but suitable marriage prospects
weren't plentiful. Oh, there were the usual
cattle drovers who came through town,
bringing their longhorns up from Texas to
ship them out by railheads. Of course, the
travel-worn herders were always looking for
female companionship. But Charity despised
their slovenly ways and drunken antics. They
carried on like the devil himself. Their cattle
brought them a good price back East, but
Charity wanted nothing to do with such men.
They were rovers and drifters, and she
needed a man who'd stay around for a while.

But she was going to have to find someone
soon or lose her claim by this time next year.

She sighed in despair and turned her face
upward, as she did increasingly these days.

"Well, it's up to you, Lord. I'm at the end of my row."

The lone rider slowed his horse beside the stream and paused to let the animal drink his fill. The man was unkempt and dirty. A dark blond stubble marred his formerly clean, handsome features. He seemed older than his twenty-eight years. Fatigue lined his face, and nature hadn't been kind. The sun had cooked his skin to a dark, golden bronze, and blue eyes that had once danced with merriment now stared in blank acceptance of a life that no longer held purpose.

Beau knew he looked bad.

He didn't eat the way he should. He was at least forty pounds lighter than he had been a year ago. During that time, he'd rambled down one winding road after another, going wherever the next road took him. He'd just tried to get through one day and then the next and then the next. Sometimes he'd notice when he crossed a state line, but if anyone had asked him where he was, Beau wouldn't have known or cared. Life was just one long dreary day after the other.

Betsy had been gone a year now, or close to it. Beau didn't know what month it was, but it seemed to him the heat was letting up some, so it was probably September again.

He smiled at the memory of his wife. Their

baby would've been almost a year old by now. Wonder if it would've been a boy or girl? Suddenly, he realized he'd never let himself ask that question. Well, it didn't matter now. Nothing mattered anymore.

He slid from his horse. Reaching into the stream, he cupped his hands for a cool drink of water. When he finished, he splashed a handful of wetness down his neck to ease the heat.

Straightening, he prepared to mount again when his horse began to shy nervously. "Whoa, girl, easy." Beau gripped the reins and pulled himself into the saddle as the mare whinnied and sidestepped again. "Easy . . . easy. . . ." He glanced toward a wooded area, and a strange wariness came over him.

"What's the matter, girl?" Once more, his eyes scanned the area. Suddenly, Beau felt a tightness in his stomach. Standing not twenty feet away, partially hidden in the undergrowth, was one of the biggest timber wolves he'd ever seen.

The horse trumpeted in alarm and started to bolt. The wolf's lips curled back above his fangs, and he gave a low, ominous growl. His eyes had a bright, feverish sparkle to them, and his back paw dangled limply.

Beau could see fresh blood dripping from the wounded paw onto the dusty ground.

The wolf had been caught in a trap, Beau

surmised. Slowly, he backed his horse out of the stream, taking pains not to make any sudden moves. The wolf would be in no mood for socializing, and neither was Beau. He could shoot it, but his draw would have to be lightning quick, and he didn't want to chance it.

Before Beau could choose his next move, the decision was out of his hands.

With one tremendous lunge the wolf sprang from his hiding place as the horse reared wildly in fright.

Beau tried to control his horse and reach for his gun at the same time, but the wolf charged, and suddenly the air was alive with the screams of man and crazed animals pitched into a life-or-death struggle. Angry snarls and shrill squeals of rage and terror surrounded Beau as the wolf viciously tore into the meaty flank of the horse. Swearing violently under his breath, Beau managed to pull his gun from his holster, but the wolf sprang again. This time he took the rider out of the saddle, and Beau went down into the water, trying to shield himself from the wolf's ferocious jaws.

Man and animal thrashed about in a frenzied battle as the wolf repeatedly ripped and slashed Beau's body. The water swirled and churned and turned red with blood.

Some three hundred yards away a young woman stopped kneading bread and cocked her ear toward the open window. The dogs were setting up a howl on the front step, and in the distance she could hear what sounded like animals in some sort of terrible fight.

Charity wiped the flour from her hands and moved to the mantel. Darn pesky coyotes, she thought irritably, reaching for the rifle. They'd probably attacked a stray dog or calf.

The noise increased in intensity as she stepped out of the soddy and started toward the stream.

She'd be forever grateful to Ferrand for choosing this particular piece of land. In this part of Kansas, a shortage of rain, coupled with high winds and low humidity, sometimes left a pioneer at a serious disadvantage. But the Burkhouser soddy was built near an underground spring that provided a stream of cool, clear water year round.

Charity's footsteps quickened as she heard a horse's shrill squeal rend the air. Good heavens! Something had attacked a horse!

Her feet faltered as she entered the clearing, her eyes grimly taking in the appalling sight. Before her, a large timber wolf was ripping a man apart as his horse danced about him wildly.

Regaining her composure, Charity hefted the rifle to her shoulder and took careful aim. Seconds later, a loud crack sliced the air, and the wolf toppled off the man into the water.

The gunfire spooked the horse, and it bolted into the thicket as Charity hurriedly waded into the stream.

She flinched as she edged past the fallen wolf, but the gaping bullet hole in the center of its chest assured her that her aim had been true. The first thing Ferrand had taught her when they'd moved here was how to be a deadly, accurate shot. She'd learned her lesson well.

Kneeling beside the injured man, she cautiously rolled him on his side in the shallow water and cringed as she heard him moan in agony. He was so bloody she could barely make out the severity of his wounds, but she knew he was near death.

"Shhhh . . . lie still. I'm going to help you," she soothed, though he could neither see nor hear her. As his eyes began to swell shut from the nasty lacerations on his face, he passed out.

She glanced around, trying to determine whether to hitch Myrtle and Nell to drag him out of the water. He was a tall man, but pitifully thin. Though she was small and slight, she was a lot stronger than when she'd first arrived in Kansas. She decided she wouldn't need the oxen to move him from the water.

It took several tries, for he wasn't as light as he looked. She tugged and heaved inch by inch, pausing periodically to murmur soothing words of encouragement when he groaned in pain. Though she handled him as carefully as she could, his injuries were so great that he suffered excruciating pain.

Once she had pulled him onto the bank, she hurriedly tore off a small portion of her petticoat and began to clean his wounds. He tossed restlessly, fighting her when her hands touched his torn flesh.

"Please, you must let me help you!" she urged.

Charity was accustomed to patching wounds on her stock, but she grew faint looking at his injuries. In her whole life she'd never seen such mutilation of a human body, but she shook off her queasiness and administered to his needs.

As her hands worked, she studied him carefully and recoiled not only at his injuries but at his general condition; he was so unkempt, so dirty, so . . . slovenly. She wasn't used to that. Ferrand had always kept himself clean and neat. No doubt this man was a drifter, or perhaps one of those drovers. He certainly hadn't had a bath in months—maybe even years—and he was in need of a shave and a haircut.

She peeled away his torn shirt and washed the blood from the thick mat of dark blond hair that lay across his chest. Though his chest was broad, she could count his ribs. Obviously, he hadn't had a square meal in a long time. With more meat on his bones he'd be a very large man . . . powerful . . . strong. . . . Strong enough to build a barn and set fence and work behind a team of oxen all day. . . . Her hands stilled momentarily.

Good Lord. A man. Here was a man—barely alive perhaps, but a man all the same. He could be the answer to her problems.

Her hands flew about their work more feverishly. She had to save him! Not that she wouldn't have tried her best anyway, but now no matter what it would take, by all that was holy, she'd see to it that this man survived.

As far as men went, he wasn't much . . . disgusting, actually, but she reminded herself she wasn't in a position to be picky.

She'd nurse him back to health, and once she got him on his feet, she'd trick him into marrying her. No, she amended, she wouldn't trick him . . . she'd ask him first, and if that didn't work, *then* she'd trick him.

But what if he has a wife? an inner voice demanded.

Don't bother me with technicalities, she thought irritably. I'll cross that bridge when I get to it.

Her hands worked faster, a new sense of confidence filling her now. He *would* live. She just knew he would. The good Lord wouldn't give her such a gift and then turn around and snatch it back, now would he?

He moaned again, and Charity lifted his head and placed it in her lap possessively.

He was a gift from God.

She was certain of that now. Who else would so unselfishly drop this complete stranger at her door?

Once more she looked down at her unexpected gift, and her face lit with a radiant smile. Closing her eyes, she lifted her face heavenward, and sighed with relief. Maybe now she would be able to claim her land after all.

Then in her most reverent tone, she humbly asked for the Lord's help in making this man strong and healthy again, at least strong enough to drive a good, sturdy fence-post.

She closed her petition with heartfelt sincerity. "He's a little . . . well, rough looking, Lord, but I'm sure not complaining." She bit her lower lip thoughtfully as she studied the ragged, dirty, bloody man lying in her lap. With a little soap and water, maybe he'd be tolerable. She shrugged, and a big grin spread across her face. "I suppose if this is the best you have to offer, Lord, then I sure do appreciate your thoughtfulness."

Chapter 3

Charity dragged the stranger up the ravine, and then the quarter of a mile or so to the soddy. By the time she managed to pull him onto her bed, she was gasping for air.

Sighing, she surveyed his pitiful state. The nearest doctor was over an hour's ride away. The stranger would die before she could make it to Cherry Grove and back.

No, if his life were to be spared, she'd have to use whatever skills she possessed, and she had to admit they were deplorably few.

It would take a lot of nursing, and the mercy of a higher power, to see him through this, she realized.

Though he remained in a fortunate state of unconsciousness, the man's face was swollen and contorted with pain.

The angry six-inch gash across his chest was oozing blood in a red stream, and Charity knew the stranger would bleed to death if she didn't tend his wounds soon.

Rolling up her sleeves, she moved to the hearth. Without hesitation she tore an old petticoat into soft bandages and filled a wash pan with scalding water from the kettle.

She'd stitched up livestock, she reminded herself, as her hands automatically went about her task. When Sally had gotten tangled in Ansel Latimer's fence last year, Charity had been the one who'd cleaned the torn flesh and stitched it back together. From her sewing basket, she took her scissors and a needle. Of course, Sally's wound had been nothing like this poor man's, but the ox had healed beautifully.

And she'd assisted with a few births. Right now, she decided, helping a woman have a baby seemed easier than sewing a man together after he'd been mauled by a wolf. She selected a spool of black thread and absently closed the lid on the basket. Doctoring wasn't her favorite thing, but then she had no choice if she wanted the man to survive.

It took a half hour to cut away his clothes. As she began bathing his wounds in cool water, her stomach lurched ominously, and she rushed to the window. Drawing deep breaths of fresh air helped to quell the urge to empty her stomach. His wounds were ghastly; tender flesh was torn open in large, gaping holes. The front of her dress was splattered with his blood, and she nearly gagged as she rubbed her palms across her apron and saw huge red stains.

Charity wasn't sure she could go on. Most likely the man would die in spite of her efforts. No one could survive such injuries, she told herself. Then she thought of her own miserable plight and resolved again to save his life.

Inhaling deeply, Charity strode to the washbasin. The water turned a bright red as she washed her hands. Determinedly, she refilled the basin and resumed her gruesome task.

A laceration across the middle of his back was the deepest, she decided. Grimacing, she carefully rolled him onto his stomach and cringed as she poured a small amount of carbolic acid into the wound as an antiseptic. The man stiffened and screamed in anguish as he tried to knock her hands away. But Charity held firm, throwing her slight weight against his large frame, pinning him down until he drifted back into unconsciousness.

She found herself biting her lower lip till she could taste her own blood as her hands worked feverishly to stitch the wound. When she finished repairing his back, she rolled him over and continued to stitch the other wounds. At any moment he could wake up and overpower her, and then what would she do?

The darning needle, which she'd held in the fire, slid in and out, in and out, in and out . . . until she thought she'd surely faint. The room was stifling, and flies buzzed about her head, lighting on his wounds. She shooed them away and dipped a cloth into the bucket of clean water and pressed it to her flushed features. After the lightheadedness had passed, she continued.

Her damp clothes clung to her as her hands mechanically went about pulling flesh together and carefully sewing it into place. Her stitches were neat and small, and she was surprised to feel a rush of pride as she gazed at her work. He might not live, but if he did, he'd have few scars.

The afternoon shadows began to lengthen. Charity's back felt as if it would break, but she worked on. She heard Bossy standing near the front door, bawling to be milked.

"Not now, Bossy," she called out softly, hoping the old cow would wander away.

It was nearing dark when she finally finished. Tears stood in her eyes as she listened to the sounds of his suffering. She dropped weakly into the rocker and stared unseeingly at the dying embers, numb with fatigue.

She'd felt every agonizing prick the needle had made in his bruised flesh as surely as if she'd been the one injured.

Her body, as well as his, was sticky with sweat and blood, and she knew she must bathe the both of them before she could rest.

The man began to mumble and thrash about on the bed, and Charity feared he'd reopen his wounds. If he did, she wasn't sure she'd have the strength to sew them again.

There was nothing to ease the stranger's agony except the bottle of brandy Ferrand had kept for special occasions.

If this wasn't a special occasion, Charity thought desperately, she didn't know one. Hurriedly, she pulled the bottle from the cupboard. She scooped his head from the pillow and cradled it in the crook of her arm. Tipping the bottle to his lips, she let the strong brown liquid trickle down his throat.

When he started to choke, Charity set the bottle aside and patted him soothingly. He screamed in torment as the wound across his chest threatened to escape the bounds of the slender thread she'd so meticulously sewn.

When he regained his breath, she tipped the bottle again, and the nerve-racking choking began again. It took several minutes to get enough of the liquor down him to dull his senses.

He'd fought her with a strength that was

surprising for a man so gravely injured. Twice he'd nearly knocked the bottle out of her hand, but Charity was as determined as he. As the liquor took full effect, he lay so still that Charity leaned forward to be sure he was still breathing.

Assured that he was, she released a long sigh and absently tipped the bottle to her mouth. *He's going to make it,* she thought. *He has to.* If she could clean and stitch his wounds without fainting, then by all that was holy, he could live! She took another long sip from the bottle and eyed the unconscious male lying in the middle of her bed.

He sure was a pitiful sight. His chin was covered with dark stubble, and his ribs poked through his sides like those of some half-starved animal.

But it didn't matter, she reminded herself, trying to bolster her sagging morale. He *was* a man, and she was going to see to it that he lived. He obviously needed someone to take care of him, and she needed a man. Surely a satisfactory arrangement could be worked out, once he regained his health.

She tipped the bottle again. The harsh liquid stung her nose and burned her throat, bringing a rush of tears to her eyes. She coughed and thumped her chest solidly, then paused to observe his condition. He was still breathing, she confirmed, taking comfort in the thought. By morning he'd be awake, and she'd find out who he was, and where he'd come from.

Mustering up enough strength to walk to the woodbox, she tossed a couple of logs on the fire, then stumbled back to the rocker and dropped into an exhausted sleep.

Chapter 4

The wind whistling down the chimney penetrated Charity's dulled senses. Her eyes opened to slits, then closed shut again.

For three nights, she'd hovered over the stranger, alternately bathing him in cool water and changing the bandages.

His wounds didn't look good. The long, angry lesions were beginning to fester, and Charity's heart pounded with fear every time she looked at them.

The man was hot and feverish—delirious at times, calling out for "Betsy." If Charity had known a Betsy, she'd have gladly fetched her. She'd try anything to ease his torment, but nothing seemed to help.

Only once had he shown any sign of consciousness. Last night, when she'd been sponging his burning forehead, his eyes had opened to stare at her with a blank plea in the deep, tormented pools of indigo.

Charity had smiled and spoken to him in soft, reassuring tones, running the damp cloth gently across his reddened skin. "There, now, you're going to be fine."

Her heart had skipped a beat when his eyes had grown incredibly tender as he'd returned her smile.

It had been so long since a man had looked at her that way. Then she realized that it wasn't Charity Burkhouser he'd been seeing but his "Betsy," as his feverish mind had continued to play tricks on him.

The stranger had grasped Charity's hand and brought it to cradle lovingly against his stubbled jaw. His eyes had slid shut, and she'd heard him whisper faintly, "Bets, I knew you'd come back, darlin'." Charity watched with an aching heart as tears rolled from the corners of his eyes to the pillow.

Slowly his eyes had opened again, and she'd caught her breath as he pulled her head down to meet his.

Charity had been transfixed as their lips touched and lingered. Because he was so ill, the kiss had lacked passion, but nothing could have disguised the love he'd been transferring to her. His kiss had caused her pulse to flutter erratically, and she'd felt herself growing weak all over.

When their lips parted, Charity had seen a look in the stranger's eyes that she'd seen before in Ferrand's.

It had been a look of love . . . and desire . . . desire so strong that Charity felt warmed by the heat shimmering in the tormented depths. Then he smiled at her again and said softly, "Bets, I love you."

Charity had never seen such striking eyes, clear, vibrant blue . . . the color of morning glories on the trellis beside the porch when the first rays of daylight nudged them gently awake.

Instinctively she knew those eyes bright with fever could sparkle with merriment during better times.

Despite his pitiful condition the stranger was the handsomest man she had seen in a long while.

And he loved a woman named Betsy, Charity realized with a sinking heart.

The wind was rising, and Charity noticed a slight chill in the air as she rose to throw another log on the fire. Stoking the glowing embers, she thought of the stranger again, and a frown played across her features. Maybe he wouldn't be able to help her after all. Then what would she do? She'd lose the homestead after everything she'd done to keep it.

Her thoughts wandered back to Ferrand and how hard they'd worked together to build the soddy. It hadn't been easy traveling to the Great American Desert, as Kansas was sometimes called.

Charity remembered the steamboat they'd taken part of the way. My, what a glorious time that had been, churning up the wide Missouri on a big old paddle-wheeler. By then, Ferrand had convinced her that an exciting new life awaited them; all they had to do was reach out and take it.

Charity walked back to the rocker and sat. It was still early; the sun wasn't up yet, so she could dawdle for a spell before she milked Bossy. Rocking back and forth, she let her thoughts remain on the past.

Lordy, how she'd loved Ferrand Burkhouser.

When they'd arrived in Kansas, they'd immediately found a piece of land, staked their plot on good level ground, and stripped the spot of grass. They'd worked from daylight to dusk, smoothing the site with a spade, then packing the dirt down to form an earthen floor.

From sunup to sundown, they'd cut the heavy sod into blocks to build the one-room soddy. She smiled, recalling the way she'd followed Ferrand behind the plow, carrying a sharp spade to cut the strips of earth into individual blocks, one foot wide, two feet long, and four inches thick. After the blocks had been cut, she'd loaded the heavy bundles into the spring wagon. Ferrand had driven Myrtle and Nell as they pulled the grasshopper plow that sliced the strips of sod from the earth.

At times, Ferrand had stopped to wipe the sweat from his brow, and feeling playful, he'd picked up a handful of sod and tossed it at Charity. With her impish grin she'd returned the barrage, and soon they'd lost a good hour. When they'd paused to catch their breath, Ferrand's expression had changed, and he'd carried Charity to the large old walnut tree where they'd made love.

Tears sprang to her eyes as Charity remembered how happy they'd been. Dabbing her eyes with a corner of her apron, she tried to push her memories aside.

What good did memories do her anyway, she scolded. Ferrand was gone, and crying wouldn't bring him back. She wouldn't cry again. She was just feeling tired, that was all. Sitting up with the stranger for three nights straight had taken its toll.

She walked to the bed and touched the man's forehead. Still hot. She didn't know how much longer the fever could rage before it either disappeared or killed him. It had to do one or the other soon.

As she settled back in the chair, memories

returned. She sighed wistfully. Ferrand seemed to hug the fringes of her mind this morning. Perhaps, she conceded, it was because he'd always loved this time of day. Charity let herself think about his quiet strength, and somehow that eased her pain.

Leaning her head against the smooth wood, she thought about how he'd made the rocker and given it to her on their first Christmas together. She tried to remember Ferrand's eyes . . . blue, like the stranger's . . . no, they were hazel, weren't they?

The slow creak of the rocker paused momentarily. Blue . . . no, hazel. She frowned again. Blue or hazel? Which one was it?

Strange, she couldn't seem to recall. Setting the chair in motion again, she thought about how tall and handsome Ferrand Burkhouser had been.

She could remember clearly what an attractive man he was. Oh, he might not have had a broad-shouldered frame like the stranger, but Ferrand had had a gentleness about him that she'd cherished.

And he'd held his own when it had come to working the land. He might've been raised in a home where servants had done all the back-breaking chores, but Ferrand hadn't been afraid of hard work.

The sod blocks had been heavy and burdensome, and Charity had thought her back would surely break in two, but Ferrand had helped her lift them, and daily the pile of earth bricks had grown.

Earthen bricks had been stacked with the grass side down, one layer after another to form walls two feet thick. Since they'd had no mortar or nails, they'd packed loose dirt and mud into the cracks and crevices. They'd covered the walls with a simple frame of cottonwood poles and willow brush, topped with the rest of the strips of sod. When they'd finished, Charity had felt sure there wasn't a finer house in all of Kansas.

Charity's eyes wandered lovingly around the room. The soddy was all she had left of Ferrand, and if she lost it, she feared she'd lose what remained of his memory.

Oh, she knew this house they'd built with their hands wasn't fancy like her ancestral home in Virginia. The soddy was dark and it lacked proper ventilation. When it rained, mud dripped down on the few pieces of furniture she had.

Charity's gaze surveyed the meager furnishings. Not much, that was for sure: an old, worn cowhide carpet on the floor, a wooden bed with a straw-filled mattress, some goods boxes fashioned into tables, and a few barrels Ferrand had shaped into chairs.

But she'd managed to save enough egg money to make some pretty gingham curtains, and the two richly patterned patchwork quilts that had once belonged to her grandmother brightened the room.

All things considered, Charity loved this house. That's why she had to keep the stranger alive. He might be pitiful, but if she could enlist his strength after she built him back up, he could help save her homestead. She didn't know how she'd make him stay after he recovered, provided he did recover.

This "Betsy" would be an obstacle, but perhaps the stranger could be persuaded to help out while he was mending. It would take a long while for him to regain his full strength, Charity thought.

Suddenly she slapped the arm of the chair as her frustration erupted. Oh, it cut her to the core to depend on someone else to bail her out! Everything should have been so different. Damn the war! Damn the miserable, senseless act of war that had snatched Ferrand away from her!

The wind whistling down the chimney added to her fury. While she was cursing everything, she thought angrily, she might as well include the Kansas grasshoppers, tornadoes, and blizzards, along with the incessant wind that had withered what little crops she'd planted.

Wearily she rose from the chair and blew out the tallow candle on the kitchen table.

The sun was up now—a new day. Maybe this one would shine more favorably on her and the stranger.

Pouring water into the washbasin, she washed her face and hands, then pulled the pins from her hair. The soft black cloud fell like a silk shawl around her shoulders as she picked up a brush and began to pull it through the tangled locks. She paused and stared at her reflection in the mirror. Frontier life had been hard, and she feared her beauty —what there was left of it—was fading quickly.

Her hand absently fingered the faint crow's feet around her eyes. Come next month, she'd be twenty-three years old. Twenty-three years old! It was hard to believe.

Most women her age were busy raising families and tending husbands, but Charity had neither. Instead she had a dead husband, a small piece of land, a few chickens, a few old sows, a dog, a cow, two oxen, and a sick stranger about to go to his final reward. Sometimes life was so unfair.

The sound of a buckboard rumbling into the yard caught her attention. Charity hurriedly repinned her hair, wondering who could be calling at this hour. She surveyed herself one final time in the mirror, then quickly smoothed the wrinkles on her dress and answered the knock.

She was surprised to find her neighbor, Ansel Latimer, standing on her doorstep, his face pale, his mouth set in a grim line.

"Good morning, Ansel," said Charity, peering on tiptoe around his large frame. "Is Letty with—"

"Letty sent me to fetch you," Ansel interrupted curtly. "She's—she's feeling right poorly this morning, and I don't know what to do for her."

"Oh, my. Is it the baby?"

"I don't know. It ain't time for the youngun to be born, but Letty—she's been hurtin' all night."

Ansel and Letty Latimer had been Charity's nearest neighbors until a few months ago when the Swenson family had staked their new claim.

The Latimers lived a good five miles away, but Letty and Charity visited back and forth once a month, happily planning for Letty's new baby due in late November.

Being about the same age, the two women had developed a close friendship while the Latimers and Burkhousers homesteaded their properties. Ansel and Letty were the closest thing to family Charity had, now that Ferrand was gone.

Charity was reaching for her shawl when she remembered. "Of course I'll come, Ansel, but will you step in for a moment?"

Ansel removed his hat and walked into the cool interior of the soddy, trying to adjust his eyes to the dim light as he spoke. "We'd best hurry, Charity. I hate to leave Letty alone any longer than need be."

"Of course. I'll only take a moment." Charity motioned for him to follow her to the bed. "I want you to see something."

Ansel Latimer strode across the room. He was a tall man, still handsome at forty-three, with brown eyes and dark hair streaked with gray. He was twenty years older than Charity, and she valued his intelligence and common sense. Many times she'd gone to him with her problems since Ferrand's death. If anyone would know what to do about the stranger, Ansel would.

Slowly his puzzled gaze surveyed the man lying deathly still, and a frown crossed his rugged features. "Who is he?"

"I don't know. Three days ago I found him in the stream where a wolf was attacking him. I shot the wolf and managed to drag him to the house."

Ansel leaned forward and lifted one of the bandages, and Charity watched his frown deepen. "Infection's set in."

"I know," Charity confessed in a low whisper. "I've tried to keep the wounds clean, but they look worse each day."

Ansel lifted the other bandages and shook

his head as he viewed the angry, pus-filled lesions. "He needs a doctor, but even then, I don't believe he can make it."

"I know. Oh, Ansel, what should I do?" Charity pleaded, her voice trembling. "I'm afraid he's going to die!"

Ansel patted her shoulder reassuringly. "Looks to me like you've done about all you can, girl." Ansel had never seen a better job of stitching. "But the man's wounds are too serious. It'd be better to let him go to his reward in peace."

Charity's eyes filled with tears as she stared down at the stranger's flushed features. His face was pathetically swollen and hot with fever. She felt such a closeness to the man, yet she couldn't explain why; he was a complete stranger. But she'd fought so hard to save his life that it seemed impossible to let him go.

Still, she knew Ansel had spoken the truth. Wouldn't it be kinder to let him pass away? In three days she'd managed to get only a few drops of water and a couple spoonfuls of broth down his throat, and he hadn't kept it down.

Though she sat next to the bed, the man was so weak Charity could barely hear him whispering for Betsy. She wondered how much longer she could bear to watch his suffering.

Ansel gently touched her arm. "Let him go,

Charity. You've done all you can. He's in the Lord's hands now."

Charity nodded, tears of resignation beginning to trickle down her cheeks. Ansel was right. She had to let the stranger go. There was no mercy in letting him suffer this way.

"Come with me, Charity. We'll tend to Letty, then I'll bring you back this evenin' and help you bury him," Ansel said, certain the stranger would be dead by sunset.

Charity nodded, reaching to tuck the sheet tenderly over the man's chest. "I know it's best, but it . . . it seems awful just letting him pass away, alone." Her voice caught as her tears began to run in swift rivulets.

"Nothing more you can do," Ansel comforted, putting his arm around her shoulders and leading her away from the bed.

She knew he was right. Ansel was always right, but it seemed wrong, leaving a man like this. Charity wanted to be with him when it happened. . . .

"Letty needs you," Ansel reminded her gently, as if he could read her thoughts.

"Oh . . . yes, Letty . . . of course." Charity had almost forgotten her friend. Letty should be her first concern, but Charity's eyes raced back to the still figure lying on her bed as Ansel helped her with her shawl.

"Best bundle up real good. Chilly out this morning."

"Please put plenty of wood on the fire. I—I don't want him to be cold."

Ansel did as she asked, then opened the door and commanded quietly, "Charity, Letty needs our help, girl."

"Yes . . . yes, of course, Ansel." Charity glanced one final time at the bed before she turned and walked through the door.

"May the mercy of the Lord be with you," she whispered, wishing desperately that Betsy could be there to see him home.

Chapter 5

The old buckboard rumbled along the rutted road, bouncing Charity back and forth on the wooden seat uncomfortably, but she barely noticed. Her thoughts were still with the stranger as she wondered how long it would be before he went to meet his maker.

He could be dead at this instant, she realized, and the thought made her shiver in her shawl. At another time a ride in the crisp fall morning would have been a source of pleasure, but not today.

The roadbed ran along Fire Creek, and Charity found herself recalling the times she, Ferrand, Letty and Ansel had enjoyed picnics here on Sunday afternoons after church.

The riverbank was lined with willow trees, grapevines, and hazel bush. Charity and

Letty used to spend hours gathering the wild-flowers that grew in colorful profusion along the roadbed, while the men discussed their crops.

A killdeer sang his tuneless note, and a meadowlark called as the old buckboard lumbered across the shallow stream and rattled up the steep incline toward the Latimer homestead.

Charity noticed Ansel had said little during the ride, commenting only occasionally on the weather. His face remained pensive, and the worry lines were grooved deeper at the corners of his eyes.

Charity knew how much Ansel loved Letty, and she sympathized with his concern for his young wife. She knew he and Letty had looked forward to their first child like young-sters waiting for Christmas. Charity sighed deeply, wishing she and Ferrand had had a child.

Her thoughts drifted back to her friend. Charity couldn't imagine what was ailing Letty this morning. She'd seemed fine at church on Sunday. After the service Letty and Charity had lingered outside, discussing the new dress they'd make for Letty after her baby was born. They'd use the fine blue and yellow sprigged calico they'd dawdled over the last time Charity had ridden to Cherry Grove with the Latimers for supplies.

Charity suspected Letty's weakness for green apple pie was the source of her discomfort, but she didn't think Ansel was in any mood to hear her opinion.

The buckboard clattered along the prairie, and soon Charity could see the sod chimney of the Latimer dugout poking out of the ground. Whenever Charity visited Letty, she always came away thankful that Ferrand had built a soddy instead of a dugout.

Letty was forever complaining about her home being dark and damp year round, and she said it was practically impossible to keep her home clean with dirt from the roof and walls sifting down on everything. Whenever it rained, water came pouring in through the roof and under the door, and Letty had to wade through the mud until the floor could dry out.

Bull snakes got into the roof made of willows and grass, and Letty said sometimes a snake would lose its hold at night and fall down on the bed. On those occasions Ansel would jump up, take a hoe, and drag the snake back outside.

Charity shuddered at the thought. There were no snakes in her soddy. In summer it was cool as a cavern; in winter, a snug, warm refuge from the howling Kansas blizzards.

"Looks like Letty's let the fire burn down," Ansel remarked uneasily as he drove the buckboard alongside the dugout and drew the horses to a halt. Only a faint wisp of smoke curled from the chimney.

Ansel set the brake, jumped down, and lifted Charity from the wooden seat. "I'll bet Letty will have dinner waiting," she predicted, trying to ease the worried look on his face.

But when Ansel and Charity stepped inside the dugout, Charity's optimism began to fade. It took a moment for her eyes to adjust to the small room. A ray of sunshine filtered through the one window in the room, and Charity squinted to locate Letty, who lay on the bed, her hands crossed over her swollen stomach, her lips moving silently.

Charity moved swiftly across the room and knelt beside the straw-filled mattress, reaching out to smooth back the damp tendrils of carrot-red hair. "Letty, it's me, Charity."

For a moment she thought Letty hadn't heard her. Then Letty's lips moved, and Charity leaned close to understand her words. "Ansel . . . make him go outside. . . ."

"What?" Charity's heart started to hammer. Something was terribly wrong. This was far more serious than a case of eating too many green apples. Charity touched her friend's delicate hand reassuringly and discovered it was unusually cold. "Ansel's here,

Letty, and so am I. Can you tell us what's the matter?"

"Ansel . . ." Letty's voice was stronger this time. "Make Ansel . . . go outside," she repeated weakly.

"But, Letty . . . why?"

Letty's tears fell across cheeks sprinkled generously with girlish freckles. "Just make him go, Charity . . . make him leave. . . ."

Charity turned in bewilderment to face Ansel, who was standing quietly in the shadows of the room. "She wants you to leave."

"I heard." Without questioning his wife's unusual request he turned and walked out.

Charity turned to Letty and began smoothing the rumpled sheets. "Now, let's get you comfortable." She paused and frowned when she felt a warm, sticky substance on the sheets. A jolt of shock moved through her as she stared at the blood on her hand.

Gently, Charity moved Letty's body. The girl was pitifully thin except where she was swollen with child. Charity pressed her hands to the bottom sheet and discovered it was saturated with Letty's blood. Her gaze flew back to Letty's pale face as the young woman on the bed whispered softly, "It's the baby, Charity. It's comin' . . . and there's somethin' wrong."

Letty cried out, then bit her lower lip and muffled an agonized scream as she reached to grasp Charity's hand. Letty held on tightly until the spasm passed.

Charity grabbed a cloth from the basin on the floor beside the bed and gently sponged Letty's flushed face while she spoke in low, soothing tones. "There now, everything will be fine," she promised. "The baby might be a few weeks early, but I'm sure it'll be strong and healthy. Perhaps Ansel should go for the doctor?"

Letty reached up and halted the movement of the wet cloth, her dark eyes fraught with anxiety. "There isn't time, Charity. Something's wrong."

Charity smiled assuringly. "Nonsense, Letty. I'm sure everything's fine. You're just nervous about having your first baby."

Charity hushed as another violent seizure racked Letty's slender frame. Sweat broke out across the girl's brow, and she buried her face in Charity's shoulder to muffle her scream. "Don't . . . want . . . Ansel . . . to . . . hear," Letty panted as the spasm slowed.

"Don't worry about Ansel," Charity soothed. When the pain abated, she ran the wet cloth across Letty's pale features again. "How long have you been in labor?"

Letty shook her head as she stiffened with the onset of another contraction. This time the seizure was so violent, so savage, that

Letty screamed and clung to Charity's hand so tightly that Charity bit her lip to keep from crying out. The baby was very near, she thought frantically. She needed to tell Ansel to stoke the fire to bring the kettle to boil. . . .

But Letty's amber eyes grew wide with fear, and her body began to shake convulsively as she called Charity's name. Still trembling, Letty began the Lord's Prayer with whispered fervor, "Our Father, who art in heaven . . . hallowed be Thy name . . ."

Charity's hand flew to her mouth as she watched blood pour from Letty onto the sheet and gather in crimson pools.

". . . Thy kingdom come . . . Thy will be . . . done . . ." continued Letty until she screamed again and clutched the sides of the bed.

Charity couldn't think straight. She knew it shouldn't be happening this way. She'd assisted at other births, and they hadn't gone like this.

". . . Give us the day . . . our daily . . ." Letty whispered till another contraction seized her. "Ansel!" she pleaded in a high-pitched wail.

The door to the dugout flew open and Ansel rushed into the room, his eyes wild with fear. "Letty . . . my God!"

"Leave!" Charity tried to shield him from

the pitiful sight. Letty was thrashing wildly on the bed, screaming Ansel's name over and over as her life's blood gushed from her and ran down the side of the bed onto the dirt floor.

"My God—do somethin' for her!" Ansel watched his wife in stunned horror. Letty's body was consumed with spasms as his child was pushed from the confines of its mother's womb.

". . . And lead us . . . not . . . into . . . temptation. . . ." Letty murmured, stopping to pant, her eyes squeezed tight in torment. "Ohhhh . . . Ansel, help me!"

Throwing her full weight against his frame, Charity tried to shove Ansel toward the doorway, hoping to spare him from what was happening. "Go outside," she pleaded, raising her voice above the sound of Letty's terrified pleas. "I'll tend to her. She'll be fine . . . she'll be fine. . . ."

Ansel let Charity push him through the doorway, and he stood outside as she slammed the heavy wooden door in his face. "My God, she's dyin'," Ansel mumbled hoarsely to himself. "Letty's dyin'."

He sagged against the door frame, then slid down in a crumbled heap on the dirt stoop. He threw his hands over his ears to block out his wife's screams, tears of helpless frustration rolling down his cheeks.

Inside, Letty was splitting apart with the pain. Charity's hands reached to support the baby coming out bottom first.

Letty's screams ran together as she clawed the sheets, her eyes bright with terror. "I'm goin' to die, Charity. Take care of . . . my . . . baby . . . take care of my baby. . . ."

"No!" Charity protested, her own voice rising in hysteria. She couldn't permit Letty to die! "You have to hold on, Letty—you have to fight!" The baby was nearly out now as Charity grasped the small mound of flesh and pulled, blinking back her tears.

"Tell   Ansel . . . I . . . love . . . him . . . take care . . . of . . . baby!"

Before Letty could finish another plea, she convulsed violently one final time as the baby slid free of her body into Charity's waiting hands.

"It's a girl, Letty! You have a daughter! Look! She's beautiful!" Charity held the squalling, red-faced bundle up for Letty to see, her words slowly dying in her throat.

She blinked back sudden tears as she realized Letty would never know she had a fine, beautiful daughter.

She lay peacefully in the folds of the bloody linen, her screams finally stilled.

Ansel wasn't sure how long he'd sat before the door finally opened again. He glanced up and saw Charity holding a bundle in her arms. He could see she'd been crying.

"Ansel?" she spoke softly, her eyes welling into emerald pools.

"Yes?"

"You have a lovely baby daughter." She carefully pulled back the folds of the blanket and held the baby so that her father could inspect her.

Ansel stared awkwardly at the tiny wrinkled face. "A little girl?"

"Yes. She looks real healthy."

Ansel's eyes slowly lifted to meet Charity's expectant gaze. How young and vulnerable he looked, she thought. "Letty?"

Charity shook her head as tears trickled down her cheeks. For a moment the anguish in Ansel's eyes was more than she could bear.

Two tears rolled out of the corners of his eyes and he looked at Charity, heartbroken. "She's . . . gone?"

Charity could only nod, her own tears blinding her.

His sad gaze dropped to the baby. "A little girl. Me and Letty was hopin' for a boy," he said thoughtfully, all trace of emotion suddenly gone from his voice.

"Would you like to hold your new daughter?"

"Oh . . . no . . . not now. . . ." He turned and nearly stumbled off the porch in his grief. His shoulders slumped as he moved away. "Think I'll take a walk right now," he murmured.

"Ansel, are you all right?" Charity's heart was breaking. She wanted to go to him and lend him comfort, but she hesitated. He needed time to grieve.

"Oh . . . yes. I'll be all right. You'll—you'll see to my wife's needs, won't you?"

"Of course." Charity would bathe Letty and dress her in her Sunday best for viewing.

"Good, good." Ansel stopped and took a deep breath, looking up into the sky. "My, it's a fine day, isn't it? Couldn't ask for any finer. Letty would have found it real enjoyable."

"Ansel." Charity watched numbly as he ambled off alone. She looked down at the tiny bundle in her arms and saw Letty's pug nose and thatch of bright red hair. Letty would live on in this child, she thought with sad jubilation. Letty would live on, but what would happen to poor Ansel?

She lifted her tearstained face to the glorious blue sky—and as if Letty could hear her, Charity finished Letty's last thought in a heartfelt whisper. "For Thine is the kingdom, and the power, and the glory . . . forever . . . amen."

Chapter 6

The door to the soddy swung open slowly, a head popped around the corner, and a pair of coal-black eyes traveled intently around the room.

The gaze, dark as midnight, surveyed the chairs, the table, the mirror over the washstand, then moved reluctantly to the cold ashes in the fireplace. Then the eyes moved slowly back to the bed where a large mound lay still in the middle.

"White Sister sleep."

The door creaked open and an Indian squaw moved into the room, followed by a second squaw. Both were unusually large in stature and impressive in girth. Many buffalo had been consumed by these women in their respective thirty-one and twenty-nine summers.

The first squaw, Laughing Waters, crept silently toward the bed to see if White Sister was sleeping soundly. It was unusual for White Sister to be asleep while the sun was still up.

Laughing Waters and Little Fawn knew they could quietly browse as they pleased, examining every nook and cranny, satisfying their natural curiosity, and White Sister wouldn't scold them.

She'd let Laughing Waters and Little Fawn come into the soddy many times without invitation. The two Indians would pop in every week or so for an unscheduled visit.

They'd peek at the cooking utensils, pry open the storage bins, and if White Sister wasn't busy, she'd let them watch her work the big wheel by the fireplace that spun round and round throwing pretty yarn into a basket.

Sometimes White Sister would snip a piece of yarn or colorful ribbon and give it to them, and the two squaws would leave delighted with their new treasures.

The women drew the red blankets they wore around their massive bosoms and crept closer to the bed. The cabin was chilly, and Laughing Waters was puzzled. Was White Sister sick?

Moving closer, the two women peered intently at the form lying on the bed. Then Little Fawn looked at Laughing Waters and frowned. "This no White Sister," she whispered.

Laughing Waters was just as surprised as Little Fawn to find a strange man lying in White Sister's bed. She leaned closer and suspiciously eyed the man, whose face looked as if it had been pecked by a buzzard.

Little Fawn looked at Laughing Waters expectantly, then laid her head on the white man's chest and listened. When she was certain she'd heard a faint heartbeat, she looked up at Laughing Waters and grinned, displaying a wide, toothless gap beneath her upper lip. "Gold Hair lives, but sick."

"Ohhhhh, big sick," clucked Laughing Waters maternally as her hands gently peeled back one of the bandages on the man's chest. She shook her head sadly as she viewed the infected wounds. "Heap big sick," she agreed.

Little Fawn thought the man, despite his illness, was the handsomest white man she'd ever seen. Her sharp gaze ran admiringly over the powerful, broad shoulders. His hair reminded her of the golden stones she'd found in the stream one day. The sun had shimmered and danced on the rocks, mesmerizing Little Fawn with their unusual beauty. She couldn't imagine where White Sister was and why she'd left behind such a treasure.

Her hands touched the long, golden locks, stroking them carefully. "This good man," she told Laughing Waters. *"Good."*

"Man White Sister's," Laughing Waters reminded her sternly.

Little Fawn shook her head stubbornly, her two long braids fanning out in the air. "White Sister gone. She leave Gold Hair to meet Wahkun-dah alone. I take care. Make Gold Hair strong again." Little Fawn looked lovingly at the man on the bed. Gold Hair mine, she thought fondly. He fine, strong buck. When he well, Little Fawn call him Swift Buck with Tall Antlers. He be good father, make many papooses.

Laughing Waters recognized the determination in her little sister's voice and knew it would do no good to argue with her. Little Fawn wouldn't let Gold Hair pass on to the Great Hunting Ground in the Sky without doing her best to prevent the journey.

Besides, Laughing Waters thought Gold Hair fine man too. She make white man well. Then he be hers, and she call him Brave Horse With Many Wounds. He and Laughing Waters make many strong papooses.

Little Fawn turned to Laughing Waters and spoke rapidly in Kaw, the native language of their tribe. Laughing Waters listened, nodding her head as Little Fawn outlined her plan to save this splendid specimen.

Both women hurried into action. Laughing Waters slipped out of the cabin to gather the roots and herbs they would need for the healing poultices, while Little Fawn rushed to get the fire going again.

Beau stirred uncomfortably on the bed. Damn! It was hot.

He wanted to force his eyes open, but the effort was too painful. Every inch of his body ached, and his mouth was so dry he could spit cotton.

Where was he? He willed his legs to move but found them so heavy they refused to budge. A trickle of sweat began to run down the side of his head, and when he tried to wipe it away, he realized his hands wouldn't move.

Paralyzed. He was paralyzed! The image of the wolf with its slobbering jaws came rushing back, and Beau realized with a sinking sensation what had happened. He was dead. The wolf had killed him.

The thought was strangely painful to him. Beau had to admit that he hadn't wanted to live since Betsy's death, yet he hadn't necessarily wanted to die either. But that must be what had happened.

Beau drew a shaky breath and found the air stifling and arid. A new, even more disturbing thought came to him. If he was dead . . . and it was this hot . . .

He groaned and willed his eyes to open. If he was where he thought he was, he might as well face it.

Slowly, his lids fluttered open, and he looked around in the dark. He was lying in some sort of bed . . . in a room. His heart began hammering, and he felt the sweat roll in rivulets down his forehead and drip into his eyes.

The rosy glow of red hot flames danced wickedly across the wall in front of him, and he groaned again and clamped his eyes shut tightly. Oh, God, thought Beau, feeling limp with fear. So that's where he was—in hell.

Well, it wasn't fair, he thought dismally, resenting the fact that he hadn't even had a chance to explain the bad things he'd done in life—not that there'd been all that many.

There had been a few times when he and Cole had been with some pretty questionable women.

And he had fully intended to pay that hundred-dollar gamblin' debt, once he got back to Missouri. . . .

It was his understanding that he'd at least have a chance to tell his side of the story, even if He did have all transgressions written down in some big book.

No, it just wasn't fair, he railed silently. Ma

had taught him to obey the Ten Commandments, and with a few minor exceptions, he hadn't been all that bad. Cole had been worse.

Beau wondered if he could talk to someone to get this mess straightened out. He hadn't seen anyone when he'd opened his eyes. Maybe he'd been left down here to roast all alone.

He carefully opened one eye and moved it slowly around the room, surprised to discover hell looked much like the inside of a dirt soddy. Of course, he'd never stopped to think what hell would look like, since he'd never had any intention of going there.

But damn, it was *hot* down here. Preacher Slystone had been right about that.

Again he tried to wipe the sweat off his forehead with the back of his hand, only to discover he was wrapped tight as a tick in some sort of blanket. He moved around, trying to jerk his hands free of the cocoon. Suddenly he glanced up, and his heart jumped into his throat.

Standing over him was the biggest Indian he'd ever seen. On closer examination he saw it was a squaw, and she was smiling a wide, toothless grin at him.

"Gold Hair wake. Good."

Beau grinned back lamely, wondering if he was supposed to say something, though preferring not to. He might be in hell, but he didn't have to socialize with the other residents this soon.

A second Indian woman suddenly loomed above him, her massive bulk blocking the flickering flames on the walls as she began unwrapping the tight blanket.

Beau groaned and jerked away. "No! Don't!" he pleaded weakly. They were going to finish him off before he could state his case to the proper authorities. "Listen, there's been a mistake."

"No talk, Gold Hair," the second woman grunted. "Save strength."

Beau's eyes widened as the first woman reached out and touched a lock of his hair, smiling as she fingered the silken softness. "Pretty, like rocks in water."

"Listen, who's in charge here?" Beau demanded. He wasn't sure what was happening. A terrible stench filled his nostrils as the second woman hurriedly stripped off the blanket, blatantly baring his naked body in the light of the dancing flames.

Beau self-consciously jerked the blanket back over himself.

"No hurt, Gold Hair. We make well," Little Fawn soothed.

Amid Beau's indignant protests the women tossed the blanket aside again, then dipped their large hands into a pail beside the bed and slapped moist, vile-smelling mud all over his body.

Beau gagged and winced as a series of sharp, excruciating pains ricocheted through him like stray bullets. He realized frantically that this must be part of his eternal punishment, though he'd never have imagined it would be administered by a pair of Indian squaws.

Preacher Slystone had never mentioned any such thing. That neglectful omission was Beau's last rational thought before he mercifully slipped back into sweet oblivion.

Chapter 7

Friday dawned dark and dreary. A cold gray mist fell from the leaden sky and surrounded the travelers riding silently in the buckboard.

The young woman held a small bundle in her arms. Occasionally she crooned to the tiny infant as the man beside her drove the team of horses with methodical movements.

Had it been only two days since she'd traveled this same road? To Charity it seemed an eternity had passed since Wednesday, the day Ansel had come to fetch her for Letty.

Dear, sweet Letty. It was still hard to comprehend that the fresh mound of dirt behind the Latimer dugout was all that remained of her friend.

LETICIA MARGARET LATIMER, BELOVED WIFE, MAY SHE BRING AS MUCH JOY IN

HEAVEN AS SHE BROUGHT HERE ON EARTH. With a sad heart Charity had watched Ansel lovingly carve the inscription onto a wooden cross and place it on Letty's grave that morning.

Charity had dressed Letty in her wedding gown, made of the finest ivory silk. Unpacking the dress, she'd found a tiny pair of kid shoes tucked beneath the folds. Slipping the shoes on Letty's feet, Charity had thought of Letty's well-to-do family back East, who'd married their daughter to Ansel Latimer in grand style.

When Letty's hair had been brushed until it was the color of a fiery sunset, Charity tied a cameo brooch at the base of her neck, remembering that Ansel had given the cameo to Letty on their first Christmas. It had been Letty's most cherished possession.

As she gazed down at her friend, Charity's eyes filled with tears. Letty looked so small, so young . . . so helpless.

Charity had draped the kitchen table with Letty's grandmother's lace tablecloth. She'd called Ansel in from the lean-to, where he'd been building the small pine box.

As Ansel stepped hesitantly into the room, Charity had slipped past him to go outside, giving him time alone with his wife.

Later, the two had hoisted the simple pine box onto the middle of the table. Gently they'd placed Letty in it. Charity lit a single candle that burned until Letty's burial the following day.

Charity stood for a few moments looking down at her friend, fondly recalling how they'd sat around that same table, laughing and giggling like two schoolgirls. For hours on end they'd made plans for the new baby, stitching tiny gowns, lace bonnets, and knitting booties. So many dreams had come to an end with Letty's death; so many hopes would be buried with her.

The funeral was small. Only a handful of neighbors stood in a circle around the open grave, singing "Amazing grace, how sweet thy sound, that saved a wretch like me. . . ." The haunting strains still echoed in Charity's head as the baby began to fret. Charity looked up at Ansel. "She's hungry again." Without the benefit of her mother's milk the infant seemed insatiable.

It bothered Charity that the baby hadn't been named yet. When she'd mentioned the subject at breakfast, Ansel looked at her blankly. Instead of answering her he'd responded vaguely about his crop for next spring.

Letty had wanted to name the baby Mary Kathleen, if she should have a girl, but Charity wanted Ansel's blessing on the name.

Ansel glanced down at the baby, and Charity wondered if he was aware it was his child. At times, she didn't think he knew. Leaving the sole care of the baby to Charity, he'd barely acknowledged that the infant had been born.

She was sure Ansel was acting strangely because his grief was so profound. He didn't cry or express his sorrow overtly. Charity was almost certain that if he'd just hold his new daughter, somehow a small part of Letty would return to him.

The babe looked so much like her mother, Charity could swear those were Letty's laughing, amber-colored eyes staring back at her.

"We'll be at your place soon," Ansel said quietly, his tone unchanged by the noises of the baby sucking loudly on her tiny fist. "The child can eat then."

Charity shifted the baby to her shoulder and bounced her gently. The soothing motion stilled the baby's fretfulness for the moment. Charity worried how Ansel would care for the child alone, once he returned home. Perhaps, she sighed, it would be good for father and daughter to be on their own. She'd promised to help Ansel find a woman to live in and care for the baby, but she knew that could take time.

In some ways, though, she felt that might be for the best. Ansel could become acquainted with his daughter, and Mary Kathleen could help fill the void in his life.

The baby began to whimper as the buckboard topped a rise and the Burkhouser soddy came into view. Charity's thoughts turned to another, even more perplexing problem: the stranger in her house. He would have to be buried immediately. She'd been gone much longer than she'd expected to be, and his remains would have to be disposed of quickly.

She glanced at Ansel and prayed he'd spare her the unpleasant task. Her heart still ached from having left the man to die alone.

When the buckboard rumbled into the yard and Ansel brought the horses to a halt, Charity noticed a heavy plume of smoke coming from the sod chimney.

Ansel jumped off the wagon and lifted Charity and the baby to the ground. "Someone has built a fire," she remarked, glancing in puzzlement at the rising smoke.

Could the stranger still be alive? she wondered. A thrill of expectation shot through her though she quickly suppressed that improbable hope. There had to be a more reasonable explanation for the fire.

She glanced around the yard, looking for a clue. The stack of firewood next to the house was the exact height it had been when she'd left two days ago. The oxen and old Bossy, her bag heavy with two days' milk, grazed in the small pen beside the lean-to. A few sitting hens roamed outside the soddy, scratching in the dirt and clucking contentedly.

Gabriel and Job lay in front of the door, wagging their tails lazily, waiting for Charity to come scratch behind their ears.

Everything seemed exactly as she'd left it, except for the strong smell of woodsmoke in the air.

She turned to ask Ansel how he'd explain the strange occurrence and was surprised to see him climbing back onto the seat of the buckboard.

"Oh, Ansel, why don't you rest for a spell before you unhitch the horses," she urged, knowing he'd need the wagon to carry the stranger's remains to the gravesite.

"No, thank you, Charity. I'd best be gettin' along." Ansel picked up the reins and released the brake.

Charity stared at him open mouthed. "But, Ansel," she protested lamely, trying to make sense of his behavior. "You can't be leaving!"

"You take care now, you hear?" Ansel whistled and slapped the reins across the horses' broad rumps. The buckboard began to roll noisily out of the yard amid the jangle of harness and creaking leather.

Charity watched in stunned silence as the wagon moved off in the direction it had just come. She glanced from the bundle in her arms to the cloud of boiling dust. Great balls of fire! He *was* leaving, she thought frantically.

"Ansel, wait!" she shouted, running after the wagon. "You forgot your baby!" But in a few moments she was out of breath, and her footsteps began to falter. The buckboard disappeared over the rise and was completely out of sight.

Charity let out an exasperated sigh and stared down at the infant in her arms. If this wasn't a fine kettle of fish! How dare Ansel ride off and leave the child in her care!

The baby began to cry, thrashing her fists angrily in the air, demanding her dinner as Charity started trudging toward the soddy, wondering what in blue blazes had gotten into Ansel! Surely he'd have the good sense to remember he'd forgotten his baby and come back; meanwhile, she was left to care for the infant and face the unpleasant task of burying the stranger by herself.

As if her thoughts weren't disconcerting enough, the baby was screaming at the top of her lungs when Charity finally reached the soddy. She pushed the door open and sucked in her breath as a blast of hot air nearly knocked her off her feet.

"What in . . ." Charity pushed the door wider and stepped into the room, trying to adjust her eyes to the dim light. Once she could see, Charity surveyed the scene before her with amazement.

Two Indian squaws sat beside the fireplace, chanting and passing a large pipe back and forth between them. They had built a roaring fire, and the flames were licking wildly up the chimney.

Charity wrinkled her nose, her attention momentarily diverted as she noticed the several large pans of herbs and roots bubbling on the stove, filling the room with a vile odor.

The stranger lay on the bed. Swathed tightly from head to toe in a bedsheet, he resembled a picture of an Egyptian mummy Charity had once seen in a book.

The room was so stifling hot she could barely breathe, and the odor coming from the stove made her stomach lurch. She stood at the door, clutching the baby against her bosom.

When Little Fawn caught sight of Charity, she gave her a wide grin. "White sister return?"

Then Little Fawn wondered what Charity's return would mean to her claim on Gold Hair. Her smile faded as she scrambled to her feet, dragging Laughing Waters behind her.

"Little Fawn? Laughing Waters?" Charity surveyed the two disheveled squaws with growing bewilderment. The heat in the soddy had flushed the women's face to a bright red.

Their buckskin dresses clung to their massive frames. Sweat rolled from beneath their dark hairlines, and the tailfeather in Laughing Waters's hair was cocked at an odd angle.

"What on earth is going on here?" Charity glanced to the bed where the stranger lay, writhing in agony. Her heart leapt when she heard him moan weakly as he tried to break free of the bindings. Realizing he was alive, she went weak with relief.

Little Fawn, seeing the unmistakable joy on Charity's face, crossed her arms over her ample bosom, and a combative glint came into her eyes. "We make Gold Hair better."

Charity could hardly believe he was still alive. It was nothing short of a miracle, but the man *had* survived. "He's better . . . he really is? Oh, thank God!"

Laughing Waters grunted. *"Little Fawn and Laughing Waters* make Gold Hair better," she clarified curtly, lest Charity misunderstand who'd actually saved the man's life.

Charity hurried to the bed, trying to control her rapid pulse. Yes, he was alive, though only his eyes, open now and staring at her wildly, were visible through an opening in the sheet.

"Why is he wrapped so tightly?" she asked in a whisper, unaware that the man was fully conscious.

"Make medicine work," Little Fawn explained. She scurried to the bed and edged Charity out of the way with her large hip. Her fingers picked up a stray lock of his hair, and the man's eyes widened fearfully as she smiled and stroked the golden strand. "Pretty, like rocks in water. Me keep."

The man groaned and clamped his eyes shut. "I think he's trying to say something." Charity reached to unwrap the bandage wound so tightly under his chin that it prevented him from speaking, but Little Fawn's hand shot out and stopped her. The squaw sent Charity a stern look. "*We* help Gold Hair!"

Charity glanced up, surprised to detect the possessive note in her voice. Laughing Waters and Little Fawn visited her often. They were the last of a friendly band of Kaw Indians who camped about five miles on the other side of Fire Creek. For months the two squaws had made a habit of visiting the soddy, making themselves at home whenever they came.

Apparently they'd happened to visit two days ago and discovered the wounded man. But Charity certainly hoped they didn't think he'd become their property!

"Thank you very much for tending . . . Gold Hair . . . while I was away," she said carefully, hoping she could convince them that the man was hers, not theirs.

"Gold Hair heap good man," Little Fawn proclaimed with another grin.

"Oh, yes . . . yes, I can see that. He's very . . . nice, and he's . . . mine."

Little Fawn's face fell.

Laughing Waters's eyes narrowed. "Why you leave Gold Hair? Heap big sick."

"Yes, I know he is." Charity wasn't sure how much they understood but sensed they were waiting for her explanation. Remembering the baby, she smiled and unwrapped the blanket and proudly displayed a grumpy Mary Kathleen. "See? I've been away helping my friend have her baby. That's why I had to leave Gold Hair."

The women lowered their heads in unison and looked at the child. "Oh, papoose," Little Fawn crooned, tickling under the baby's chin.

Charity noticed Laughing Waters wasn't impressed. "Gold Hair heap big sick. We fix; we keep," she calmly announced.

Since the Indians had never seemed threatening to her, Charity didn't feel alarmed. Apparently the two squaws had been able to do for the stranger what she hadn't, and she was grateful.

But not grateful enough to let them have him. "No, you see, my friend was very ill. She was about to have her baby, and she needed my help," Charity explained patiently. "Since Gold Hair was asleep, I thought it would be all right to leave to help my friend." That wasn't exactly true, but Charity knew the women would have no way of knowing otherwise.

Laughing Waters was clearly skeptical. "Where mother of papoose?"

"She . . . died," Charity admitted painfully.

Laughing Waters still wasn't convinced that Charity should have first claim to the man. "Where papoose's father?"

"He's . . . not here right now . . . but he'll be back soon. Because my friend died, I was gone longer than I intended to be. I'm thankful to see you and Little Fawn have taken such good care of Gold Hair."

Little Fawn and Laughing Waters exchanged a noncommittal look. "If you'll show me what to do, I'll take over now," Charity bargained, praying they'd buy her story. "You see, he was attacked by a wolf, and I haven't been quite sure how to care for him. I see you have him on the mend."

Laughing Waters grunted disgustedly, and it seemed unlikely the two would relinquish their rights to the white man. They went off into a corner of the soddy and gestured animatedly as they whispered to each other.

While Charity held her breath, she glanced over at the bed and found the man eyeing all three of them warily. His eyes were as blue as she remembered them, and she tried to reassure him with a nod.

Laughing Waters returned and grudgingly handed Charity a large cup of vile-smelling tea. "Make Gold Hair drink."

Charity nodded and released a sigh of relief. "Thank you, I will."

"We be back Big Father's Day," Little Fawn stated firmly.

The baby began to fuss, and Charity nervously rocked it back and forth in her arms. She thought she'd faint from the heat. "Sunday? Yes, Sunday will be fine," she said agreeably, realizing the squaws were not going to give him up so easily.

"Keep fire going. Heap big sweat. Make Gold Hair better."

"Yes . . . yes, of course," Charity promised, wondering why she hadn't thought to try and sweat the poison out of him herself.

"Put medicine on hurts."

Charity stared at the bucket of herbs and roots next to the bed. "I will."

Little Fawn walked back to the bed and touched a strand of golden hair once more. As Beau looked up helplessly, she gave him a flirtatious wink and proudly displayed the wide gap of missing front teeth.

"We go now," Laughing Waters announced.

"I'll take good care of . . . Gold Hair," Charity promised.

Laughing Waters started past her, then paused to look at the baby again. "Gold Hair make stronger papoose," she grunted.

Charity watched as Little Fawn and Laughing Waters opened the door.

"We be back Big Father's Day," Laughing Waters warned again.

"Yes, fine. We'll be here."

The door slammed, and Charity sank weakly onto a chair as the baby began to scream. What a disagreeable day, she thought numbly. Most disagreeable.

Chapter 8

Though she knew the stranger needed attention, Charity warmed a bottle and fed Mary Kathleen. At the moment, the baby was more demanding than the man, and he seemed momentarily comfortable.

Casting worried glances toward the bed, she rushed around the soddy, trying to soothe the baby's wails, which were growing more frantic by the minute. No doubt about it, Mary Kathleen had turned hostile.

Even the warm bottle of milk Charity tried to feed her did nothing to appease the baby. She screamed at the top of her lungs, her tiny face turning red as a raspberry as Charity paced the floor, jiggling her up and down in her arms.

The more Charity jiggled, the louder Mary Kathleen cried.

Beau, still trussed up like a Christmas goose, lay on the bed calmly watching the growing ruckus.

When the infant suddenly flew into a full-blown tantrum, holding her breath until her tiny features turned a strange, bluish white, the woman panicked and broke into tears of frustration. Both woman and baby were sobbing noisily as Beau cleared his throat, hoping to get the woman's attention.

He'd felt relief after discovering he wasn't in hell—at least he wasn't in the huge fiery pit described in the Good Book. But just exactly *where* was he? he wondered.

Wherever it was, it was strange. Two Indian squaws fussing over him, slapping foul-smelling mixtures on his wounds had been bad enough; now he was faced with a baby howling like a banshee and a woman who obviously didn't know the first thing about raising a child.

Again Beau cleared his throat loudly and squirmed about, but the woman and baby were too busy sobbing to notice. Glancing around, Beau focused his gaze on a tin cup filled with tea sitting on the stand beside the bed. Slowly, he inched his way across the mattress and nudged the cup with his shoulder, knocking it off the table.

The contents splattered on the bed, leaving a dark stain on the white linens, but the cup had the desired effect of hitting the floor with a resounding clatter.

Both Charity and the baby ceased their wailing at the same instant. Charity glanced at the bed through a veil of tears, and saw the man motioning with his eyes for her to remove the tight bandage confining his chin.

Deciding the loud interruption didn't concern her, Mary Kathleen resumed screaming while Charity hurried to the side of the bed.

"Were you speaking to me?"

"Ohmmhgtynm."

"You want me to untie the bandage?"

"Ohmmmhgtynm!"

"Oh . . . yes, of course."

With one hand Charity began loosening the knot in the bandage, while trying to converse over the baby's screams. "I'm sorry, I know we're disturbing you, and I'm *trying* to get her to hush, but she just won't!"

The knot came undone, and Beau felt as if he'd been released from a bear trap. He worked his jaws back and forth, wincing at the painful stiffness yet grateful for the blessed freedom.

"I just don't know what's gotten into her," Charity apologized. "Nothing seems to help."

"Get the scissors and cut me out of this damn sheet," Beau whispered hoarsely.

"Oh, I don't think I should. Little Fawn and Laughing Waters said—"

"I know what they said!" Startled by the snap in his voice, the infant screamed louder. "Just get me out of this!"

"You're scaring the baby." Charity patted Mary Kathleen on the back, to no avail; the baby only cried harder. "If I remove the sheet, it'll disturb your wounds." Pleased the stranger was improving, she didn't want to do anything to hinder his recovery.

Trying not to frighten the baby again, Beau made a conscious effort to lower his voice and speak calmly. "Just get me out of this, and I'll help you with the baby."

Those were the magic words. At this point Charity would have done anything to stop the baby's crying. Quickly she took scissors in hand and snipped away at the sheet as Mary Kathleen lay on the bed beside Beau, kicking and bellowing at the top of her lungs.

When the last of the cloth fell away, Charity blushed and averted her eyes. He was completely naked, and the sudden sight of his superb male body flustered her more than the baby's cries.

"Your . . . bandages need changing." Her hands were as shaky as her breathing. Beau sucked in his breath as Charity lifted the fabric Little Fawn and Laughing Waters had carefully placed over the tender wounds.

"Damn! That hurts. Take it easy!"

"Cursing won't make it any better." Gingerly she peeled away another bandage.

"You let a damn wolf gnaw on you for supper and see if you don't feel like swearin'. Ouch! Dammit, woman, that hurts!" There was a time when he would have apologized for swearing in a woman's presence, but much had happened to change Beau Claxton in the past year. So he swore again and gritted his teeth in renewed agony as his raw wounds were exposed to the air.

"There, now . . . just one more. . . ." Charity removed the last bandage and chanced another glance at his bare body before averting her eyes.

Beau sat up slowly and jerked the blanket over the lower half of his body. Charity knew he was watching her. Moreover, she knew he'd seen her looking at him. She had to break the awkwardness and tension surrounding them. "You remember the wolf?" she asked, staring at a far corner of the room.

"I try not to." He winced as the baby's howls continued. "Hand her to me."

Charity glanced at him in surprise. "You feel like holding her?"

"I can hold her better than I can stand to listen to her."

She hurriedly gathered the baby in her arms and carefully handed her to him. Beau caught his breath when Mary Kathleen's flailing fist hit one of his wounds.

"Oh, I'm so sorry!" Charity started to remove the baby, but Beau shrugged her away and eased the tiny bundle into the crook of his arm. He laid his head back on the pillow limply. The exertion of the past few moments had broken a fine sheen of sweat across his forehead. Mary Kathleen promptly ceased crying and snuggled deep against his side.

The room became quite peaceful as Beau gazed down at the infant in his arms. "You know, little one, you're pickin' up some bad habits," he said softly. "Some man's gonna turn you over his knee someday if you don't control that nasty temper."

Mary Kathleen hiccuped, then stuck her fist in her mouth and began sucking it loudly.

"She's hungry," Beau pronounced.

"I know she is, but she refuses to take her bottle."

"Give me the bottle."

Charity fetched the bottle and handed it to him. In moments the baby was contentedly sucking the contents dry.

"How did you do that?" She was awed by the way he handled the infant.

Mary Kathleen nestled snugly next to his large frame, her big amber eyes beginning to droop with exhaustion.

"I've always been good with kids. I have a

nephew I used to visit every day. We got along real well." Beau refused to think about the child he'd lost.

Charity watched with amazement as Mary Kathleen slowly dropped into a peaceful slumber. "Would you like me to move her?"

"No." Beau tucked the baby's blanket around her snugly. "She'll be fine right here."

"I need to put clean bandages on your wounds."

"In a while."

Charity tried not to stare at his chest, but her eyes kept wandering back to the bare expanse of masculine flesh. It was impressively broad, covered in a cloud of light-brown hair. She felt an unexpected rush of desire when she remembered how protected, how wonderful, she'd felt when he'd held her, even if he had thought she was his "Betsy."

She suddenly realized that she missed having her own man, missed being held and kissed, and made love to.

After Ferrand's death she'd sworn she'd never love another man, never again risk the hurt he'd caused her by going off and getting himself killed in that senseless war.

It occurred to Charity that she'd been angry at Ferrand for a long time. Now she could feel that anger subsiding.

For the first time since his death she found

herself thinking that maybe it would be possible to love again.

She wanted to be made love to again, to be a cherished wife and bear a man's child. Her gaze drifted wistfully back to the stranger, and she wondered again why she found him so attractive. His hair was shaggy, he hadn't shaved in weeks, and his large frame was whipcord thin. The two large wounds across his middle were covered with a thick, sticky poultice, and his ribs were poking through his skin. Still, she found him extremely desirable.

Charity found the admission disturbing. Would her growing feelings for him only serve to bring her new heartbreak?

"I guess we should introduce ourselves." She willed herself to take one step at a time. She drew her palm across her dress to dry the moisture from it, and extended her hand. "I'm Charity Burkhouser. I shot the wolf and brought you here."

The man glanced at her extended hand, but made no effort to take it. "You shouldn't have bothered."

"Oh . . . no bother." Charity was puzzled. She thought he'd be immensely grateful she'd saved his life. She paused, waiting for a thank-you, but when it appeared she'd have to wait all night, she let her hand drop to her side.

"What did you say your name was?" He hadn't said, but she thought it only decent he supply some sort of information about himself.

"Claxton."

Charity smiled. "Just . . . Claxton?"

"Beau. Beau Claxton."

"Beau. That's nice. I'll bet your mother chose that name." Charity noticed he was losing interest in the conversation.

"Well, Beau, I must admit, there were times when I thought I'd never know your name." She watched his eyes begin to droop with fatigue. "Are you from around here?"

"No." His voice sounded weaker than before.

"Oh. I'm sorry I had to leave you, but Letty —the baby's mother—she needed my help. I'm so thankful Laughing Waters and Little Fawn happened along when they did."

Beau wasn't sure he was thankful, but he was too weary to think about the horror of the past few days.

"How long have I been like this?" he murmured.

"Almost a week, but you're getting better." It was relief to see his wounds weren't looking so angry.

He was silent for a moment. "You said the child's mother died?"

"Yes, I'm afraid she did."

"That's too bad. A baby should have its mother."

The image of Betsy, heavy with child, drifted painfully back into Beau's thoughts. God, he didn't want to think about Betsy again . . . he didn't want to remember it could have been his child tucked safely against his side. . . . He could feel a weight of sadness that had been his for over a year creep back into his heart.

"Would you like some broth? I see that Laughing Waters and Little Fawn left some on the stove for you."

"I'm not hungry." Just tired. Bone tired.

"Well, just rest a spell. We can talk later." Charity leaned to tuck the sheet around him and the sleeping baby. His eyes drifted closed as she stood and gazed fondly from the baby to him. After a moment they were sound asleep, his large arm wrapped protectively around Mary Kathleen's tiny shoulders.

I sure hope there's no Betsy waiting for you to come home, Charity found herself thinking. Startled by her errant thoughts, she realized how selfish she sounded.

Of course, if he was married, Charity would write and inform his wife of her husband's injuries. It would only be right. And yet . . . As she reached to brush his hair from his forehead, she sighed.

Perhaps Betsy was his sister? But no, he wouldn't kiss a sister the way he'd kissed her the other day, she realized. Maybe Betsy was just an acquaintance? Even that possibility sent a pang of jealousy through her.

Well, no matter who Betsy was, Beau Claxton was a fine man, Charity decided. If there was no legal Mrs. Claxton, there'd be one soon —if she had anything to say about it.

Chapter 9

Beau awoke to the tantalizing smell of cornbread baking in the oven. The tempting
aroma drifted through the soddy, making his
empty stomach knot with hunger. How long
had it been since he'd last eaten?

He glanced down at the small bundle cud-
dled protectively against his side, and a smile
formed at the corners of his mouth. The baby
was still sleeping peacefully.

Without disturbing the infant, Beau shifted
around to ease his stiffened joints. The ma-
neuver hurt him, but not as much as before.

Settled more comfortably, he let his gaze
drift toward the window, where he noticed
the last rays of sunshine glistening on the windowpane. It must be late afternoon, he
thought, realizing this was the first time he'd

been able to distinguish the hour of day since his injury.

His gaze moved on, roaming aimlessly about the room. The bright gingham curtain hanging at the window looked freshly washed and ironed. The buffalo rug covering the floor was swept clean, and everything was tidy.

The room had all the signs of a woman's touch, he reflected. The colorful red-and-blue patchwork quilt draped across the foot of the bed reflected long hours dedicated to the intricate rows of tiny stitches.

Beau knew little about such womanly pursuits, but he'd watched his mother sit beside the old lamp in her parlor, working late into the night on a coverlet much like the one he was saw now.

The sound of a woman's voice humming "Dixie" momentarily distracted him. His head turned slowly on the pillow, seeking the source of the clear, sweet notes filtering through the room.

He saw a young woman standing at the stove, stirring a large pot with a wooden spoon. Instead of the foul-smelling brew the pot had contained before, there was a delicious aroma of meat and vegetables.

Who was this girl? Beau searched his memory for her name. Charita? Cherry? He couldn't remember.

"Well, hello. You've finally woken up."

Charity's voice interrupted his thoughts as she set the spoon aside and wiped her hands on her apron. "Dinner will be ready soon. I hope you feel up to eating a bite."

"Yes, I think I can." His gaze drifted back to the pot on the stove. The smell of the simmering stew made his mouth water.

"Well, good!" Charity brought her hands together enthusiastically. His returning appetite was the most encouraging sign of recovery so far. She immediately began ladling the thick stew onto a plate. She added a piping hot wedge of cornbread and a slab of freshly churned butter, then arranged everything on a tray along with a large glass of milk.

The baby was beginning to stir as she approached, so she sat the tray on the small table beside the bed and gently scooped Mary Kathleen into her arms. "Best you eat slow," she cautioned, fearing the rich food might upset Beau's stomach.

"Aren't you going to eat?" His eyes were on the cornbread. It was thick and crusty—just the way his mother used to make it.

"I'll feed the baby, then I'll eat." She returned to the stove and removed the bottle of milk she'd warmed earlier. "You and Mary Kathleen had a nice long nap," she remarked.

Beau picked up the piece of cornbread and took a cautious bite. The exquisite flavor made him close his eyes with pure pleasure.

It'd been a long time since he'd tasted anything so good.

"Looks like rain to the west." Charity sat in the rocker and held the baby, who was eagerly sucking from the bottle. "Sure could use a good soaking. It's been real dry."

Beau took another bite of the cornbread and chewed it slowly. "What time of the year is this?"

"October." Charity cocked her head to one side. "Why?"

"No reason." Beau picked up the spoon and brought a bite of stew to his mouth. God, he'd been wandering for over a year! The realization astounded him, and he felt a pang of guilt. His family must be sick with worry. "Exactly where am I?"

"In my soddy."

"No, I mean, am I still in Missouri?"

Charity laughed warmly. "No, you're in Kansas. Not far from a town called Cherry Grove."

"Kansas?"

"Yes. Are you from Missouri?"

"Yes."

Charity thought his questions odd and wondered if his memory had been affected by the accident. In a way, it would be to her advantage if he didn't remember his past. If he couldn't remember who he was, then he might be more easily persuaded to stay and help her. She decided to face her biggest obstacle first.

"Who's Betsy?"

The stew in his mouth suddenly tasted sour. He lifted his head slowly, and a defensive light came into his eyes as he met her inquiring gaze. "Who?"

"Betsy. You kept calling for her while you were unconscious." Charity held her breath, praying Betsy would be anyone but his wife.

A tight knot formed in the pit of his stomach, and Beau pushed his plate away though he'd barely touched it.

"You're finished already?" Her tone rang with disappointment.

"I've had enough."

"But you barely touched your food."

"I lost my appetite."

Charity hated to hear that. If he didn't eat properly, she knew he'd be slow to regain his strength. "Perhaps if I put your plate in the warming oven, you'll feel like eating more later."

Beau seemed to ignore the suggestion as he settled back on the pillow and closed his eyes again.

When Mary Kathleen finished the bottle, Charity lifted her to her shoulder and patted her back gently, savoring the sweet fragrance of the baby's skin. Once more her thoughts turned to Ansel, and where he could be.

All afternoon she had been expecting him to return for his daughter, but it was getting dark, and she feared he wasn't coming. If he didn't show up tomorrow, she wasn't sure what she'd do. Send someone to fetch him? She didn't know who it could be. And it would be impossible to leave Beau and the baby alone.

Grief had made Ansel temporarily forgetful, she tried to reason. It was the only explanation she could come up with for his puzzling behavior.

Surely tomorrow he would return for his daughter.

Turning back to the present, Charity remembered that Beau hadn't answered her question about Betsy. Was it an oversight or had he deliberately avoided her question? There was only one way to find out: she could be what Ferrand had always called downright nosy. She decided to chance it.

"You never told me about Betsy."

This time, Charity was sure he was deliberately avoiding her question. He lay on the bed, eyes closed, hands folded peacefully across his chest—totally ignoring her.

The baby burped loudly, filling the silence that had suddenly crowded the room, but Beau said nothing.

"Well?" Charity prompted.

Finally he took a deep breath and opened

his eyes. With pained resignation he met her gaze across the room. "Betsy is my wife."

Disappointment ricocheted like heat lightening across Charity's face. She'd known it was a possibility he was married, hadn't she? Hadn't she warned herself not to get her hopes up? But nothing could dull the dismal feeling of frustration closing in on her.

"Oh . . . I—I thought maybe that's who she might be." Her voice sounded high and hollow even to her own ears.

Well, Charity, *you've no one to blame but yourself for getting the foolish idea in your head that he was sent to you as a personal gift,* she scolded silently. It was plain he wouldn't be any use to her now. He had a wife named Betsy waiting for him when he recovered.

She sighed and squared her shoulders. "First thing tomorrow morning, I'll write your wife about what's happened and where you are."

Beau stared at the ceiling for a moment with expressionless blue eyes, and then Charity thought she detected a veiled sadness began to creep into them. "Yeah, you can do that, but I don't see how you're going to have it delivered," he said softly.

"Shouldn't be too hard. It's about time to go into town for the mail. I'll send the letter then."

Beau said the words slowly, as if trying to make himself believe them. "No, you can't do that. Bets is dead." It was true. Betsy was dead and a year was a long time to wallow in self-pity. His wife had been taken from him, and, like it or not, he was going to have to accept it.

Charity's gaze lifted expectantly to his. "She is?"

"Yes."

Dead. Betsy was dead! Relief surged through her, and she was instantly ashamed of herself for being so heartless and selfish. It was plain to see from the look on his face that his wife's death had been unbearable for him. "Oh . . . I'm very sorry," she apologized, the sincerity of her tone indicating she truly was.

"Yeah." He took a deep, ragged breath. "So am I."

"How long ago?"

"Over a year."

Strange, this was the first time Beau had been able to talk about Betsy's death without weeping like a child. To say her name didn't even hurt as much as it once had. "She was carrying our baby, and a rattlesnake . . . bit her," he continued cautiously.

Charity knew this couldn't be easy for him. Memories of Ferrand's untimely death flooded back as she listened to Beau talk about his wife's accident in quiet, almost reverent tones.

"It—it didn't take long for her to die. . . ." His voice broke momentarily, then he cleared his throat. Charity was stunned to see him reach for his plate again. He calmly picked up the spoon and ladled a bite of vegetables into his mouth. He chewed for a moment, absently savoring the flavor of the stew. When he glanced back at Charity it was almost as if he'd forgotten she was there. "I loved my wife very much."

"Yes, I'm sure you did," Charity said softly, feeling his pain as deeply as she'd felt her husband's loss. "It's hard to get over something like that. I lost my husband three years ago."

"Oh?" Beau was surprised that with each bite, his appetite increased, and his spirits lifted. "The war?"

She nodded. "Ferrand was riding with Sterling Price's Confederate raiders in the fall of sixty-four. When the Confederacy made its last offensive west of the Mississippi, Curtis Stewart, with the help of Alfred Pleasonton's calvary, whipped the Confederates and drove them back into Arkansas. Ferrand was killed near Westport, Missouri."

"The Confederacy?" Beau glanced up. "Your husband fought for the South?"

"Yes. Ferrand's decision was very hard—

especially on me. But I understood his reasons. Naturally, there was a lot of talk. You must remember, in the Civil War Kansas sent a larger number of Union soldiers to the field, in proportion to its population, than any other state. But my husband and I came from Virginia, and your upbringin' is hard to forget. Our families still live there. Ferrand was torn at first, but when it came right down to it, he felt he had to fight for what he believed in. Of course, all he did was go and get himself killed."

"It must have been hard on you," he murmured sympathetically.

"It was," she said with a sigh. "We had barely started homesteading this piece of land when Ferrand decided to join up. For a long time after his death I didn't know what I should do. My family wanted me to move back to Richmond, and that would probably have been wise. But Ferrand always said I was as stubborn as a Missouri mule when it came to holding on to what's important to me. After all the hard work we'd put into this soddy, it sure seemed frivolous to walk away and leave it for someone else."

"You been tryin' to work the land by yourself?" It wasn't unusual to find a woman homesteading land—the war had left many widows as heads of their families. But Beau couldn't imagine this tiny woman driving a team of oxen.

"I've been doin' a miserable job of it," Charity wasn't too proud to confess. "The fences are mostly down, I haven't had a decent crop in two years, and I haven't begun to make the improvements required by the state to grant me a title." She looked down at the baby thoughtfully. "I must admit, I was near my wits' end when you happened along."

Beau finished the stew and cornbread and drained the glass of milk. The meal was sitting easily in his stomach, and he felt his strength slowly begin to return.

From what he could tell, she was still young. Seemed to Beau that she was pretty enough to land another man. She was small and slender, with hair the color of a raven's wing, nice green eyes, and a wide, generous mouth—certainly nothing about her appearance to turn a man away. He suddenly realized he hadn't noticed whether a woman was good looking or not for a very long time. "Why haven't you remarried?"

Charity shrugged. "We have a real shortage of men out here, Mr. Claxton. Besides, other than Ferrand, I've never met one I'd want to share my bed—" Charity caught herself, then cast her eyes down to the baby shyly. "Never met one I'd want to have underfoot all the time," she corrected.

"Yeah." Beau knew the feeling. "Since Bets died, I haven't been with a woman—" He caught himself quickly when he realized what he was saying. "Well, I guess it doesn't matter. I'm never going to marry again."

Charity arched her brow slightly. "Oh?"

"Yeah, I loved Bets. No one could come close to taking her place."

"Oh, yes. I feel the same way." Somehow his pessimism gave her a feeling of foreboding. "Do you have family in Missouri that should be notified about your accident?" She wondered where his roots lay.

"I have family, but you don't need to bother gettin' in touch with them. I've been wandering around ever since Bets died." He paused for a moment before continuing. "I'll write and let them know where I am, soon as I'm up and around."

"You've just been driftin' all this time?"

"Yeah, just driftin'."

Glancing at Mary Kathleen asleep on Charity's shoulder, he seized the opportunity to change the subject. "Where's the baby's father?"

"I'm not sure. Ansel brought me home yesterday, then just up and disappeared."

"Disappeared?"

"Yes, and I don't know what to make of his

strange behavior. You see, Ansel's wife, Letty, died giving birth to the baby a few days ago. Now Ansel seems so lost—not like himself at all. When he brought me home yesterday, I thought naturally he'd take the baby with him, but he didn't. He just climbed back in the buckboard and drove off." Charity shook her head, still puzzled by Ansel's peculiar actions. "But I figure once he comes to terms with his grief, he'll be back for the baby."

Charity rose and walked over to lay the baby at the foot of Beau's bed, her mind returning to what Beau had said about no other woman ever replacing his wife. She didn't know why his statement bothered her. It was natural for him to feel that way, she reasoned. She wouldn't be asking for his love. All she wanted was his strength and stamina for the next few months to clear her land and set fences.

After all, it was just as likely that no other man would ever replace Ferrand in her heart. She supposed if he'd agree to marry her, they'd be starting out even. And she supposed she shouldn't be beatin' around the bush about her intentions either. Now was as good a time as any to involve him in her plan.

"Mr. Claxton," she began formally.

"Just call me Beau." He'd closed his eyes again, wanting to doze. He felt relaxed and comfortable, ready for sleep.

"I understand how you feel about the loss of your wife, and I can sure sympathize with your feelings about not wantin' to marry again. I loved Ferrand with all my heart. But I've discovered that sometimes you have to put personal feelings aside and go on with life. . . ." Her voice trailed off anxiously.

"Yeah, that's what they say." Beau knew it wouldn't be easy, but he was going to have to try to make a life for himself again. Life went on, whether a man wanted it to or not, and the time had come for him to stop grieving. As soon as he got back on his feet, he'd head back to Missouri. Maybe he'd bring his mother and their housekeeper, Willa, home to live with him. They could help tend the house while he worked the fields. It wouldn't be the rich, full life he'd had before, but it would be livable.

Charity was trying to gather enough courage to proceed with the conversation. Asking this man to marry her was going to be one of the most brazen things she'd ever undertaken, but she'd never before faced losing everything either.

Necessity could override her fear in this instance, and she knew she had him at a certain disadvantage. He was still too weak to get up and walk out on her if he didn't take to the idea right away. If he did balk—and she was fully braced for that possibility—she would at least have a few days to try and make him change his mind.

"What are you wondering about?" Beau finally asked.

The heavy meal had made him feel complacent and drowsy. He was thinking how good it was to carry on a simple conversation again. He'd been on the trail for over a year, and although a few months earlier he would have argued otherwise, he felt beholden to this woman for saving his life.

Charity took a deep breath and shut her eyes. There was no easy way to approach it. She'd simply have to be blunt and forthright before her courage failed her again. "Well, I was wondering . . . would you marry me?" Her voice suddenly sounded downright meek.

For a moment her words failed to register. Beau's eyes remained closed, his head nestled deep within the pillow.

"Ordinarily I'd never be so brazen," she rushed on, determined that he wouldn't think her a sinful, immoral woman. "But I'm afraid I'm in a terrible quandary." Her voice picked up tempo, as she interpreted his continued silence as a hopeful sign. "You see, if I don't make the required improvements on my land within a year, I can't claim title to my homestead. To be blunt, Mr. Claxton, I need a man. That's why I think it was fate—you know, the way I found you in my stream. I dragged you back to the soddy, and worked day and night to save your life—although I suppose most of the credit should go to Little Fawn and Laughing Waters. Nevertheless, I worked just as hard, and if it hadn't been for Letty needing my help so desperately, why, I would never have dreamed of leaving you here alone . . . to die. . . ." She paused and sighed. "But, of course, you didn't die, and I'm tremendously grateful you didn't. Now" —she paused again for air, preparing to make her next recitation in one long breath— "you'll find I work hard, cook decently, bathe regularly, and make a good companion." She hurried to the side of the bed and sat down, sounding more enthusiastic as she explained her plan. "You see, I figure if you'd be so kind as to marry me, then at the end of the year, I can claim my land and you can be on your way."

Beau's eyes remained closed, and she prayed he hadn't fallen asleep. "Of course, I realize I'm asking you to spend the whole winter here, but I think it will take a while for you to fully regain your strength. In the meantime we can make the needed improvements on my land. Naturally, I'm prepared to pay you well for your time and effort," she promised. "While I'm not a rich woman, I do have a small nest egg, and I can assure you I'll see that your generosity is handsomely rewarded." She paused, leaning closer to see if he was listening at all. She couldn't tell. "It wouldn't take very long, and I'd be most grateful for your assistance."

Beau's left eye opened very slowly.

Charity held her breath. If he refused, she wasn't sure what she'd do next.

Both eyes opened wide, staring at her in disbelief. "Marry you!"

"Yes." Her smile began to wilt as she realized she might have been a bit hasty in revealing her plan. Maybe she should have waited a few days, let him get to know her better. . . . "I realize this may have come as a bit of a shock, but you see, Beau—"

"Mr. Claxton," he interrupted curtly.

Her chin tilted stubbornly as she ignored his frosty attitude. After all, she understood this might be disconcerting for him. She *was* a complete stranger. "Mr. Claxton, I'm afraid my unfortunate circumstances have forced me to come directly to the point, though to be honest, I don't know any other way to be. Now, I've been truthful by revealing to you why I'd make such an unusual suggestion, and, while I can't fault you for being taken by surprise, I don't think you have the right to act like I've escaped from an asylum for the insane. It's just that I'm . . . desperate." Her tone had gone from meek to pleading.

Beau found the sudden turn of conversation incredible. "Let me understand . . . you're *seriously* asking me—a complete stranger, a man you know nothing about—to marry you?"

How ludicrous, he thought. Why, for all this woman knew, he could be a worthless drifter, a debaucher, a hired killer, and there she sat innocently offering to be his wife—and pay him for the privilege?

"I am, indeed," Charity stated firmly. "I need a man."

He shook his head with a frown. "Can't you find someone to—"

"I don't *need* a man, not in that way," she shot back, her face flushing scarlet with his bold insinuation. "I need a man's strength, not his . . . you know. . . ."

"No, I *don't* know. Why in the world would you ask a complete stranger to marry you? Are you addlebrained?" Now that Beau had regained his composure, he was angry. A woman should never ask a man to marry her, no matter *what* the circumstances.

"I'm not addlebrained, and I told you why," she returned calmly. "I don't want to lose my land, and I'm going to unless I come up with a man soon."

"So you propose marriage to the first man you meet?"

"You're not the first man I've met. You're

just the first *available* man I've met," she corrected.

The baby began to fret, and Charity rose to pick her up. "Besides, you're not a stranger—not really. In fact, I feel rather close to you." There wasn't an inch of his body she wasn't already familiar with, and the thought of his masculine, naked physique made her stomach turned fluttery. "I know your name is Beau Claxton, and I also know that once you've recovered from your accident, you'll be a strong, healthy man—healthy enough to clear land and set fence posts and drive a team of oxen. I know you come from Missouri, you're widowed, and, because of your injuries, you're going to be laid up here for a while." Charity turned and smiled at him. "That's all I need to know, Mr. Claxton."

"This is the most ridiculous thing I've ever heard." The woman *had* to be addlebrained, Beau thought irritably. "You don't know a thing about me, and I just told you, I don't plan on ever marrying again, let alone to a woman I've just met."

"Are you refusing my offer?" She had the sinking feeling he was.

He looked at her again in disbelief. "Of course I am."

"Oh. You won't at least think about it?"

Beau shut his eyes again, trying to dismiss the entire unpleasant conversation. He felt obligated to her for saving his life, but not enough to marry her. "Certainly not."

The room grew silent for a moment as Charity tried to digest his words. He wasn't going to marry her, that was plain as the nose on her face. Well, she hadn't wanted to take advantage of the situation, but he was leaving her little choice.

Beau glanced over at the rocker and found his temper simmering again. She had no right to ask him to marry her, but that damn whipped-dog look on her face annoyed him even more. "Look, if you're so desperate for a husband, what about Mary Kathleen's father? Seems to me he could sure use a wife right about now." The silence had grown ominously thick.

"Ansel?" Charity looked up in surprise. She had never considered Ansel. He'd be the logical choice, but it would be months before he could think of taking another wife. No, she quickly discarded the idea. Ansel was out of the question. She needed a man *right now.*

"No, Ansel isn't my answer." Charity hated to resort to underhanded tactics, but it seemed clear she'd have to force Beau's hand. At this point she wasn't above double-dealing.

"Then I'm afraid you're up a creek without a paddle," Beau predicted.

"I guess so, but I figure you're in about the same shape."

Beau looked at her sternly. "I don't see how you figure that."

"Well, if you won't at least consider my proposal, I'll have no other choice than to turn you over to Little Fawn and Laughing Waters."

Beau's eyes widened. "Those two women who—"

"The Indian squaws who took care of you in my absence," she confirmed, feeling almost shameful for being so mean. Almost. "They're very enamored of you, you know. I had a terrible time convincing them you're my . . . man. They feel they have a certain claim to you since they had a part in saving your life."

"I'll be damned if they do!" Beau's chin jutted stubbornly. This mess was growing more ridiculous by the moment.

"I know it's disconcerting." Her tone was soothing, but she planned to be just as heartless as he if he wouldn't cooperate. "But I'm afraid if you don't marry me, then I'll have no alternative but to give you back to them. They're returning Sunday, you know, and I'll just tell them you're not my man after all. They'll take you back to their camp, nurse you back to full health, and then—" Charity's eyes narrowed, and her voice dropped ominously low— "you'll be on your own, Mr. Claxton, because they *both* want you for a husband." All traces of pleasantness had suddenly evaporated. She straightened her back with a satisfied smile. "Of course, if you'd prefer being a husband to Laughing Waters and Little Fawn to staying here and helping me save my land, then I suppose there's no point in talking."

Feeling he had to get out fast, Beau struggled to the side of the bed. As he sat up, his head suddenly started spinning, and he felt so weak he couldn't keep his balance. He groaned and toppled back on the pillow. If those two squaws got hold of him again, he didn't know what he'd do. He didn't have the strength to outrun them . . . and yet, by the same token, he refused to be cornered like a damn rat by this woman!

"I could still die," he threatened.

"Oh, I don't think so. You've already missed your chance. Besides, I can't understand why you find marrying me so offensive. You obviously don't have anything else to do; you said so yourself."

"This is blackmail, you know." His voice was muffled in the pillow. "And I'll be damned if I'm going to let you get away with it!"

"Suit yourself." Charity walked to the rocker and sat down. She gently rocked the baby back and forth as she hummed "Dixie."

She knew she had him. He was sensible enough, she thought, just a mite stubborn, that was all. When he thought it over, he'd prefer marrying her to facing his fate with Laughing Waters and Little Fawn.

"I mean it!" Beau eyed her sternly. He was sitting up again, his head bobbing weakly back and forth. It didn't take much for him to see that she hadn't given up yet. She was a mean, pigheaded woman. "I'm not marryin' anyone, let alone two crazy squaws or an addlebrained girl."

"We'll see. You do know what day this is, Mr. Claxton?"

Actually, he didn't have any idea. "No."

"Saturday." Charity sent him a smug look. She should be ashamed of herself; he was still very ill and could do little about the circumstances facing him. But she was desperate, and he was the only available man she knew.

"So?"

"Big Father's Day is tomorrow." She began humming softly.

Beau slumped back on the pillow, her words sinking in. He vaguely recalled the two Indian women saying they'd return on "Big Father's Day."

Tomorrow was Sunday.

His hand absently touched his hair as he remembered how the Indian squaws had constantly fussed over him. Damn. His gaze shot back to Charity, and he saw that she was ignoring him.

Well, fine. Let her, he thought. She could threaten all she wanted, but she couldn't make him marry her. She was bluffing, that was all.

Just bluffing, and he wasn't about to fall for it.

Chapter 10

The next morning the sun rose earlier than Beau would have liked. He'd lain awake most of the night, trying to figure a way out of this entrapment. Sleep would have been impossible anyway: the baby had screamed the entire night.

Beau had to admit he felt sorry for Charity. She'd paced the floor, trying everything she could think of to quiet the baby. Nothing had worked. The infant had only stiffened in anger and cried all the harder.

The birds outside the soddy began to chirp noisily when Mary Kathleen finally dropped into an exhausted slumber. Charity placed the infant in the small crib she'd fashioned from a drawer and tiptoed to the rocker, dropped numbly into it, and fell into a sound sleep.

Beau lay quietly staring at Charity, feeling renewed resentment at the predicament she'd gotten him into. Still, he couldn't say he didn't feel sympathy for her own unpleasant predicament.

Stranded on the Kansas frontier with a seriously injured man and a baby who wasn't hers didn't seem rightly fair. With her tending his needs and the baby's, she'd barely had time for her other chores.

And not only did he sympathize with her, he was beginning to feel guilty because he'd permitted her to sleep in the rocker the past two nights, allowing him the luxury of the soft, straw-filled mattress.

Of course, neither of them had gotten any rest, he recalled, what with the baby crying all the time.

As he watched Charity awaken and begin to move around in the soddy, it occurred to him again how unjust it was that so much misery could fall on one woman. However, he wasn't about to let compassion overrule common sense. Her marriage proposal was out of the question.

While he could pity her plight, he wouldn't permit himself to become part of it.

And as far as her threatening him with those Indian squaws was concerned, she was downright crazy if she believed she could *scare* him into marrying her.

She wouldn't actually turn him over to them, and he knew it. He figured no one would be that callous. He was a sick man, unable to defend himself. No matter what, she wouldn't do that to him.

As soon as he was able, he was going to hightail it out of here and head for Missouri. At least the women back there were sane.

Charity served Beau his breakfast, and they both carefully avoided the subject of marriage. Still, Beau kept one ear tuned to the door, listening for signs of Laughing Waters and Little Fawn.

He agreed to keep an eye on the baby while Charity went to the stream for fresh water.

After she returned with the buckets full, she set out to gather chunks of dried dung left by grazing cattle and buffalo. The chips would be fuel for the cooking stove, along with dry twigs, tufts of grass, hay twists, woody sunflower stalks, and anything else she could find to burn.

Later, while Beau and Mary Kathleen napped, Charity built a fire outside the soddy and set a large black kettle over it. With a bar of lye soap and a washboard, she scrubbed the baby's diapers, then hung them to dry.

Normally she'd never dream of washing on Sunday, but this Sunday was different. She had very few diapers for Mary Kathleen, and the baby's needs came first.

By the time Charity had finished the wash, the baby was awake and demanding to be fed again.

"I'll do that," Beau offered, as Charity warmed the bottle and bounced the baby on her hip to still her hungry cries.

Charity glanced at him gratefully, her hair hanging limply in her face. "Are you sure you feel up to it?"

"I'll manage."

Beau thought it was the least he could do. He didn't suppose Charity felt much better than he did after the morning she'd put in.

When Charity placed the baby in Beau's arms, Mary Kathleen quieted down immediately. "She seems to like you." She handed him the warm bottle of milk and tucked Mary Kathleen's blankets around her snugly.

"You're gonna squeeze the life out of her," Beau complained. "Give her room to breathe." He began loosening the blanket, and Charity could have sworn Mary Kathleen heaved a sigh of relief.

"I don't want her to take a chill," Charity fretted.

"She won't. Babies don't need so much mollycoddlin'." When Beau put the bottle in the baby's mouth, she began nursing hungrily.

"She's real cute, don't you think?" she asked.

The woman always smelled fresh and

lemony . . . and feminine, Beau thought as Charity leaned over his shoulder and peered at the baby with maternal pride. He studied Mary Kathleen's wrinkled, reddish face and decided it reminded him of a scarlet prune. "Not really . . . but she might be, given a few more weeks."

"Oh, what would you know about babies?" Charity teased as she moved to the stove and began preparing their dinner.

"I told you: my brother Cole, and his wife, Wynne, have a baby." Charity noticed a tenderness lit his eyes when he talked about his family. "Jeremy must be gettin' nigh on to three years old now."

"Do they live in Missouri?"

"They have a piece of land not far from my place."

"Is your brother taking care of your farm while you're gone?"

"He said he would." He gazed down at Mary Kathleen thoughtfully. "Don't you think someone should see about getting the baby's father to assume his responsibility?" Beau didn't think it was fair for Mary Kathleen's father to have waltzed off and left the baby with Charity, even if he was grieving over his wife. If his and Betsy's baby had lived, Beau was certain he'd have seen to its care.

"I thought Ansel would be here by now." She sank down wearily in a chair by the kitchen table and began peeling potatoes. "I'll ride over to his place this afternoon while the baby's napping—"

There was a sudden knock on the door and both Charity and Beau looked up.

"Maybe that's Ansel now." Charity hurried to the door, and Beau held his breath, praying it wouldn't be Laughing Waters and Little Fawn.

When Charity found Ansel on her doorstep, hat in hand, a pleasant smile on his face, she gave a sigh of relief. "Ansel, where in the world have you been?" Her voice sounded more critical than she'd intended, but she was bone tired.

"Morning, Miss Charity. I hope I'm not disturbin' you?"

"Of course you're not disturbing me," Charity said curtly. "I've been worried about you, Ansel. Where have you been?"

"Worried about me?" Ansel looked at her blankly. "Why?"

"Why? Because you rode off yesterday and left Mary Kathleen with me."

"Who?"

"Mary Kath—oh, never mind. Come in, Ansel." Charity ushered him into the soddy and closed the door. She could explain the selection of the baby's name later.

Ansel saw Beau lying in the bed and

glanced back at Charity with a puzzled look. "Didn't know you had company."

"Company?" Charity eyes darted around the room expectantly. "I don't have company."

Ansel's gaze returned to Beau accusingly. "Who's he?"

Charity glanced at Beau, then back to Ansel. "He's the man I found in the stream." Charity was more confused than ever by Ansel's odd behavior. It was as if he'd forgotten all about the stranger. "You know—the one the wolf attacked?" *And the one you left* ME *to bury,* she wanted to add but didn't.

Ansel walked to the table and sat down, seeming to dismiss Beau for the moment. "It's cold out this morning."

"Ansel, are you all right?" Charity moved to the table and knelt beside his chair. "I've been so worried. Where have you been?"

"Been? Why, I've been at home, why?"

"Home . . . well, I've wondered . . . Are you sure you're all right?"

Ansel looked at her and smiled. "Yes, Letty, I'm just fine. How are you today?"

"I'm fine." She frowned. She'd noticed he had called her Letty. "And the baby's fine, Ansel. Would you like to hold your daughter?"

Ansel's face brightened. "Why, yes, I think that would be nice."

Charity felt encouraged. This was the first

time Ansel had shown any sign of wanting to hold his daughter. She hurried to the bed to retrieve Mary Kathleen from Beau's arms.

Charity hurriedly introduced Ansel to Beau, who'd been watching the exchange with interest.

"I know you'll be glad to hear Mr. Claxton is doing fine now. When I got back, I discovered he was being nursed by Little Fawn and Laughing Waters—I think I've mentioned them to you before. The two women happened to find Mr. Claxton and knew exactly what to do." Charity settled Mary Kathleen in Ansel's arms. "There now, isn't she beautiful?"

Ansel looked down at the tiny bundle in his arm, his face growing tender with emotion. "Oh, she's real pretty."

"She truly is." Mary Kathleen opened her eyes and stared at her father angelically. He returned her smile and hesitantly reached to touch his forefinger to her rosy cheeks. "She looks like you, Letty. Just like you," he whispered softly.

Charity wasn't sure if he was speaking to her or his deceased wife. "Yes, she does look exactly like Letty. She has the same eyes, the same color of hair. . . . Letty would be proud," Charity acknowledged tenderly.

"Yes, yes, she would." Then, as quickly as he'd accepted the baby, Ansel handed Mary

Kathleen back to Charity and stood up. "Well, I mustn't overstay my welcome. My chores need tendin'."

"You're always welcome, Ansel, but I understand your wanting to get back home." She began gathering the baby's belongings. "She's a bit fussy at night, but I think you'll get along fine. She's been eating about every two—"

The sound of the front door slamming shut caused Charity to whirl around in disbelief.

The room was empty, except for Beau and herself—and Mary Kathleen. Charity faced Beau. "Where'd he go?"

He shrugged.

Charity raced to the door and jerked it open just in time to see Ansel's buckboard rattling out of the yard. "Hell and damnation! What in tarnation is wrong with that man?" Charity slammed the door shut, making the baby jump with fright. Mary Kathleen puckered up like a thundercloud and began squalling.

Beau tried to quiet the baby while Charity stormed around the soddy, mumbling under her breath about the injustices of life. She slammed the iron skillet on the stove and angrily dug a large spoon of lard from a can and flung it into the pan.

"I *can't* imagine *who* he thinks he is to leave

me with his baby! I *can't* take care of a baby
and fix fences and drive oxen and—Letty was
my friend, but there's a point—*hell* and damnation!" Charity irritably questioned Ansel's
sanity—and her own—as she chopped potatoes and onions and dropped them into the
sizzling fat.

Beau managed to calm Mary Kathleen but
left Charity alone. He figured only a fool
would try to talk to her now.

He had no idea what was going on, but it
was plain to him that Ansel wasn't in full control of his faculties.

The realization did little to soothe Beau's
jangled nerves.

If Ansel Latimer had gone off the deep end
because of his wife's death, Beau was going to
be left as the only candidate to help Charity
save her land, and that grim prospect made
him even more uneasy.

As if she understood his turmoil, Mary
Kathleen burst into tears again.

Beau heaved a weary sigh as Charity sent a
bowl clattering on the table and began mixing
a batch of cornbread, still mumbling heatedly
under her breath.

"I know just how you feel," he confided to
the baby dryly. "It's a hell of a mess, isn't it?"

And, as if he didn't have enough trouble,
Laughing Waters and Little Fawn appeared
right after dinner.

Chapter 11

Laughing Waters and Little Fawn arrived in their usual unpretentious manner.

Beau had just drained the last of his coffee when the front door to the soddy opened wide. Heart plummeting, he stared mutely at the dark outline of two large squaws silhouetted starkly against the noonday sun.

Both women had their arms piled high with firewood.

The memory of Charity's earlier threat closed in on him: *If you won't marry me, I'll have no other choice but to hand you over to Laughing Waters and Little Fawn. . . . They are enamored of you. . . . They both want you for their husband. . . .*

"Laughing Waters, Little Fawn, how nice to see you!" Charity turned from washing dishes to cast a pointed look at Beau. Wiping her sudsy hands on her apron, she stepped forward to greet the two women.

"We come. See Gold Hair." Little Fawn stated their purpose, and Laughing Waters's stern, austere expression reinforced it.

"Well, how nice. Please come in." Charity smiled pleasantly at Beau as she reached for her shawl hanging on the hook beside the door.

Beau shot her a warning look, but she ignored him. "While you visit with Mr. Claxton, I'll feed the chickens and gather the wash."

"Charity!" The sound of her name snapped authoritatively across the room.

"Yes?" Charity faced Beau with a look of wide-eyed innocence.

"You have company. It's not proper for you to go gather the wash." Though his voice remained firm, there was a distinct plea in it as well. "Besides, the baby will be wakin' up anytime now."

"Little Fawn and Laughing Waters aren't here to see me." She paused to tie the strings on her sunbonnet. "They've come to visit you, Gold Hair," she pronounced carefully, "and don't worry, I'll listen for the baby. You just go right ahead and enjoy your visit." She smiled graciously at the two squaws. "Make yourselves at home, ladies."

Laying their bundles of wood by the doorstep, the squaws solemnly entered the soddy and stood by silently as Charity reached for her egg basket. Knowing the women had brought wood as a gift to please Beau, Charity smiled at them. "The wood is nice. I'll see that Gold Hair is warmed by it."

Beau couldn't believe Charity was callous enough to desert him! "Charity . . . now, wait a minute!"

"Papoose asleep?" Laughing Waters asked suddenly.

"Yes, she's sleeping soundly. Would you like to see her?" Charity invited.

The squaws edged toward the table where Charity had placed the baby's makeshift crib. Intently their dark eyes surveyed the infant until their curiosity was satisfied, then they slipped back to stand quietly at the doorway.

"Well, I'd best get to my chores," Charity announced.

As soon as Charity slipped out the door, Little Fawn, with a wide grin, began creeping toward the bed.

Beau winced, realizing he'd just been unsympathetically thrown back to the wolves.

Gold Hair heap better, Little Fawn was thinking, rejoicing that Beau was no longer so pale. He looked healthier now, and he was still handsomer and stronger than any other warrior. Her dark eyes moved to Beau's hair, and her fingers wiggled involuntarily, itching to touch the soft yellow mass.

While the men of other tribes let their hair grow long, it was the custom of Kaw men to shave their heads, leaving only a well-curved tuft on the crown where they could wear their warrior's eagle feathers.

Only when grieving a death would a tall, raw-boned Kaw suffer his hair to grow as proof of his inconsolable sorrow. But Little Fawn had never once seen such striking golden hair on any man. Her heart beat faster with anticipation. Soon, Swift Buck with Tall Antlers would be hers, and she would give thanks to Wah-kun-dah, the "All Powerful," for sending her such a fine, strong brave.

Beau saw the possessive light in Little Fawn's eyes, and began to draw back into his pillow defensively.

The squaw's toothless grin always made him uneasy. He knew something about his hair fascinated the two, but he wasn't sure what.

"Now, don't you go messin' with my hair," he warned in a voice that brooked no nonsense.

"Gold Hair speak! See! See! Gold Hair speak!" Laughing Waters quickly joined Little Fawn at Beau's bedside, and the two smiled down at him.

"Ohhhh, Gold Hair heap better," Laughing

Waters proclaimed, thinking it wouldn't be
long now before she and Little Fawn could
take Brave Horse With Many Wounds back to
their camp. Laughing Waters eyed Beau
proudly. She knew that White Sister claimed
Gold Hair, but the two squaws, after much
discussion, had decided that would change.

They reasoned that they'd helped save
Gold Hair's life; therefore, he belonged to
them as much as he belonged to White Sister.

Laughing Waters and Little Fawn had been
without a man's protection for too long.
Speckled Eye, Little Fawn's husband, had
died of smallpox during the past winter.
Handsome Bird, Laughing Waters's husband,
had ridden off on a buffalo hunt three years
before and never returned.

The squaws had made a pact. They weren't
going to relinquish their claim to this male
just because White Sister wanted him too.

No, Gold Hair was theirs by all rights, and
they planned to have him. So they'd con-
cocted a clever plan.

Everything was set. They'd make Gold
Hair drunk, then carry him off to their camp
before he knew what was happening.

The plan was a simple one, and it had
nearly worked on at least one other occasion.

But this time, it couldn't fail.

If White Sister tried to prevent them from
taking Gold Hair, they would run like the

wind, and Laughing Waters and Little Fawn knew Charity wouldn't be swift enough to overtake them.

Then Gold Hair would be theirs.

"We bring you gift," Little Fawn announced.

"Now listen, ladies." Beau knew he had to put a stop to their ambitious interest and quickly, or he could find himself running around half naked, hunting buffalo for the rest of his life. "I don't want to hurt your feelings, but—"

Laughing Waters slyly withdrew a bottle from beneath her red blanket and handed it to him. "We bring *pi-ge-ne.* Make you heap better!"

Beau cautiously took the bottle of amber liquid and examined it closely. "What's this?"

Little Fawn proudly displayed another toothless grin. *"Pi-ge-ne*—firewater!"

"Whiskey?"

Laughing Waters and Little Fawn bobbed their heads enthusiastically.

"Where'd you get this?"

"Trade pony and two buffalo robes," replied Little Fawn.

Beau couldn't deny that a shot of whiskey would ease his pain and anxiety, but he knew he couldn't accept their gift. He had a feeling there'd be strings attached. He quickly handed the bottle back to Little Fawn. "Listen, I appreciate the thought, but I can't drink this."

In unison their faces fell. "You no like *pi-ge-ne*?" Little Fawn asked.

"Sure, I like," Beau hedged, "but I can't accept your gift."

"White Sister no like *pi-ge-ne*?" Laughing Waters prodded.

"Yeah, that's it. White Sister no like *pi-ge-ne*."

Why not pin the blame on Charity, he decided. After all, if it hadn't been for her, he wouldn't be in this mess. She wasn't listening, so what could it hurt? He figured if he let the squaws think he belonged to "White Sister," they'd be on their way and out of his hair. Literally.

Little Fawn turned to Laughing Waters, her eyes frankly puzzled. "Gold Hair no want *pi-ge-ne*."

The gift had cost them one pony and two buffalo robes, no small sacrifice for two lone women.

Beau could see the squaws were distressed by his lack of gratitude, and he began to feel guilty. Despite their absurd infatuation with him, he had to admit that if it hadn't been for their dedicated care, he'd probably be dead by now. They'd been good enough to stay with him in Charity's absence, applying the healing poultices to his wounds, stoking the damn fire until it'd nearly melted the walls, and here he was, treating them unsociably.

The least he could do was take a drink of their "*pi-ge-ne*" to show his appreciation. But he'd make it clear from the start: the idea that he belonged to them because they'd saved his life was totally out of the question.

"Okay ladies, now listen. I'll drink your *pi-ge-ne*, but I'm not going to marry either one of you." Surely, he thought, if he were brutally frank, there'd be no misunderstanding.

The squaws looked at each other, startled that he knew of their intent. "White Sister tell," Little Fawn whispered sharply to Laughing Waters.

"She no fair," Laughing Waters complained. Dark eyes suddenly riveted on Beau as Laughing Waters immediately turned sullen. "Gold Hair no be husband to Little Fawn and Laughing Waters?"

"No," said Beau firmly. "I'm beholden to both of you for savin' my life, but as soon as I'm able, I'll be movin' on. I'm not going to marry anyone."

"No be husband to White Sister?" Little Fawn asked, reluctant to abandon hope of snaring this fine brave.

"No, no be husband to White Sister," Beau confirmed, noticing the squaws' faces swiftly light with renewed expectation. *"No be husband to anyone,"* he stated. "But if it will make you feel any better, we'll drink some of the *pi-ge-ne*, then you can be on your way," he offered in a more conciliatory tone.

It was as charitable as he could be, under the circumstances.

"Drink *pi-ge-ne*." Little Fawn nodded enthusiastically at Laughing Waters, and her sister's head bobbed cheerfully.

Now they were getting somewhere.

The squaws weren't ignorant of the effect strong liquor could have on Gold Hair. They knew firewater would not only make him docile and willing to accompany them to their camp, but Laughing Waters and Little Fawn knew the *pi-ge-ne* could make a man amorous, a condition they would not be at all averse to in Gold Hair's case.

"Heap good, Gold Hair. You like." Laughing Waters snapped the cork off the bottle with her gums and grinned as she handed the bottle to Beau.

He accepted the bottle cautiously. "One drink, then you go . . . and not come back," he added.

Little Fawn and Laughing Waters nodded agreeably.

Keeping his eyes trained on the squaws, Beau wiped the rim of the bottle with the corner of the sheet, then carefully tipped it to his lips and took a swig. The strong whiskey brought a rush of tears to his eyes as he took a couple of swallows. Slowly, he lowered the bottle.

"Heap good?"

"He-a-p g-o-od," Beau agreed, his voice breaking off in a suffocating strangle. He rolled to his side to catch his breath.

The squaws grinned knowingly at each other. Little Fawn handed the bottle to Laughing Waters, who promptly took a long, noisy swill.

When it was Little Fawn's turn, she drank deeply, and Beau was astounded at their amazing tolerance. Neither of them had even blinked an eye.

"Good!" Little Fawn wiped her mouth with the back of her hand and extended the bottle to Beau again, who by now had recovered his composure.

He took the bottle and carefully wiped the rim again. He hoped the second swig would go down easier than the first.

The warmth of the liquor snaked its way down his throat pleasantly, and he could feel his veins begin to hum.

He glanced out the window and saw Charity throwing corn to the chickens.

Smugly, he thought how shocked she was going to be when she discovered how easily he'd outfoxed her and the two squaws. She really thought she'd backed him to the wall with her threats of "marry me or else." He smirked. Well, once more, he'd proved you couldn't tangle with Beau Claxton and come out on top. At least, not a puny little woman like Charity Burkhouser.

The bottle made the rounds again, and by the time Beau had drunk his fill a third time, he was relaxed and enjoying himself.

"*Pi-ge-ne* good, Gold Hair?" Little Fawn couldn't resist reaching out and touching Beau's hair.

He drew back defensively, but the liquor was beginning to make him feel mellow, so he tried to be diplomatic. "Don't touch my hair, ladies." He flashed them both a winning grin. "Just drink your firewater and leave my hair alone."

Laughing Waters grinned. "Goooood *pi-ge-ne*, Gold Hair?"

Beau's grin was a bit uneven. "Yeah, not bad." He blinked, noticing his words seemed slurred. But when Little Fawn handed him the bottle again, he decided he'd imagined it. Actually, he felt better than he had in months. He gave the squaws a lopsided grin. "Thank youuu, laaadies. You are most kind." He winked at them, his blue eyes shining, then tipped the bottle and took another long swallow.

A few minutes later, Little Fawn's hands

crept up to touch his hair again. This time he smiled tolerantly, deciding he didn't mind her affections all that much. So she wanted to touch his hair, what could it hurt?

"Pretty," Little Fawn cooed.

"Thanks." His eyes locked on the sway of her massive bosom, and he felt a hint of uneasiness. Damn, was he getting drunk? The squaw was beginning to look good to him—at least, from the neck down.

In another ten minutes the bottle was empty.

Where'd those ugly squaws disappear to? Beau wondered. In their place were two beautiful Indian maidens, with hair as black as night and dark mysterious eyes that made his blood sing.

They sat by his bed, smiling and twining locks of his golden hair between their nimble fingers. Beau felt a quick, long-suppressed tightening in his loins.

"Wheeers Liitle Fwam and Laughin' Waters?" he asked, grinning stupidly at the lovely apparitions that had magically appeared from nowhere.

They were the most exquisite creatures he'd ever seen!

Little Fawn and Laughing Waters looked at each other, covered their mouths, and giggled girlishly.

As they'd planned, the firewater had paid back its cost.

At this moment the *pi-ge-ne* was worth more than *four* ponies and *six* buffalo robes to them.

Chapter 12

Charity was beginning to feel guilty about leaving Beau with the squaws. Although she was desperate for a man's help, her conscience told her it hadn't been right to leave him to the mercy of Little Fawn and Laughing Waters.

Her hand dipped into the corn bucket. As she scattered the kernels on the sunbaked ground, she admitted she'd been heartless to threaten him with the squaws if he didn't marry her.

Ferrand would have been ashamed of such underhanded tactics. He'd always said a person was only as good as he was honest. Charity had to face it; she'd seriously jeopardized her integrity lately.

She'd apologize to Beau for behaving so

brazenly. Furthermore, she'd assure him that she wouldn't hinder his return to Missouri, once he'd recovered.

Perhaps she would even consider asking Ansel Latimer to marry her. She knew he was strong and kind. After he weathered the initial shock of losing Letty, he'd need someone to help him raise Mary Kathleen, and Charity would love the child as dearly as if it were her own.

But in truth, Charity knew a marriage to Ansel would be disappointing. He'd never make her stomach turn upside down the way Ferrand had. No, she thought, no one would ever give her that delicious, giddy feeling again, and she might as well accept that.

Ferrand could just smile a certain way, and her pulse would race with heady anticipation. . . .

But Ansel would be good to her, and she knew Letty would be pleased to know Charity was raising her daughter—her thoughts broke off and she glanced up as she heard a door open.

She stared open mouthed, watching Laughing Waters and Little Fawn haul Beau out of the cabin spread eagle. His backside nearly dragged along the ground, and he had a silly, stupefied grin on his face.

The corn pail rattled to the ground as Charity sprinted toward the soddy.

The squaws wasted no time in their wily escape, their short, squatty legs pumping, their flat feet thundering across the crusty ground.

"Hold it!" Charity skidded to a stop and brought her hands to her hips, sternly.

At the sound of Charity's voice both squaws glanced her way but made no effort to slow their rapid departure up the hillside.

Beau grinned at Charity and waved happily. " 'Lo, Mrs. Burkhouser!"

"Ladies! I said, wait a minute!" Charity's feet went back into motion when she realized the squaws had no intention of stopping. She couldn't imagine what was going on.

She'd been fully aware that Little Fawn and Laughing Waters were smitten with Beau, but she'd had no idea they'd carry their whimsy to this appalling extent!

And Beau! Beau not only appeared unconcerned about his abduction, but it looked to Charity as if he was a willing participant in the escapade.

"We go, White Sister," Little Fawn puffed over her shoulder. "One sleep, come back," she lied.

Finally overtaking the two, Charity reached out and jerked Laughing Waters to a sudden halt. "Now see here! You can't just come in here and tote this man away like a sack of flour!"

"Gold Hair no mind." Laughing Waters stubbornly planted herself in front of Charity, keeping a firm hold on Beau's bare feet. Charity was relieved to see that the women had at least had the forethought to put trousers on him.

"Well, we'll just ask Gold Hair if he minds or not!" She leaned over Beau's limp body. The strong smell of liquor assaulted her nostrils as he leered up at her drunkenly.

"Hallo there, Mzzz. Bursshouser. Didja feed all them chickens?"

"You're drunk!"

"Me?" Beau looked properly insulted. "I certaaainly am not! I've jusst been havinng a litttle *pi-ja-nnee* with thesse twoo bootuful maidens." He flashed Charity an apologetic grin when he saw she wasn't buying his explanation. "Wall, maybe I have had . . . jest a little too much . . . but they made me—"

"I can't believe this!" Charity confronted the two squaws again, her sudden anger making red flags bloom high on her cheeks. "You carry him back into the house—immediately!"

Laughing Waters and Little Fawn had no intention of obliging her wish, and their stoic expressions proved it.

"Gold Hair come with us," Laughing Waters proclaimed, lifting Beau's foot as a signal to Little Fawn to move on.

"Hold on." Charity spread her feet and blocked their path. "He can't go with you. I thought I made it clear: Gold Hair is *mine*."

Little Fawn looked to Laughing Waters for direction.

"Gold Hair say he no marry White Sister," Laughing Waters announced.

"But he no marry Laughing Waters or Little Fawn either," Charity reasoned.

"Ladieees, ladieees, don't fight. I no marry any of you," pronounced Beau in a lofty slur.

Charity could see the squaws had their hearts set on having Beau, and she knew he'd give her no assistance in saving himself in his disgusting condition.

It was clear: if Beau were to be delivered from this fiasco, it would be solely up to her. She frantically searched her memory for a bartering tool. She had so little left.

The brooch. Ferrand's grandmother's emerald brooch. It had been his gift to Charity on their wedding day, and Little Fawn and Laughing Waters had admired it extensively since the first day they had discovered it in the tin box she kept under her bed. It was her greatest treasure, but she couldn't idly stand by and let the poor man be abducted this way, especially since he wasn't even aware he was being abducted!

"Ladies, let's hold on a minute. Surely we can come to some satisfactory solution."

The squaws held their ground and watched Charity suspiciously.

"What White Sister mean?"

"I agree you helped save Gold Hair's life, and I suppose you could argue that he is partly yours."

Laughing Waters eyed Beau possessively. "We save Gold Hair. We like. We take."

"But I saved Gold Hair too."

"You leave Gold Hair to meet Wa-kun-dah, alone."

"But I had good reason. I was called away to help the papoose's mother, remember? She was very ill too."

They remembered, but didn't care to.

"Gold Hair heap good man. We want," Laughing Waters repeated sullenly.

"True, that's why I'm prepared to make you a trade."

Little Fawn hurriedly shook her head. "Gold Hair make good papooses. We keep."

Charity glanced at Beau and frowned. "Yes, I'm sure he would . . . but I'm prepared to offer you my brooch. The one in the tin box. Remember how much you liked those pretty green stones? You said they looked like sky sparkling at night?" Charity glanced down at Beau, who was dozing, and scowled. The nerve of the man. His very future hung in the balance, and he was asleep!

Laughing Waters exchanged a dubious look with Little Fawn but then curtly nodded.

Charity smiled sadly. "I will trade you my emerald brooch for Gold Hair."

"Green rocks for Gold Hair?" Little Fawn's eyes immediately lit up. She was a complete fool when it came to bright, shiny things, and White Sister's green rocks sparkled like morning dew on the grass.

Drawing a deep breath, Charity closed her eyes and repeated again, before she lost her nerve, "The brooch for Gold Hair."

Little Fawn and Laughing Waters knew they'd have at least to consider her tempting offer.

"We talk. White Sister stay."

The squaws dropped Beau's limp body in the dust, and he landed with a resounding thud, bringing him wide awake.

"Damn!" Irritably he sat up and rubbed his smarting backside. "What is going on?"

"Serves you right," Charity snapped. "Because of your foolishness, I'm going to have to give up Ferrand's grandmother's brooch."

"Whose what?" Beau was befuddled, and his head was splitting.

"Ferrand's grandmother's . . . oh, never mind." Charity knew he couldn't possibly understand anything in his sorry state. "You'd just better hope they accept the trade or you're in serious trouble, Mr. Claxton!"

Beau looked around him in a daze. "What?" He wished somebody would make some sense. What was he doing sitting in the middle of the road? It was hot, and suddenly he didn't feel well at all.

Charity glanced over worriedly to Laughing Waters and Little Fawn still conferring in hushed tones beneath a large thorn tree.

Occasionally, one would raise her voice, and the other would shake her head and wag her finger angrily.

The tense conversation went on for a full ten minutes, and Charity was beginning to despair. If they refused the brooch, she didn't know how she'd prevent them from taking Beau away.

Beau had curled up in the road and was sound asleep again, blissfully ignorant of what was taking place. Gazing at him sourly, Charity wondered if he was really going to be worth giving up her brooch for.

Finally, Little Fawn raised her arms, shook her hands in the air in exasperation, and stalked away. With a satisfied smile Laughing Waters scurried back to Charity. "We trade Gold Hair for roach."

"Brooch."

Laughing Waters grinned. "Yes. Roach."

Charity heaved a sigh of relief. "Good. And Little Fawn? Does she agree?"

"She no care."

Charity seriously doubted that. "Now, when we make our trade," she warned, "it's final. You must leave Gold Hair alone, for he will be all mine."

"Laughing Waters no see Gold Hair again?"

"That's right, and Little Fawn must agree to relinquish her claim as well."

Laughing Waters thought for a moment, then smiled agreeably. "Me tell Little Fawn: Gold Hair White Sister's. We no take."

"Very well."

They reached down in unison and picked up Beau's feet and hands.

"We make good trade," Laughing Waters proclaimed proudly as they started carrying Beau's limp body back to the soddy; but Charity found it hard to be as optimistic.

After all, she had just given away her prized brooch, and she wasn't one inch nearer to saving her land.

But at least her integrity was back in place, and for that, she was grateful.

Chapter 13

The old rooster stretched, flapped his wings, and loudly crowed in another new day. Mellow rays of dappled sunlight spilled through the window of the soddy, spreading a warm golden path across the wooden floor.

With a groan Charity stirred on her pallet, reluctant to face the new morning. She knew it was late, but Mary Kathleen had cried most of the night. Finally the baby had quieted at dawn, giving Beau and Charity their first opportunity to sleep.

Charity willed her eyes open and glanced toward the bed. She was relieved Beau was still sleeping soundly. He was lying on his stomach, his golden hair tousled appealingly like a small boy's. His face was burrowed into the pillow, and his arms were wrapped snugly around it, revealing tight bunches of corded muscles in his forearms.

Her stomach danced about lightly. His sleeping position was a simple, masculine one, and yet somehow, though she had no idea why, it made a slow, languorous warmth spread sweetly through her body.

Memories of making love in the early morning flooded her mind until she struggled to block the stinging reminders. She warned herself it would be sheer tomfoolery to become physically attracted to Beau; still, she couldn't deny that she found him more fascinating every day. After making certain he was fed properly, she couldn't help but feel a twinge of pride as he began to shed his pitiful gauntness, and his body grew strong and sinewy again.

And every day he seemed more thoughtful. They'd taken turns walking the floor with the baby during the night and she'd been so grateful for his help. She thought again how thankful she was to have him around. Trading her emerald brooch had been such a small sacrifice for such a large reward.

A smile curved her mouth again. It had been a month since Laughing Waters and Little Fawn had attempted his abduction. Rolling over, she hugged her pillow to her tightly, her smile widening as she remembered how grateful Beau had been when he'd learned

Charity had intervened and saved him from living like a Kaw brave.

He'd been too intoxicated to know he'd been captured or how Charity had accomplished his release. He couldn't remember anything beyond the first few swallows of potent *pi-ge-ne* he'd shared with the two squaws.

She thought of how sick he'd been afterward. He'd suffered a splitting headache for three days. Of course, she figured it only served him right. She couldn't imagine how he'd gotten drunk enough to let the squaws carry him off with his grinning approval!

She sighed. She couldn't blame Laughing Waters and Little Fawn for their infatuation with Beau Claxton. He was bathed, clean shaven, and breathtakingly handsome now.

He was truly an exceptional man.

And now that he was up and about, getting stronger all the time, Charity was achingly aware of how handsome and masculine he was. His tall, imposing frame loomed over her small one as they moved within the confines of the soddy. Although she warned herself not to, she found herself feeling content and secure again, the way she'd felt when Ferrand had been close by.

At times she caught Beau's blue eyes studying her as if he felt the same sort of contentment—or maybe that was only wishful thinking on her part. Regardless, he was polite and a joy to be with. They'd talk for hours on end, passing Mary Kathleen back and forth between their laps when she became fussy.

It was then that Beau would confide in her how he was looking forward to returning to his family in Missouri. He spoke fondly of his brothers, Cole and Cass, and told her of the stunts they'd pulled together on Willa, their family housekeeper.

He talked about his ma's biscuits and Willa's chicken and dumplings, and how much he loved them both. One evening he asked Charity to help him compose a letter to his family, informing them of his injury, yet assuring them he was healing properly. They moved to the table, and while Beau talked, Charity penned the letter in her neat, legible hand. The following day, Charity made the long ride into Cherry Grove and mailed the letter.

Charity sighed again, recalling how she had felt unusually lonely after that particular conversation.

When Beau had fallen asleep, she'd slipped outside the soddy and sat for a while, listening to the lonely wind on the prairie, broken occasionally by the howl of a coyote or the gentle whish of the tall prairie grass.

She found herself sinking even lower into self-pity as she reviewed her own gloomy circumstances. She missed her mother and father unbearably, and she thought it would be sheer heaven to curl up on her old feather bed beside her sisters, Hope and Faith, and pour her heart out to people who really cared. Then, after a visit with her family, and a good long cry, it would be nice to return to her homestead and find a man like Beau waiting for her.

Perhaps they could never love each other the way they'd loved Ferrand and Betsy, but it wouldn't be hard for her to adjust to living with a man like Beau, with his kind ways and gentle nature. In time, she felt sure their mutual respect could bring them a union that would be, if not passionate, at least comfortable.

Charity opened her eyes again, wondering why she was thinking such nonsense. The very best she could hope for from Beau Claxton would be an act of mercy in her behalf, not love and undying devotion, with a passel of golden-haired babies thrown in.

Still, she knew that once Beau was gone, there'd be a large void in her life again.

The sun went behind a cloud, and the room suddenly turned a dreary gray, as gray and sad as Charity felt this morning. She found herself deliberately dawdling as her mind turned to another weighty problem that only served to drag her sagging spirits even lower.

Something had to be done about Ansel. For the past week he'd visited the soddy daily. Though she hated to admit it, she'd concluded that Letty's death had left Ansel temporarily unstable.

At times he acted as though Charity were Letty. On other occasions he was totally at a loss as to where his wife had gone. He still paid little attention to Mary Kathleen, behaving at times as if he resented the child.

His continuing confusion worried Charity, but she didn't know what to do about it.

Once, she'd thought about asking Ansel to stay with her so she could take care of him until he could cope again, but she knew that would be improper; besides, the soddy couldn't shelter another person besides Beau and the baby.

On top of everything else, Beau's suggestion that she marry Ansel to get the help she needed with her land kept popping into her mind. Apparently, that was her only alternative. Once he returned to his old self, perhaps she could approach him with a reasonable offer of marriage. She realized she was trying desperately to persuade herself that it was the only solution left, since Beau wouldn't marry her.

Ansel was a reasonably young and vital man, and, once he got past the shock of losing Letty, he would be a good provider.

Ferrand surfaced in her mind, Ferrand making love to her during the long cold, winter nights. . . . She admitted she missed that part of her life. She and Ferrand had been shamelessly attracted to each other, making love at the most outrageous times. But performing such an act with another man? The thought was frightening.

Charity rolled to her right side, her eyes drifting over to the man on the bed.

She studied his sleeping form, trying to visualize what it would be like to be Beau Claxton's woman. She felt an ache growing deep within her, a painful reminder of how long it had been since she'd had the pleasure of knowing a man.

She knew she shouldn't be thinking of Beau this way—surely it was sinful, and disrespectful to Ferrand's memory, but her mind seemed bent on tantalizing her.

She imagined lying next to Beau, cradled within his arms. She could almost feel the thick mat of hair on his chest brush against her flushed skin. She thought of his mouth moving on hers, possessively molding and exploring. His hands would excite and demand, lifting her into a storm of passion that would—

A brisk rap on the door interrupted her fantasy. Charity bolted upright and guiltily pulled the blanket up to cover her budded breasts.

Beau stirred on the bed. "Someone's banging on the door," he mumbled after the knock sounded loudly again.

Charity glanced at him and blushed, hoping he couldn't read her mind. "I can't imagine who it would be."

"Better answer it before they wake the baby." He rolled to a sitting position and scratched his head.

He looked so masculine, so tempting, that for a moment Charity could only stare at his chest, the same chest she'd imagined herself being held against. She swallowed dryly.

The rap came again, and Beau glanced up to see what was keeping her. "You want me to get it?"

Charity sprang to her feet, forgetting for the moment that she wore only a thin muslin gown. "Oh . . . no. I'll get it."

Beau eyes reluctantly followed her as she scampered barefoot across the floor and reached for her wrapper hanging on a peg.

His breath caught in his throat as the morning light turned her gown transparent. He warned himself to look away, but found his gaze wanted to linger on the outline of her slender body blatantly displayed through the gossamer fabric. He felt an undeniable stirring of desire. It had been a long time since any woman had aroused him, and he found the feeling pleasant.

His eyes skimmed her high, firm breasts, her slender waist, her shapely thighs. There was a delicate, breathtaking beauty about her he'd never noticed before, and, for an instant, he wondered what it would be like to make love to her.

The idea astounded him. Since the day he'd married Betsy, he'd never speculated about another woman.

Charity was unaware of Beau's scrutiny as she pushed her heavy mass of dark hair over her shoulder and pulled the door open a crack.

Her mouth dropped open when she saw Reverend Olson and his wife standing on her doorstep, smiling at her warmly.

"Good morning, my dear. I hope we're not disturbing you." Reverend Olson's kind face reminded Charity of her father, and she was always glad when the reverend and his wife made their monthly visit.

But not this morning.

Charity was reluctant to reveal Beau's presence. Once the neighbors found that he was staying with her, gossip would be inevitable. As far as she was aware, only Ansel knew about Beau, and she preferred to keep it that way.

Cherry Grove was a small community, and

its residents were unyieldingly straitlaced.
For them, right was right, and wrong was
wrong, and there was no middle ground.

While Charity thought her neighbors
wouldn't judge her harshly for nursing an injured stranger, she knew there would still be
some who'd argue that it wasn't proper for a
man and woman to live under the same roof
without the sanctity of marriage, especially
when the woman happened to be a pretty
young widow like Charity Burkhouser and
the man was a handsome stranger like Beau
Claxton.

"Reverend Olson . . . Mrs. Olson. How
nice to see you." Charity felt trapped. Her
fingers nervously plucked at the collar of her
wrapper. "You must forgive me, I'm afraid
I've overslept this morning."

"We heard you've been quite busy, dear."
Mrs. Olson leaned forward, her blue eyes
twinkling as she spoke in a soft, compassionate tone. "Has your unexpected visitor been
keeping you awake nights?"

Charity smiled lamely. They already knew
about Beau. "Yes . . . some . . . but I don't
mind."

Reverend Olson looked hopeful. "Well,
may we come in to see her?"

"Her?" Charity stared at him vacantly.

"The Latimer babe. We understand you're
caring for Ansel's child." Reverend Olson in-

clined his head. "We were wondering if we might see the little girl."

When she realized they'd come to see Mary Kathleen, Charity felt limp with relief. "Oh . . . of course! But she's still asleep—perhaps you could stop by another time?"

For an instant she'd forgotten her main concern—Beau. If the Olsons came in, they'd find him. And what would they think, she fretted, when they discovered she and Beau were still wearing nightclothes in the middle of the morning?

Reverend Olson glanced from his wife to Charity with a benevolent expression. "I'm afraid that would be most inconvenient, dear. We plan to make several calls today. But I promise we won't take up much of your time, just a few minutes."

"But I'm not dressed."

"We'll wait in the buggy while you get yourself together," Mrs. Olson suggested brightly. It was plain to Charity, the elderly couple would not be easily deterred.

"Yes, well, I'll only be a moment." Charity gave them a hesitant smile, then, closing the door, she sank to the floor in despair.

Now what was she going to do? Reverend Olson and his wife would discover she was caring for a man in her house and then brows would lift with suspicion.

"Who is it?" Beau's voice drifted across the room, breaking into her frantic thoughts.

"It's Reverend Olson and his wife!" The fire in the grate had died, and Charity felt goose bumps rising on her arms. She hurriedly crossed the room to stoke the dying embers into a rosy glow.

"What do they want?" Beau discovered he was strangely disappointed that the wrapper she was wearing concealed her fully now.

"They want to come in and see Mary Kathleen. I don't know how they found out I have her, but they did."

Realizing the impropriety of his presence, Beau asked quietly, "Do you want me to hide?"

She added a couple of logs to the fire and turned back to face him. She knew she couldn't complain about the incriminating position she'd found herself in. It wasn't his fault, and nothing could be done to correct it now. She would just have to bluff her way through the visit and hope for the best. "No, that's impossible. Where could you go? We'd better get dressed. They're waiting."

Ten minutes later Charity opened the door and smiled cheerfully at the reverend and his wife, who were sitting patiently in their buggy. "You may come in."

For the occasion Charity had put on her

best yellow calico and tied a matching ribbon in her hair.

Reverend Olson helped his wife from the buggy, and they hurried toward the soddy.

Rebecca Olson was making lively chatter as they stepped inside. "I just love the crisp snap in the air this morning and the glorious autumn leaves! I saw a field of ripe pumpkins on our ride from town. The reverend just loves pumpkin pie, don't you, dear?"

"My favorite."

Charity clasped her hands tightly and braced herself as Rebecca stopped short and gasped, catching sight of Beau.

Standing in front of the fireplace, he wore a pair of Ferrand's faded denim overalls and a dark cotton work shirt. To Charity he seemed unusually tall and handsome this morning. She suddenly wished he looked fifty years older, six inches shorter, with eyes that were pale and nondescript instead of vivid cornflower blue.

It would make her explanation much more credible.

"Why . . . hello." Rebecca smiled hesitantly and offered her small gloved hand to Beau. "You didn't mention you had company, Charity." The reprimand in her soft voice was unmistakable.

"How thoughtless of me," Charity apologized meekly.

"Good morning, ma'am." Beau stepped forward and took Rebecca's hand. "Pumpkin pie happens to be one of my favorites too." His voice dripped charm like molasses off hot biscuits.

Rebecca glanced at her husband again. "It is difficult not to like pumpkin pie."

Charity took a deep breath, unclasped her hands, and stepped forward.

"Reverend Olson, Rebecca, this is Beau Claxton. He's—he's been my guest for the past two weeks."

"Oh?" Rebecca's smile slowly faded. "Your guest, dear?"

"Yes, you see, Beau had the misfortune of meeting up with a wounded wolf in the stream, and, as a result, he was gravely injured. I've been looking after him until he regains his health." Charity tried to sound breezy and carefree, and as if it were the most natural thing in the world for Beau to remain with her.

Rebecca glanced at her husband. "Oh . . . do tell."

"Why, that must have been a terrible experience. It's a miracle you survived, young man." Reverend Olson reached out to clasp Beau's hand. "I guess that explains the bandages."

"I'm afraid without Mrs. Burkhouser's ex-

cellent care, I wouldn't be here right now,"
Beau admitted.

"Oh, dear." Rebecca's eyes anxiously surveyed the bandages still visible on Beau's
face. "I do hope you're feeling better, Mr.
Claxton."

"Yes." He flashed her a melting smile. "And
please, call me Beau."

Rebecca blushed and her face turned three
shades of rose. "Beau, what a lovely southern
name. Are you from around here?"

"No, ma'am. I'm from Missouri."

"Missouri? How nice. I have a sister in Kansas City." Although the elderly couple was
trying to be cordial, Charity saw the wary
glances Rebecca was sending her husband.
She knew they were unnerved by Beau's
presence.

"Well, my, my, why don't we all sit down
and have a cup of coffee?" Charity invited
nervously, wishing she could smooth over the
uncomfortable situation.

"A cup of coffee would be nice," Reverend
Olson agreed. "But we mustn't stay too long,
Rebecca. We do have other calls to make."

"Yes, dear. We'll only be a minute." Rebecca turned back to Beau. "Exactly where in
Missouri do you come from, Mr. Claxton?"

"It's a small town, River Run—not far from
Springfield." Beau held a kitchen chair for
Rebecca, and she slipped into it graciously.

"Now, we'll only stay a minute," Rebecca reiterated as Charity began to pour coffee. "Claxton . . . Claxton—you wouldn't happened to be kin to the Claxtons of Savannah, would you?"

"As a matter of fact, I am." Beau smiled. "My father's family is from Savannah."

"They are?" Rebecca glanced at the reverend expectantly. "Did you hear that, Reverend? He's a Savannah Claxton."

To Charity's dismay Rebecca's minute proceeded to drag into an hour, then two, and before Charity realized it, suppertime was drawing near.

Rebecca had become enamored of Beau, as throughout the afternoon he entertained her with exciting war tales about his brother and himself and stories of the Savannah Claxtons.

Charity and the reverend shared Mary Kathleen, periodically changing diapers and warming bottles.

While Charity prepared the evening meal, Reverend Olson gave up on an early departure and dozed peacefully in the chair before the fire.

During supper the conversation was cordial, but Charity occasionally caught a renewed note of disapproval about Beau's remaining at the Burkhouser soddy while he recovered.

"The Reverend and I would be happy for

you to stay with us until you're well. Isn't that
right, Reverend?"

"Hummph . . . uh . . . well, of course,
dear." Reverend Olson cleared his throat and
reached for a third biscuit. "Mr. Claxton
would be most welcome to share our home."

Beau glanced at Charity and saw her start
to protest, and he intervened softly. "I surely
do appreciate your offer, Rebecca, but I'd like
to stay here awhile longer. I notice Mrs.
Burkhouser has a few fences down, and I
thought before I went home, I'd help out a bit
to repay her for my keep."

Charity glanced up from her plate in surprise. Their eyes met and held for a moment
as she tried to convey her gratitude. Why
would he do this? Did it mean he actually
planned to stay on and help her with the land,
or was he only trying to pacify the reverend
and Rebecca? Charity felt her pulse increase
its tempo as she smiled at him, and he smiled
back.

"But, Beau, dear. You're not going to be
able to mend fences for weeks." Rebecca was
clearly appalled that he'd consider remaining
with Charity.

"I'm doin' better every day, ma'am, but I
thank you for your concern." Beau's gaze slid
easily away from Charity's and returned to
the food on his plate. "Another week or two
and I should be up to earning my keep."

Charity decided a change of subject was in order and promptly mentioned Ansel Latimer, inquiring whether the Olsons had noticed Ansel's strange behavior since Letty's death.

They said they had, and Charity discovered Ansel had told the Olsons of Mary Kathleen's whereabouts. She was relieved when they devoted the remainder of the supper conversation to that topic.

It was late when the reverend and his wife finally prepared to take their leave. Charity walked them to the buggy, while Beau put Mary Kathleen down for the night.

"He's a fine man," Rebecca remarked. "So tragic about his young wife."

"Yes, he loved Betsy very much."

Reverend Olson helped his wife into the buggy, then ambled around to check the rigging while the two women continued to chat.

Charity wrapped her shawl tighter in the crisp autumn air and smiled. "I'm so glad you stopped by, Rebecca."

"Why, thank you. We didn't intend to take up your whole day."

"We didn't mind at all." Charity was surprised how easily she'd begun to include Beau in her statements.

Rebecca glanced hurriedly toward the front of the buggy. Seeing her husband still busy adjusting the harness, she turned to

Charity. "Dear, I don't know how to say this
. . . but I feel as if I must."

"You know you can say what's in your heart,
Rebecca."

At that moment Reverend Olson walked
back to the buggy. "All ready, dear?"

"Well," Rebecca fretted, "I was about to
remind Charity that while you and I find Mr.
Claxton a perfectly delightful man, there will
most assuredly be others in the congregation
who'll question the propriety of this—this unusual arrangement. Don't you agree, papa?"

"Hummph . . . well, yes, dear, as a matter
of fact, I've been thinking the same thing," he
admitted. He turned to Charity, his faded
eyes growing tender with concern. "Now,
mind you, I'm not judging, but I'm sure
you're aware it isn't proper for two . . . uh
. . . unmarried adults to share the same roof,
no matter how innocent it may be." He
cleared his throat nervously. "Once the town
hears a man is living with you, there will be
talk, Charity, and I'm afraid it will be unkind,
my dear. Mrs. Olson and I don't want to see
that happen."

Charity lifted her chin, and a stubborn light
came into her eyes as she met his gaze. "Talk
doesn't bother me, Reverend."

"I'm aware of that, dear." He knew Charity
Burkhouser was a courageous woman with a
mind of her own, but that wouldn't prevent

the storm of gossip that would surely follow the news that Beau Claxton was living at the Burkhouser soddy. "But we must protect your reputation," he reminded her.

"We're not alone," Charity argued. "I'm taking care of Letty's baby until Ansel returns, and Beau is a sick man. What could we be doing?"

Reverend Olson shook his head sadly. "I'm afraid that's beside the point, dear. There *will* be talk, so I'd like to suggest Mr. Claxton reconsider our offer to stay with us until his recuperation is complete."

Charity lifted her chin a notch higher, determined that gossips wouldn't control her life. "Are you saying you and Rebecca will inform the town about my houseguest?"

"Certainly not!" Rebecca objected, horrified that they'd be accused of such betrayal. "But you know a thing like this will eventually leak out. We're only thinking of you, Charity. We don't want to see you hurt."

Charity's face crumpled like a child's as her brave façade slipped away. "I know . . . but it's so unfair. We aren't doing anything immoral," she insisted in a small voice.

"We know that, but other people won't be as understanding," Reverend Olson predicted. "I want you to promise me you'll talk to Mr. Claxton about moving to our place, soon as possible. I'm sure your secret will be safe for a few more days, but after that . . ."

Charity looked deeply into his eyes and understood he wasn't being self-righteous. He was genuinely concerned for her welfare, and he was right. There would be talk, and it wouldn't be pretty.

"Promise us you'll at least think about it, dear," Rebecca coaxed. "I'll take excellent care of your young man."

Charity swiped embarrassedly at the tears starting to roll down her cheeks, wondering when she'd become such a crying ninny. "All right. I'll speak with Beau about your offer," she conceded.

Reverend Olson patted her on the shoulder and reached into his pocket for a handkerchief. "I think you'll see that it's for the best, dear."

But Charity didn't see it that way. When Beau left, she would be alone.

Again.

Chapter 14

After Charity finished the dishes, she slipped outside to catch a breath of fresh air.

Reverend Olson's advice still drifted in and out of her mind. Moving Beau to the Olsons' residence would be the sensible thing to do, she realized. But could she let him go? She felt an inner peace when he was near, one that had been sadly lacking in her life since Ferrand's death. And if she wasn't mistaken, Beau felt that same harmony.

Should two lonely people be denied a friendship, a mutual understanding, merely to appease others who had nothing more to do than find guilt where there was none?

It seemed unjust to Charity that anyone should take this precious gift away from her. She and Beau weren't hurting anybody, so why, she wondered, should they be denied the pleasure of each other's company for the remaining few weeks before he returned home?

An hour later, Beau found her leaning against a bale of hay, staring up at the stars. "Mind if I join you?"

"No, I was just enjoying the night. It's lovely."

"Yes, it is." He sat, wincing as he slowly eased his injured leg into place.

"Is your leg bothering you today?"

"It stiffens up when I don't move around enough."

"But you're doing so much better." Charity wrapped her shawl snugly around her shoulders. "There's a chill in the air this evening."

"Won't be long till the first snow," he predicted.

An involuntary shiver traveled down her spine at the thought of another winter alone.

Winters in Kansas could be long and harsh, bringing numbing temperatures and unbelievable snowstorms. Charity knew a Kansas blizzard could be a terrifying spectacle. Without warning, dark billowing clouds would roar across the sky, unleashing blinding bursts of snow. The wind and snow could sweep across the plains with the force of a cyclone, taking a heavy toll on livestock and people. Communication with the outside world could be cut off for weeks at a time, and travel was impossible. Nothing moved until hundreds of men could dig openings through the drifts.

She rubbed her hands down her arms to warm them, and turned her thoughts to a more immediate concern. "Is the baby all right?"

"Yes, I think the reverend and his wife wore her out." Beau chuckled and added solemnly, "Thank God."

Charity laughed at his open candor. "I thought you liked children."

"I do, but I was under the impression they slept once in a while."

"Well, I think most of them do, but Mary Kathleen seems to be a bit confused about when she should be doing her sleeping—day or night. But with all the excitement today, we should all be able to get a good night's sleep for a change."

They were silent for a moment, then Beau looked over at her. "What are we going to do about that situation?"

"The baby?"

"Yeah, I don't mean to criticize, but it appears to me that Ansel is a sick man. Doesn't look to me like he's going to be able to care for a baby for a long time."

Charity sighed. "He's troubled, all right."

"Well, what are you going to do? Keep the baby indefinitely?"

"Of course. I promised Letty I'd take care of her child," Charity told him. "Ansel's a good man. Given a little time, he'll get over Letty's death. It was just been so sudden for him."

"I'm not sure that's wise, Charity. You're gettin' mighty attached to the baby. It might be better if he hired someone to care for Mary Kathleen until he's better."

Charity confronted Beau with mock surprise. "*I'm* getting attached? I've noticed she has *you* wrapped snugly around her little finger."

Beau's smile was guilty as sin. "She's cute, all right."

"She's more than cute, and I wouldn't feel right about anyone else taking care of Letty's baby. I love caring for her."

"Seems like a lot of work on top of everything you have to do."

"I don't mind."

They sat in silence for a while, studying the star-studded sky, sharing a contentment that neither of them questioned.

"You're quiet this evening," Beau finally remarked.

"Am I? I guess I'm just thinking."

"Oh? Must be serious," he teased. "Usually you're a real chatterbox."

Charity shrugged good-naturedly. "Nothing profound."

"Your thoughts wouldn't have anything to do with the reverend and his wife, would they?"

Charity glanced up, surprised by his astute perception. "What makes you say that?"

"I noticed they weren't any too happy about me living here with you."

"I expected their disapproval."

"But it bothers you, doesn't it?"

Charity glanced at him shyly. "Well, surely Kansas isn't all that different from Missouri when it comes to morality."

"Morality? No, but we've done nothing to be ashamed of."

"Well, I see their point, Beau. I might think the worst if I were in their place and didn't know what the true situation was."

Beau stared into the darkness. As a rule he would ignore such misjudgment, but this was different. He couldn't stand by and let Charity be judged unfairly. "Now that they know I'm stayin' here, it'll make it hard on you, won't it?"

"Reverend Olson and his wife aren't gossips, but I'm sure the news will get around. But I'm not worried. I know I'm not doing anything wrong, and Ferrand always said that's all that counts."

They sat in silence until Beau finally stood up to straighten his leg. He winced, then said calmly, "I suppose I should give more thought about taking the Olsons up on their offer to move in with them."

Charity closed her eyes and bit her lower lip, forcing herself to reply. "I suppose that would be the proper thing to do, all right."

Beau jammed his hands in his back pockets and stared at the sky, resenting the fact that he'd have to leave her and Mary Kathleen all alone. It didn't seem right. On top of trying to run her homestead without the help of a man, she'd been good enough to take him in, nurse him back to health, and care for a newborn child that wasn't hers. And now the whole town would be down on her for what she'd done, when in fact she'd been the good Samaritan.

"You always for doin' the proper thing?"

"I—I don't know. Are you?"

"Well, don't tell my ma, but I've never worried much about it in the past," he admitted.

She glanced up at him and grinned. "I never was set on it myself—except in certain cases, of course."

"You consider this to be one of those cases?"

She sighed and turned her attention back to the twinkling sky. "Not really, though I suppose we could be faulted for it."

"Well, since neither of us is any too set on me movin', I suppose we could just sit tight for a while and weather out the storm."

Charity felt her heart leap with expecta-

tion. "You mean, you think you ought to stay
. . . even if there will be talk?"

Beau gazed at her in the moonlight, watching her face grow unusually solemn. "If you
have no objections, I'd like to hang around a
while longer." He moved over to lean down
beside her, his eyes growing solemn. "Mind
you, I'd leave first light if I thought it was best
for you. But, dammit, I'd worry about you and
the baby if I up and done that. Now, I've been
doin' some thinkin' since the reverend left."
His voice softened in an attempt to spare her
feelings. "I—I can't marry you . . . not that
you wouldn't make a fine wife, but I guess
Bets was sort of it for me . . . you know."

"I wasn't expecting you to—to offer me
your love, Beau."

"I know . . . but I wouldn't marry any
woman without givin' my all to her. It just
wouldn't be proper. Marriage is . . . well,
hell, it's special, and a man and woman should
be in love before they enter into such an arrangement."

"I agree, but sometimes it doesn't work out
that way."

"Well, just because I can't marry you
doesn't mean I can't see that you're in a real
bind, and I'd like to help you out. Since I'm
goin' to be laid up awhile anyway, I could give
you a hand. I know I've never said it in so
many words, but I'm beholden to you for sav-

ing my life, Charity." The blue of his eyes deepened as he looked down on her, and she wondered if he could hear her heart trying to hammer its way out of her chest. "I'd like the opportunity to pay you back, if you'll let me."

"It wasn't all me," she reminded him.

"I know the squaws helped, but you're the one who took me in and sewed me up and sat up nights with me." He reached hesitantly and placed his hand over hers, sending a sporadic flurry of butterflies racing through her. "I won't be forgettin' what you've done for me, Charity. You're a good woman and I'd be proud if you'd let me repay your kindness before I leave. There's no reason I can't stay here till spring. By then I should have your land in good enough shape so's you can get your title. I'd be glad to do that for you, if you'd let me."

At another time in her life Charity might have refused his offer, pointing out that she neither wanted nor needed his sympathy.

But she'd discovered the hard way, no man —or woman, for that matter—could manage on the prairie alone.

She would've preferred he stay because he wanted her companionship. As it was, he would stay because he felt obligated to her. Nevertheless, she'd accept Beau Claxton on any terms he offered.

Her hand gently closed over his. "If you want to stay, I'll be grateful to have you."

Beau glanced down at her hand, and once more he felt a swift, tightening in his loins. Her touch was gentle, almost a butterfly caress. The feel of her warm flesh next to his rekindled desires of the flesh he didn't want to feel.

"You're sure? There's sure to be ugly talk when the town finds out I'm here," he promised. "Soon as I'm able, I'll be headed to town for wire to string fences. If they don't know about me by then, they'll be finding out."

"I don't care."

His hand gently squeezed hers, and he fought the overwhelming urge to take her in his arms. He was surprised to discover he wanted to, and he might have, if memories of Betsy hadn't kept appearing to remind him it wouldn't be fair to her memory. All he had left of Betsy was his memories, and Beau figured if he let those go, Betsy would be gone forever.

For one brief moment a flash of resentment shot through him. Hell, was he going to feel this way the rest of his life? Wouldn't the pain ever get any easier?

He took a deep breath, determined to clear his mind of the depressing thought. The least he could do was help Charity with her problems.

"I say we see this thing through together, if it's all right with you." He winked, and the butterflies in her stomach went crazy again.

She smiled and squeezed his hand tightly, unable to speak over the large lump in her throat. But it was more than all right with her. It was wonderful.

Chapter 15

The first snow of the season fell exactly two weeks later. As the fine white flakes sifted down against the windowpane of the soddy, the predicted trouble arrived.

But it came in a form Charity would have least expected.

Beau was feeding Mary Kathleen her first bottle of the morning, while Charity bustled around the kitchen making breakfast.

The smell of fresh coffee in the pot, buttermilk biscuits baking in the oven, and bacon sizzling in the cast iron skillet filled the small, cozy room with mouth-watering aromas.

With a fire burning brightly in the grate, the relentless wind whistling across the barren land made little difference to the small, hapless family nestled inside the warm soddy.

But outside, dwarfed by endless sky and sweeping plains, the Burkhouser homestead seemed hardly more than a clod of dust on the prairie.

Charity stole enough time away from the stove to stand on tiptoe and peer out the window at the swirling flakes of pristine white. "I love the first snow." To get a better look, she rubbed the steam from the window with her elbow.

"I thought you hated winter." Beau set the baby bottle aside. Tipping Mary Kathleen over his shoulder, he began patting her back gently.

Charity caught the endearing motion out of the corner of her eye and smiled. Beau performed the task so naturally now. Though he said Mary Kathleen was growing like ragweed, the infant looked tiny draped over his broad shoulder. And he had no room to talk. He was filling out rapidly these days, becoming an impressive man in his own right.

Charity couldn't help but feel a strong surge of pride as she watched the way her small family thrived under her care. It seemed she had to remind herself every day that they weren't really her family, only temporary gifts the good Lord had sent to see her through another long winter.

No one knew when Ansel would come to his senses and want to claim Mary Kathleen.

And when spring arrived . . . well, she didn't want to think about spring and Beau's promised departure. She'd learned long ago to live for the day, and let tomorrow take care of itself.

"I don't like winter, but there's something about the first snow," she said dreamily. "It just makes me feel good all over."

"Well, if it makes you feel that good, maybe you ought to come out and help me today," Beau teased. "No sense sitting in the house and pining away."

Though Charity had argued that he wasn't strong enough yet to work, Beau had already begun some basic improvements. The day before, he'd patched the roof and set a row of fence posts. This morning, he planned to make some much-needed repairs to the lean-to.

Moving away from the window, Charity returned to the stove to turn the bacon. "I'd be happy to help you out," she said, "but I must insist that you let me do the hard part."

"Of course. I'll hold the posts while you drive them into the ground," he agreed wryly.

Charity knew he was teasing. Beau Claxton was not a man to stand by and let a woman do a man's work, even through his injuries still caused him considerable discomfort.

But she was certain she could do more than

he permitted her to. While she couldn't wield a heavy sledgehammer to drive the posts into the hard-packed ground, she could lift the posts from the wagon and have them waiting in place.

But Beau wouldn't hear of it. He said she had enough to do taking care of the baby and running the household to keep her busy. While he was around, he'd do all the heavy work. Charity winced as she recalled one day the week before when they'd gotten downright snappish with each other concerning the subject.

Beau had been chopping wood, slowly and cautiously, until the pile beside the house had mounted steadily. Charity was sure that he was overdoing it and was bound to hurt himself, so she'd bolted outside four or five times to caution him to slow down.

"I used to help Ferrand all the time," she complained. Each time she'd appeared to give him advice, Beau had promptly, but politely, sent her back into the soddy. "Go bake bread or something," he'd said.

When she'd kept popping out the door to issue the same warning again and again, Beau had finally lost all patience with her.

He'd lowered the ax, leaned on the handle disgustedly, and fixed his blue eyes on her till the pupils had looked like pinpoints.

"Well, I'm not Ferrand," he'd stated calmly.

"And I'd sure appreciate it if you'd march your fanny right back in the house and nail your feet to the floor so I can get my work done!"

Nail her feet to the floor! Why, that jackass! Willing her voice to remain calm, she'd replied in a strained but pleasant tone. "You don't have to remind *me* you're not Ferrand. Ferrand was always a perfect gentleman. Besides, I was only thinking of your comfort. You're a fool to be working this hard so soon after suffering such terrible injuries."

"I feel fine. I want you to quit actin' like a mother hen, cluckin' over me constantly," he ordered. "I'm gonna chop wood until I get enough to last us for a few days, and I don't want to hear that back door flappin' every five minutes like a broken shutter in a windstorm. Do I make myself clear?"

Charity took a deep breath and squared her shoulders defensively. Her eyes snapped back at him. "Well, I'll certainly see to it that you're not disturbed again, Mr. Claxton." She tossed her head, marched back into the soddy, and slammed the door loudly enough to send Mary Kathleen into a howl.

Beau calmly watched her fuming departure. When he heard the door slam and the baby screech, a slow grin tugged the corners of his mouth.

Serves her right, the feisty little heifer, he

thought, but it had also occurred to him that she sure was cute when she got all flustered that way. It had been the first time he'd ever seen her lose her temper, and he'd discovered he rather liked her show of spunk.

They hadn't spoken to each other the rest of the day. By the following morning, they'd both concluded they were living too close in their tiny quarters to remain silent indefinitely, so they resumed talking.

Charity snapped herself out of her reverie to remind Beau that breakfast was on the table.

He was washing his hands as Charity took the pan of biscuits out of the oven and poured their coffee.

"Smells good," he complimented, and she realized he always had something nice to say about her cooking. He was a delight to cook for. He seemed to like anything she set before him. And since he was feeling better, he ate like a harvest hand at every meal.

"Thank you. I hope you're hungry."

"I'm always hungry for your cookin'."

As they sat down to eat, a knock sounded at the door.

"Now who could that be?" Charity glanced up from her plate with a curious frown.

"I don't know, but I'll get it." He winked at her solemnly as he pushed away from the table, sending her pulse thumping erratically.

"If it's Santa Claus arriving early, I'd hide if I were you, Miss Charity."

"And just what have I done that I should have to hide?"

"The list is too long to go into right now."

When Beau opened the door, she saw his expression change from amused to puzzled.

Ansel was standing in the doorway, looking nearly frozen to death. Beau was surprised to see that he wasn't a wearing coat, only dirty overalls and a thin cotton work shirt. His shoulders were covered with a thick dusting of snow.

Ansel looked back at Beau, as his teeth began to chatter. "I—I—I want to se-e my ba-b-by."

"Good Lord, man. Where's your coat?" Beau reached out and pulled Ansel inside the shelter as Charity hurried to assist him.

"My goodness, Ansel! What's happened to you?" Charity had never seen him looking so disreputable—or so unkempt. He was filthy, and his clothes looked as if they hadn't been washed in weeks. They hung loosely over his skeletal frame, and the strong odor surrounding him was rank and offensive. His unusually long hair was dirty. Charity found it hard to believe that this was the same Ansel Latimer she'd known so well.

"I co-me to se-e my ba-b-by," Ansel repeated, his voice taking on an almost belligerent tone.

"Well, of course you can see Mary Kathleen—"

"Who?"

"Mary Kathleen," Charity repeated softly. "That's what we've been calling the baby, Ansel. It's what Letty wanted to name her. I hope you like it."

Ansel seemed to forget the topic momentarily as his gaze quickly shifted to appraise Beau. His eyes roamed over Beau's tall frame insolently. "Who's this man, Charity?"

"Why, it's Beau. The man who was injured. Don't you remember?"

"I don't know him." Ansel dismissed Beau abruptly as he glanced around the soddy.

Charity glanced at Beau uneasily.

"Where's my baby?" Ansel's demand grew louder. "I want to see my baby!"

"Ansel, let's all sit down and have a cup of hot coffee. You must be nearly frozen." Charity was beginning to realize how much worse Ansel had become. He was acting more strangely than ever before, and she was afraid he'd suffered a total breakdown.

She reached to take his arm, but Ansel jerked away as if her touch had burned him. He looked her up and down with the same contemptuous look he'd given Beau earlier.

"You Jezebel," he accused hotly in a voice edged with hate.

Charity lifted her brows in stunned disbelief. "What?"

"You're a shameless woman, Charity Burkhouser . . . shameless!" he repeated, his eyes filled with rage.

"Now, wait a minute." Beau reached over and pulled Charity protectively to his side. "You have no right to speak to her that way."

"She ain't nothin' but trash!"

"Ansel"—Charity managed to find her voice— "what's wrong with you!" She was shocked by more than his language; she wondered what had prompted him to come with such outrageous accusations.

Ansel eyed her with disgust. "Don't try to lie to me, Charity. I've heard the talk. You're livin' in sin with this man, and you've got my baby daughter in your viper's nest," he sneered. "Well, I'm here to deliver her from the hands of Lucifer."

"Oh, Ansel." Charity sagged weakly against Beau. "I don't know what you've heard, but it isn't true—"

"Lies! Nothing but lies!" Ansel stepped back, his eyes flaring wildly. "They say this man's been livin' out here for weeks. Can you deny it?"

"He has been, Ansel, but we're not living

together—not the way those people are implying."

"Lies! Nothin' but dirty, filthy lies, you sister of Satan!" He spat the words as if they'd made a bitter taste in his mouth.

"All right, I think that's about enough, Ansel. I want you out of here, or I'll throw you out." Beau stepped forward, his fingers curled into fists.

Charity reached to prevent him from carrying out his threat. "No, Beau. He's ill—"

"I'm know he is, but he's not going to talk to you that way," Beau warned.

"I come to get my baby," Ansel said calmly as all trace of emotion suddenly disappeared. "It's time I be takin' her home."

Charity glanced urgently to Beau. "No . . . he mustn't take her!"

Understanding the terror in Charity's eyes, Beau tried to stall for time. "You can't take your baby today." He hoped Ansel had not gone completely insane. "It would be better if you came back for her after the weather clears."

"I can take my baby any damn time I please!" Ansel's chin jutted out sharply.

"Look, you're a sick man—you need help. Let me take you into town and—"

Ansel started backing toward the doorway, his eyes growing wild again. Charity held her breath as he paused beside Mary Kathleen's bed. He glanced down and saw the sleeping baby, and his face suddenly took on the plaintive look of a small child's. "Ohhh . . . Letty . . . she looks like Letty."

"Ansel . . ." Charity eased forward, hoping to divert his attention so Beau could safely scoop the baby into his arms. "Why don't you let me fix you a cup of coffee and then you can hold her and see how pretty her eyes are. They're amber—just like Letty's."

Ansel looked up. "You'll let me hold her?"

"Of course you may hold her."

Suddenly, Ansel seemed as sane as could be. He straightened his stance and moved with somber grace to sit quietly in a kitchen chair. He drank the coffee Charity set before him and chatted amicably with Beau about the weather and spring crops.

When it was time for him to hold Mary Kathleen, tears came into his eyes as he gazed down at his baby daughter. "She does look exactly like my Letty." His voice held a reverent awe.

After he'd played with the baby awhile, Ansel asked if it would be possible to bundle her tightly enough to let her experience her first snow with her father.

"I know I've been actin' real strange, Charity, but I think seeing my baby has helped me understand that Letty's gone," he confessed. "Maybe as soon as I have a few weeks to get my life back in order, I'll be able to take my daughter home and be a proper pa to her." His eyes grew misty again. "Letty would've wanted that, wouldn't she?"

"Yes, she would."

"Losing Letty . . . well, I can't tell you what it's done to me."

"I know. You don't have to explain, Ansel." Charity patted his shoulder consolingly.

"Do you think I can take the baby outside?" he asked again. "The snow's so pretty. I feel like Letty would be there with us too."

Charity was touched by the earnest look in his eyes and hurriedly went about fetching the baby's blankets to comply with his request.

Beau followed Charity across the room. While Ansel cooed and talked to the baby, Beau whispered to her out of the side of his mouth. "I don't like the way he's acting, Charity."

Surprised, she paused to glance up. "Why not? He seems like his old self, Beau."

"That's my point. He was acting crazy as a loon ten minutes ago."

"I know, and I've been concerned about him, too, but I think perhaps seeing his baby has finally helped him to accept Letty's death."

"What about the way he was talkin' to you?"

"I'm sure he realizes he was mistaken. He'll apologize before he leaves; you wait and see. He's acting like the Ansel I've always known. I think with a little time, he'll be back to normal. You heard him. He's even planning on taking the baby home in a few weeks."

Beau was still skeptical, but Charity seemed to know Ansel better than he did. "I hope you're not being foolish. I don't want you or the baby getting hurt."

She reached out and touched his arm, deeply moved by his concern. "I can't deny Mary Kathleen's father the right to be with her, and it will probably do him a world of good."

"I'll abide by whatever you decide," Beau conceded. "I just hope you're not making a mistake."

She squeezed his hand. "Thank you."

She shook her head at the irony. If she was going to be hurt, it wouldn't necessarily be Mary Kathleen who'd break her heart. Come spring, Beau would be leaving. . . . She shook off the thought and hurried to bundle the baby properly for the brief outing.

"I'll only keep her outside for a moment," Ansel promised, worriedly tucking in Mary Kathleen's stray little hand that persistently poked its way out of the blanket after Charity finally handed him his daughter.

"A little fresh air won't hurt her, but she

shouldn't be out but just a minute," Charity cautioned. "The wind's sharp today."

"Oh, I'll be careful with her."

Beau opened the door and Ansel stepped outside, still talking to his baby in low, soothing tones.

"I might as well fill the woodbox," Beau offered, reaching for his coat as Charity prepared to clear the table.

"Yes, it's getting low." She knew Beau wanted to keep a close eye on Ansel and the baby. If it made him feel easier, she wouldn't object. "Would you mind throwing these potato peels to the chickens?"

Beau crossed the room to take the small bucket out of her hand. Their fingers touched, and their gazes met unexpectedly. Charity felt her breathing quicken as she looked into his incredibly blue eyes. For an instant she found herself envying Betsy.

Strange, she thought, to envy a dead woman. But Charity realized that she'd gladly trade places with his deceased wife if, for only one second, for one brief second, Beau would look at her with the same love he had so fiercely reserved for Betsy. She knew it could never be, but it didn't keep her from wishing.

"This all you want me to take?" His voice was strained, and Charity thought his eyes looked vaguely troubled.

"Yes . . . that's all."

"I'd best see about Ansel." He started to walk away, but she saw him hesitate. He turned around and faced her, his face lined with worry. "I suppose the town is talkin' about us livin' together. That's what Ansel meant about hearing talk."

"It wouldn't surprise me."

"I don't like them thinking that."

"We agreed we didn't care," she reminded him.

"I know." He acted as if he wanted to say more, but changed his mind. "I'd better check on Ansel."

Charity watched as he walked to the door and opened it. He adjusted his hat low on his forehead, then smiled at her again. As the door closed behind him, she turned back to clearing the table.

Suddenly, the door flew open, and Beau stood looking at her, his face tight with fury. "The son of a bitch is gone."

"What?" Charity's hand flew to her throat.

Beau stepped into the room, removed his hat, and shook the snow off angrily. "He's gone, Charity. There's not a sign of him anywhere."

"Oh, dear God . . . the baby! He took the baby?"

Beau nodded curtly. "I'll saddle the horse and go after him, but I don't know . . . the snow's comin' down heavier now."

Charity moved across the room in a daze, trying to digest the meaning of his words. "Beau . . . Mary Kathleen . . ."

"You don't need to remind me, Charity. Damn it, I know he has her!"

At his sharp words Charity's composure crumbled, and as naturally as if it happened every day, she moved into the haven of his arms. He was taken by surprise and accepted her stiffly at first, until he heard her begin to cry. Then his arms folded around her, and he pulled her closely to him.

It felt unbelievably good to be in his arms. He smelled of soap and smoke and fresh outdoors. There were still traces of snow on his shoulder, and they were cold and wet against Charity's cheek as she buried her face in the warmth of his neck and cried harder. It was all her fault. She'd been foolish to let Ansel take the child, and now Mary Kathleen would pay the price of her misplaced trust.

"Now, now, there's no call to start cryin'," Beau whispered tenderly, smoothing her hair back with one large hand.

She had the same pleasant, lemony smell that always stirred him, and her hair felt like fine silk under his hand. With her small body pressed tightly against his, he could feel the gentle swell of her breasts through his coat.

"He couldn't have gotten far. I'll be able to

find him and the baby before any harm's done."

"It's my fault," Charity sobbed.

"No, it's mine. I should never have taken my eyes off him."

"I want to go with you."

He grasped her shoulders and held her away from him gently, his blue eyes locking gravely with her green ones. "I think you should stay here in case he decides to come back."

"Oh . . . yes . . . I suppose he might come to his senses and bring her back."

Beau doubted it, but he didn't want her to know that. "I'll ride out and see what I can find." The blue of his eyes deepened to cobalt. "Will you be all right?"

"Yes, I'll be fine." She dabbed her eyes with the corner of her apron. "You'd better hurry. It's so cold out there."

Beau winked at her reassuringly. "The baby's bundled tight. She'll be fine."

Though Charity tried to muster a weak smile in return, two fresh tears rolled from the corners of her eyes. "I know."

Beau reached out and caught the two tears with his thumbs, tenderly brushing the dampness away. "I have to go."

Charity nodded, too overcome by emotion to speak.

He looked at her for a moment, then very

slowly he pulled her face to his and touched her lips briefly with his own. Just as quickly, he stepped away, almost as if he had done something he shouldn't. "I'll be back soon as I can."

He turned, placed his hat back on his head, and opened the door. "Be careful if Ansel comes back. I don't think he'd hurt you, but you keep the gun close—and don't hesitate to use it if you need to."

Charity nodded, her knees still threatening to buckle from his unexpected kiss.

He went out the door, closing it firmly behind him.

Reverently, Charity's hand came up to touch her mouth while his taste still lingered. The kiss was only his way of reassuring her that everything would be all right.

She knew that.

But it was the most wonderful kiss she'd ever experienced, and she'd hold it forever within her heart.

Chapter 16

It was nearing dark when Beau returned.

Charity had spent the day alternately pacing the floor, praying, and wringing her hands in frustration. When she heard Beau's horse approaching, she rushed outside without bothering to put her coat on.

The snow was falling heavily, blanketing the ground with deep layers that made it difficult for her to walk. Beau was dismounting as Charity ran to him. Her eyes desperately searched his arms for a small bundle. When she saw there wasn't one, tears sprang to her eyes.

"You didn't find her?"

"No." Beau quickly led the horse into the lean-to, and Charity trailed behind.

"There wasn't a sign of Ansel or the baby?"

As he released the cinch and lifted the saddle, Beau glanced at her irritably. "You shouldn't be out here without a coat."

Charity wrapped her hands around her shoulders, trying to keep her teeth from chattering. The wind was whipping snow around the corners of the lean-to, making them raise their voices to be heard. "I'm all right!"

"Get back in the house!" Beau ordered.

"What are we going to do about the baby?"

Beau put the saddle away, slipped the bridle off, and pitched a forkful of hay to the horse. Without a word he drew Charity under the shelter of his arm and propelled her toward the soddy.

Once inside, he gripped her shoulders and turned her to face him. "I managed to pick up Ansel's tracks about a mile out, but then it started snowing heavier and I lost them."

"Oh, Beau!"

"He's taken shelter somewhere along the way. He knows the baby can't survive in this storm," Beau consoled.

"But he isn't thinking straight."

"I know, but he proved he can have his sane moments this morning. No, he's found shelter, and he and the baby are all right."

Beau wished he could be as confident as he sounded, but he could see Charity was near the breaking point. He had to act as if he believed what he said.

With a nod he released her, dusted off his hat, and stomped the snow from his boots. Quietly, Charity crossed the room to place another log on the fire.

When she turned around, she saw how deeply etched his face was with worry and fatigue, and she longed to go to him to offer comfort. She knew he'd grown as fond of the baby as she, yet she also realized it wasn't her place to take any liberties with him.

He moved closer to the fire to warm his hands, and she noticed his movements were stiff, as if the wounds were bothering him again.

"You must be exhausted." She stepped closer to help him remove his snow-crusted coat. "I'll dish up your supper," she said, hanging his coat on the peg.

After he'd eaten the stew and thick slices of white bread, still warm from the oven, she stood before him in the flickering firelight. Her expression silently begged him for some morsel of solace. "Well?"

"We wait, Charity."

"For what?"

"We wait until we hear something . . . one way or the other."

Mutely she stared back at him, aware he could no longer pretend that all would be well. He was being brutally frank now. He couldn't know any more than she what the next few hours would bring.

But Charity found comfort in the thought that she would not be alone during the wait. Beau would be with her.

She went silently into his arms, and they stood before the fire holding each other, trying to absorb each other's grief in the only way they knew how.

The night passed slowly. They tried to sleep, but found rest impossible.

Weeks before, when Beau had recovered enough to move about, he'd insisted Charity return to her own bed and he'd taken the pallet before the fire. Tonight, he tossed about on the makeshift bed, his mind restless and unsettled.

Charity stirred and called softly to him, asking him if he needed anything. His answer was no.

Thirty minutes later, he got up and came to sit on the side of her bed, and they began to talk. He reminisced about happier times, carefree boyhood days spent with his brothers. Charity spoke of her family, her sisters, and how she longed to see them all again.

The endless night dragged on, and they talked of many things. The wind howled and shook the soddy, and occasionally the sound of sleet hitting the windowpane caught their attention.

It occurred to Charity that neither she nor Beau had spoken of Ferrand or Betsy tonight, and the discovery encouraged her.

"How will he feed the baby?" Charity asked once, recalling the subject that was uppermost in their minds.

"He'll find a way. It's his child—a man takes care of those he loves."

By first light the knock they'd been praying for sounded at the door. Beau gently restrained Charity as she bolted forward. He went to answer it.

Reverend Olson stood on the doorstep, his kindly features lined with weariness. "I know you must be worried."

"The child?"

"She's with Mrs. Olson. Ansel brought her by late last night."

Charity joined Beau at the door, and he placed his arm around her supportively. "Is she . . . all right?"

"She was cold and hungry, but she'll be fine. Mrs. Olson is spoiling her outrageously right now."

Charity sagged against Beau's side with relief. "I'll get dressed and we'll go get her—"

"Charity"—Reverend Olson's expression changed—"may I step in, dear?"

"Oh, I'm so sorry. Of course. You must be chilled to the bone."

Reverend Olson stepped inside, and Beau hurriedly closed the door. The snow was still coming down in large, puffy flakes, and the wind was bitter cold.

"Let me fix you something warm to drink," Charity offered, and the Reverend nodded gratefully.

While they sipped hot coffee, Reverend Olson told them how Ansel had suddenly appeared on his doorstep the night before, cradling the baby in his arms as he talked wildly.

"He was talking about Beau and me, wasn't he?" Charity's gaze was level and grave.

"Yes, dear. I'm afraid Ansel is very ill. Somehow he finally realized Beau is staying here, and he was convinced you two are living in sin."

When Charity started to protest, Reverend Olson stopped her with an uplifted hand. "Surely you must know what the town is saying, dear. We discussed this at great lengths during my last visit, and, if you recall, this is precisely what Mrs. Olson and I feared would happen. But apparently you preferred to take the risk of having Beau remain in your care rather than having him transferred to our home for safekeeping."

Charity's eyes dropped guiltily, but Beau

met the Reverend's gaze straightforwardly. "We've committed no sin."

Reverend Olson's expression grew kinder as he shook his head sadly. "I know, my son, but surely you must see the impropriety of your situation. People are very narrow minded at times, and their tongues will continue to wag as long as you remain here with Charity."

"Then they'll just have to talk. We've done nothing wrong. Charity needs my help. Soon as I have her land in proper order, I'll be movin' on, Reverend—and not until then."

Charity watched Beau's eyes become as stubborn as his accuser's.

"You're making a grave mistake, young man." Reverend Olson shook his finger. "What you're doing will remain to haunt Charity long after you've taken your leave. You must consider that as well."

"Charity and I are in full agreement on what we're doing."

"Then I must warn you," said Reverend Olson, his tone turning grave, "the child cannot be returned to your care."

Though Charity had tried to remain silent, a low cry of protest escaped her now. "Oh . . . no. . . ."

"Ansel has left the child in my care, and I cannot, in good faith, let her be returned to such an atmosphere."

"Just exactly where is Ansel?" Beau demanded. "He has no right to take the child and give her to you! Charity has been the only mother Mary Kathleen has known. You have no authority to take her away from her."

"I'm not sure where Ansel is, but he has every right to place the child where he feels she will be properly cared for, Beau. He is Mary Kathleen's father."

"But he's insane," Beau argued heatedly.

"I certainly hope that isn't the case. I prefer to think he's a very troubled man, but, regardless, we have a search party looking for him at this moment. He was barely lucid when he brought the child to us last night. He wasn't even wearing a coat. The townsfolk are concerned he won't survive the storm unless we find him."

"I still don't see what that has to do with returning the baby to Charity. No one could give her any better care," Beau maintained.

"If she were married, there'd be no question," Reverend Olson reiterated. "Or if Ansel sees fit to return the child to her care, then I suppose there would be nothing I could say. We'll simply have to find Ansel and try to ascertain what is best for both him and the child at this point."

Charity glanced at Beau helplessly. He pushed himself back from the table and crossed the room to put on his coat. "I'll be riding back to town with you, Reverend."

"Oh, Beau." Charity stood, her features filled with concern. "You can't go out in this again. You were out all day yesterday—"

"I'll be fine, Charity." Beau cut her protest short, and she could do nothing but watch as the two men prepared to leave.

"I don't want you worryin'. I'll be fine." Beau faced her as they stood in front of the doorway a few minutes later. She handed him a sack of food she'd hurriedly assembled.

She knew her heart was in her eyes, but she couldn't disguise it. "You be careful." She handed him a warm red woolen scarf she'd knitted and given Ferrand on his last birthday. "Be sure to wear this. The wind is terrible."

Beau smiled and winked at her, his eyes silently conveying his appreciation for her concern. "Thanks. You take care too."

He tucked the sack under his arm, pulled his hat low on his forehead, and nodded to the reverend. "I'm ready if you are, sir."

The search parties had split off into small groups. Beau and Reverend Olson met up with two of the men as they rode into the outskirts of Cherry Grove.

All four men reined their horses to a halt. "Gentlemen, this is Beau Claxton," the Reverend introduced. Their horses pranced restlessly, their breath blowing frosty plumes in the cold winter air.

The two men assessed Beau silently, their expressions easily discernible. "You the one livin' with the Burkhouser woman?" Jim Blanchard finally ventured.

"Mrs. Burkhouser was kind enough to care for me while I was ill," Beau returned evenly. "And I sleep and take my meals there, but I don't 'live' with her." Though Beau spoke quietly, there was an unmistakable edge of steel in his voice.

Jim Blanchard looked at Troy Mulligan and gave him a knowing grin. Beau noted the snide exchange, and he eased forward in his saddle, casually resting his gloved hands on the horn. "And I'd appreciate it if you gentlemen would be so kind as to pass the word along. I'd not take kindly to anyone who'd say otherwise."

His smooth voice had such an ominous tone it promptly wiped the smiles from both men's faces.

"Gentlemen, we're wasting time," Reverend Olson reminded them patiently. "There's a sick man out here somewhere who needs our help."

The men agreed to search in opposite directions and meet back hourly to report any progress.

Beau rode north; the Reverend, south; Jim Blanchard, west, and Troy Mulligan headed east.

The wind continued to pick up, and icy pellets of sleet began to fall from the leaden skies. Beau rode for over thirty minutes without one encouraging sign to indicate Ansel had gone that direction. He realized even if there had been tracks, the snow would quickly have covered the trail.

The sleet stung his face, and he paused once to tie the woolen scarf Charity had given him. The faint smell of lemon lingered in the material, and Beau closed his eyes for a moment, inhaling her fragrance. The memory of her eyes, imploring him to find Mary Kathleen, lent him the strength to nudge his horse forward in the ever-deepening drifts.

It was nearing dusk, and there was still no sign of Ansel Latimer. When Beau had reported back to the other men, he found that they, too, had been unable to shed any light on Ansel's whereabouts, but they'd all agreed to keep looking.

Beau face felt numb, and he could no longer feel his hands in the fleece-lined gloves he wore. The drifts were almost up to his horse's belly now, and Beau knew he was going to have to turn back soon.

The horse topped a small rise, and Beau reined him to a sudden halt. His eyes scanned the fields below him, and he felt his heart sink.

Silhouetted against the opaque sky stood one lone tree. In the stark branches of that tree was hanging the lifeless body of Ansel Latimer.

Beau felt a crushing sense of despair come over him as he sat atop his horse on that cold rise, watching the biting wind sway Ansel's limp body back and forth, back and forth, back and forth.

God, what an awful, lonely way to die. Why had he done it? he wondered. But he knew the answer better than anyone. Ansel didn't care about living, not without Letty.

Did any man have the right to judge another for taking his own life? Beau found himself wondering as he slumped wearily over the saddle horn, staring at what once had been a vital, loving man.

He searched his soul and found he couldn't condemn Ansel. It would take a higher source than he to pass judgment on such unbearable misery, and Beau could not help but feel Ansel had found a peace most folks would know nothing about.

Beau knew exactly how deeply Ansel had suffered. Hadn't he considered the same choice, not once, but many, many times after Betsy's death? But through the grace of God and, he was sure, his mother's prayers, some inner strength had kept him going for another hour, another day, another week, always with the muted hope that the pain would eventually ease.

The only thing Beau could fault Ansel with was that, like himself, he had loved too deeply.

It only took a few minutes to ride to the tree and cut the rope. Beau gently lifted Ansel's lifeless body into his arms, and carried him to his horse. He removed a blanket from his bedroll and wrapped it securely around the body, though he wasn't sure why. Perhaps, he thought, it was because Ansel just looked so cold.

Before he tied the body securely across the back of the horse, Beau stood gazing down into Ansel's face, which was surprisingly serene.

What had been his last thoughts? Beau wondered sadly. Didn't the man realize that by committing this final, irreversible act, he was leaving behind a young child to the mercy of a sometimes cruel and heartless world?

A new, even more disturbing thought came into Beau's mind. Had his own son or daughter been born, how would the child have suffered by his father's inconsolable grief? At that moment Beau's sobering revelations served to remind him that maybe it was time he put the past behind him and made an effort to live again.

Beau reached out and touched Ansel's cheek gently. "If it helps any, I understand why you did it. And I'll do my best to see your daughter's cared for."

Beau wanted to say more, but he didn't know what to add. Surely there had to be more profound words to say at a time like this, but he guessed he'd have to leave those words to the wisdom of Reverend Olson.

He rested the body across the saddle horn and made sure the rope was tied good and tight. Then he climbed onto his horse to take Ansel home.

Chapter 17

Once again the friends and neighbors of Ansel Latimer were called upon to assemble around a gravesite. In a matter of weeks fate had set aside these particular mourners to lay to rest another victim of what seemed like a never-ending tragedy for the Latimer family.

The snow lay deep on the ground as the small group huddled against the cold wind to listen to Reverend Olson intone about the "deeply troubled soul" of Ansel Latimer.

Beau and Charity stood side by side, solemnly listening to the minister's words. A weak sun slipped in and out of mushroom-shaped clouds which promised neither rain nor shine. The icy wind whipped the mourners' hats and coats about in a hapless manner, making the forced gathering more miserable than it already was.

Reverend Olson's words seemed far away to Beau as he painfully relived the moment he'd discovered Ansel's lifeless body.

He searched for a meaningful reason why so much heartbreak should come to one family, why so much misfortune should be thrust upon one innocent child. He could find none.

Mary Kathleen was alone now.

Who would see to her needs, rejoice over her first tooth, send her to school, or walk her down the aisle when she grew into a lovely woman? he wondered. With a pang he realized how proud he'd be to do all those things for her.

Although Reverend Olson hadn't spoken again of the baby's welfare, Beau knew Mary Kathleen wouldn't be returned to Charity's care. And judging from the sadness on her face, Charity knew it too.

Beau had watched her going about her work the past two days with a quiet despondency. When he'd attempted to cheer her, she'd politely dismissed his overtures with a wan smile and her soft reprimand, "Don't worry about me."

She missed the baby. At night Beau had heard her crying into her pillow, and he'd wanted to go to her. Instead, he'd lain staring at the ceiling, feeling her misery as deeply as his own, agonizing because he had no way of easing it.

Then the guilt had set in, keeping him awake long after Charity had dropped into an exhausted sleep. Deep within his soul he knew a way to spare her this agony.

It would only take a brief marriage ceremony.

A seemingly simple solution, yet by offering to marry her, wouldn't he inadvertently be allowing her to exchange one anguish for another? Granted, the Olsons would be happy to return Mary Kathleen to Charity's care if she were properly wed, but Beau knew it would be unfair of him to marry her. While he certainly liked and respected Charity, he wasn't sure if he could ever love any woman again. Since they both had experienced good, loving marriages, would it be right for them to settle for security and companionship and never again know the depth of love they'd each shared with their deceased partners? It seemed to Beau that neither he nor Charity would be happy under those circumstances.

He knew love came in many forms. He loved Wynne, Cole's wife, but not the way he loved Betsy. If anything ever happened to Cole, Beau knew he could marry Wynne and provide a good life for her and Cole's child.

Then why was he hesitant about showing the same compassion for Charity? She'd been good to him, as good as any woman he'd ever known. He owed her his life. And since he was relatively sure no other woman could fill Betsy's void, why was he being so damn stubborn about marrying her?

If he could save her land by sacrificing a few months out of his life, why shouldn't he? Once the land title was in her hand, and he was assured she could take care of herself, he could always go back to Missouri. She would never try to hold him against his will, Beau knew that.

Beau was pulled back to the present as he heard Reverend Olson inviting the gathering to pray. Heads bowed and Reverend Olson's voice boomed out encouragingly over the frozen countryside. "The Lord is my Shepherd, I shall not want . . ." The voices of the mourners blended somberly together as they recited the Twenty-third Psalm.

From the corner of his eye Beau saw tears begin to ooze from Charity's eyes. He reached to clasp her hand and squeeze it reassuringly as his deep voice joined with hers in the moving recitation.

"Yea, though I walk through the valley of the shadow of death, I will fear no evil: for Thou art with me . . ."

Beau could see heads begin to lift as Charity absently moved into the shelter of his side. He knew tongues would wag anew, but at the moment she needed someone to lean on, and

he had about made up his mind—like it or not
—that he was the only one she had left.

The top of her head barely reached his
shoulder. The small feather on her black hat
danced frantically as she huddled against his
coat, seeking shelter from the blustery wind.
She glanced up, and their eyes met. Her gaze
searched his imploringly, crying out for his
quiet strength, and Beau was more than willing to give it to her.

The dreary day was suddenly obliterated as
he smiled, and as if they were speaking only
to each other, they recited the comforting
thought: "Surely goodness and mercy shall
follow me all the days of my life: and I will
dwell in the house of the Lord forever."

Beau believed those weren't just empty
words written a long time ago, but a firm
promise a man could depend upon, and his
eyes lovingly brought the message home to
her.

For Charity, that made Ansel Latimer's
death a little easier.

Few chose to stop by the Burkhouser buggy
to offer words of comfort after the service.
Most of the mourners conveniently dispersed
to the safety of their carriages for the return
trip.

The Reverend and Mrs. Olson paused
briefly, clasping Charity's hand. Their eyes

spoke of deep sympathy because they knew she'd lost another close friend, and their words were kind and reassuring. Charity held tightly to Rebecca's hands. They couldn't have been more comforting had they been the hands of an angel.

When the last of the mourners had gone, Beau and Charity sat in the buggy staring at the mound of freshly turned dirt.

Ansel rested beneath a large oak, and the sound of the wind rustling through the brittle branches was a lonely one. Above, the sun had disappeared behind a cloud again, enveloping the earth in a shroud of gray.

"I hate death." Charity's voice sounded small and frightened in the frosty air.

"It's as much a part of life as being born."

She turned to Beau, her face childlike now. The wind had whipped her cheeks red, and her moist eyes reminded him of pools of sparkling emeralds. He had never seen her look so pretty—or so bewildered. Since coming to the Kansas frontier, she'd seen more than her share of death, and he knew she needed to know there was more to life than this terrible, crushing sense of loss. "But it hurts, Beau. It hurts." Her voice broke and tears began to slide down her cheeks again.

"I know it does." He reached over gently and cupped her face in his large hands. His gaze, as blue as periwinkles on a summer morn, held hers soberly. "I wish I could make it easier for you."

"You do, just by being here."

She smiled through her tears, and the sun suddenly broke through the clouds in a splendid array of light, bathing the grave and the small buggy in a pool of ethereal warmth.

Or did it only seem that way because that's how Charity made him feel? he wondered. When Beau glanced up, the clouds were as dark and dreary as they'd been before.

Charity noticed that he'd been staring at her a very long time. It seemed as if he were struggling to say something, but didn't know how.

Charity waited patiently but felt disappointment when, after gently brushing her tears from her cheeks with his thumbs, he reached to pick up the reins. The horse slowly began to move over the rutted hillside and out of the cemetery.

Charity turned, watching over her shoulder as Ansel's grave grew smaller and smaller in the distance.

"I hope he's with Letty," she whispered.

Beau hoped he was too.

A stray flake of snow fell occasionally as the buggy wound its way back to Cherry Grove. Charity had mentioned she needed a few supplies and would like to stop by Miller's Mercantile before they made the trip back to the soddy.

Beau readily agreed. He needed a new hammer, and he'd welcome the opportunity to purchase a quantity of raisins.

"Raisins?" Charity's brows lifted as he mentioned his strange request.

"I love raisin pie. You know how to make one?"

"Why . . . I've never made one, but I'm sure I could."

"Good, then I'll get plenty."

But when the buggy rolled into Cherry Grove, Beau drove right past Miller's Mercantile, the Havershams' Restaurant, Dog Kelley's Saloon and Gambling House, the Parnell Clothing Store, the schoolhouse that served as the church on Sunday mornings, and the various other storefronts lining the almost deserted Main Street.

A plume of white smoke puffed out of the chimney of Miller's Mercantile, and Charity knew most of the townspeople who were brave enough to venture out on such a cold day would be huddled together around the old wood stove, exchanging tales of Ansel Latimer, and, no doubt, the scandalous Charity Burkhouser.

"You just passed the mercantile," Charity reminded him, thinking Beau had been lost in thought and missed his intended destination.

"I know."

The buggy rolled around the corner, and the horse trotted at a brisk pace down Larimore Street. Charity leaned over to assist Beau in correcting the oversight, her breath making white wisps in the cold afternoon air. "Just follow Larimore around, and it will bring you right back to Main."

"I know where I am."

"You do?" His air of confidence assured her that he did, but she didn't understand. As far as she knew, Beau had only been in Cherry Grove one previous time to purchase wire for the fences.

"How are you so well acquainted with the town?"

"I'm unusually bright for my age." He winked at her and began to whistle a jaunty little tune as he urged the horse to pick up its pace.

Charity sat back and enjoyed the ride, thinking how nice it was to get her mind off of the depressing events of the past few days. Beau seemed to be in an uncommonly good mood all of a sudden, and it made her own spirits lighter.

Still, when he pulled the horse to a stop in front of Reverend Olson's house a few minutes later, Charity glanced at him mystified.

"Are we going to visit Mary Kathleen?" She tried to conceal the sudden excitement in her voice. She knew he missed the baby as much as she did, and she didn't want to put a damper on his cheerful mood.

Beau set the brake and tied the reins to the handle. Then he got out of the buggy and turned to lift her down.

"Beau, I don't think we should drop in unannounced this way." Charity tried to slow her steps as he opened the gate on the white picket fence and ushered her hurriedly up the walk.

"A minister shouldn't be surprised by unexpected company," Beau soothed, and before Charity could protest further, he rapped briskly on the door to the parsonage.

The door was answered by Rebecca, whose face, upon encountering Beau and Charity on her doorstep, broke into a wreath of welcome smiles. "Land sake! Look who's here, Papa!"

"Who?" Reverend Olson poked his balding head around the door, and he smiled, too, when he saw the young couple looking back at him. "Well, do come in, do come in!" he invited, swinging the door open cordially.

Charity noticed he had a cloth draped over his shoulder, and signs of Mary Kathleen's recent dribblings were in evidence. "How very nice to see you!" Rebecca exclaimed as she bustled around collecting their coats and scarfs. "I never dreamed you'd stop by today!"

"Well, I had a few things to pick up at the mercantile," Charity offered lamely, never dreaming herself that she'd be standing in the reverend's parlor, inhaling the delicious smell of an apple pie simmering in the oven.

"Well, you must stay to dinner," Rebecca insisted.

"No, I'm afraid we have to be gettin' back soon," Beau refused politely. "It's startin' to snow again."

"It is? Oh, dear. I just hate winters, don't you?"

Charity nodded agreeably.

"Well, well. You must be here to visit with Mary Kathleen, but I'm afraid she just went down for her nap," Reverend Olson apologized. "She didn't sleep well at all last night. . . ."

Actually, she hadn't slept well since she'd arrived there, Reverend Olson wanted to amend, but didn't. He wasn't sure how many more nights he could walk the floor with a screaming baby and still retain a charitable attitude. The good Lord hadn't meant for old people to have babies—with the exception of the biblical Sarah, of course.

Charity was about to say they understood and would be happy to return as soon as they completed their shopping when Beau interrupted suddenly. "We'd sure appreciate seein' the baby, but that's not what we're here for, Reverend."

Charity's gaze flew up to meet Beau's expectantly. "It isn't?"

"It isn't?" Reverend Olson parroted.

"It isn't?" Rebecca echoed.

"No,   sir . . . I . . . me   and   Mrs. Burkhouser want to—to get married."

"You do?"

"We do?"

"You do!" Rebecca clapped her hands together gleefully. "Wait just a minute! I have to take my pie out of the oven."

"Beau!"   Charity   looked   at   him dumbfoundedly. Her heart was beating like a trapped sparrow, and she suddenly felt light-headed. He was going to marry her? The least he could have done was *tell* her.

"Yes. You don't have any objections, do you?" His eyes radiated that stubborn blue she'd come to recognize, and yet they looked a little sheepish too.

"No . . . I—I'm just surprised, that's all."

"Well, if you want to get Mary Kathleen back, it seems the only sensible thing to do." Beau took a deep breath and went on. "I figure since we're in town, we might as well get it taken care of."

"You—you don't mind?"

"Wouldn't be doin' it if I minded," he said abruptly.

"But, Beau, are you sure you want to do this?" Charity had no idea what had changed his mind, but she didn't want him to do something he would regret in the morning.

"I think it's the only thing left to do."

"But is it what you *want*, Beau?" She desperately wished he would say something more reassuring—anything—but could she really question his motives? If he was good enough to help her out, then shouldn't she just accept his kindness, and not worry why?

"It's all right with me, Charity, if it's what you want."

"Well, then, I suppose I don't have any objections . . . if you don't." She didn't dare press her luck by asking him if their marriage would be a permanent commitment or only a temporary arrangement. At this point it seemed immaterial.

Beau took a deep breath and straightened his stance bravely. "Then let's get on with it, Reverend."

Rebecca breathlessly returned after taking her pie out of the oven, and moments later the ceremony began.

Charity's hands trembled, and her voice could barely be heard as she nervously recited her vows. Beau's hands were steady as a rock, and he repeated his words woodenly, his voice never wavering.

How the vows were exchanged made little

difference; for better, for worse, within a scant three minutes, Charity Burkhouser and Beau Claxton had become man and wife.

"Do you have a ring to give your bride as a symbol of your vows?" Reverend Olson asked.

"I'm sorry, sir. I don't."

"No matter. A ring is only a symbol; it doesn't insure love." Reverend Olson's gaze met Beau's kindly. "It will be up to you to cultivate love and make it grow, son."

"Thank you, sir."

"I wish you godspeed. You're both good people." Reverend Olson closed the Bible firmly. "You may kiss the bride."

Chapter 18

Fifteen minutes later, Beau and Charity were standing on the opposite side of Reverend Olson's front door with Mary Kathleen once again nestled snugly in Charity's arms.

"Did you get the impression Reverend Olson was anxious to return the baby to our care?" Charity asked with a cheeky grin.

"Sure looked that way." Beau and Charity had to laugh at the almost comical way Reverend Olson had hurriedly gathered Mary Kathleen's meager belongings, while insisting Beau and Charity get an early start for home.

"I'll bet he's already curled up in bed sound asleep," Charity predicted.

"I wouldn't doubt it."

They stepped happily off the porch together and walked to the buggy. Charity waited while Beau settled the baby comfortably on the seat, making sure the child was well protected from the inclement weather. Then he turned to assist her.

He lifted her slight weight easily, his strong arms suspending her momentarily in midair as the groom's eyes met his bride's shyly. Charity grew a little breathless as she stared back at her handsome husband. His eyes were a startling blue against the stark white of the frozen countryside, and she suddenly found herself wishing the unexpected alliance between them could somehow be a permanent one. She knew she would do everything within her power to make it so. Was it possible she was falling deeply in love with Beau Claxton?

"Charity . . . about the ring . . ."

"Yes?"

"I'm sorry I didn't have one to give you."

"It's all right. I don't have one to give you either."

"And . . . I'm sorry I didn't ask you proper . . . to marry me. I . . . well, this wasn't easy for me . . . or you. . . ."

"I understand." She smiled, trying to assure him that it didn't really matter. Her mind vividly replayed the kiss he'd given her at Reverend Olson's request. It was a brief, emotionless one, nothing more than a polite ritual, but it had sent every nerve in her body tingling.

"I've been givin' the problem serious thought." He hoped to alleviate any misconception that she might have that his was a spur-of-the-moment decision. The weighty conclusion had interrupted his sleep more than one night. "I think we made the only reasonable choice."

She nodded, wondering what it would feel like to touch his hair. Would it feel soft or coarse and springy? And his mouth. It was beautifully shaped, with full, clearly defined lips that looked unbelievably warm and sensual. What would it feel like to have his mouth fully explore hers?

Her eyes widened guiltily when she realized he was aware of the way she was shamelessly regarding him. A slow grin spread across his features, the devilish smile crinkling the corners of his eyes.

For a moment he looked as if he wanted to kiss her—really kiss her this time—but the moment passed, and before she knew it, he was quickly hefting her onto the buggy seat without further ado.

The stop by Miller's Mercantile was kept short because of the worsening weather. The store was busy, and Beau offered to hold Mary Kathleen while Charity made her selections.

He carried the infant around the store, acting very paternal, pointing out various articles to the child, which Mary Kathleen could not possibly understand or appreciate the meaning of. Charity watched as he paused and whispered conspiratorially to the child about a certain rag doll Santa Claus might be persuaded to bring her, if she promised to get her outrageous sleeping schedule back in order. His endearing petition warmed Charity's heart.

When Charity's purchases were completed, the baby exchanged hands so Beau could shop. Charity browsed through the bolts of brightly colored yard goods.

"This is the finest one we have in stock," the proprietor, Edgar Miller, proclaimed as he handed Beau a heavy hammer. "The head is forged iron, and the handle is solid oak."

Beau examined the tool carefully. Assured it would serve his needs well, he agreed to buy it and turned his attention to the vast array of hoes, rakes, spades, ropes, and kegs of nails. When he'd satisfied his curiosity about all the shiny new farm implements, he moved on to examine the food staples behind the counter on long rows of shelves.

There were large containers of soda crackers, coffee, tea—black and Japanese—starch in bulk, bottles of catsup, cayenne, soda, and cream of tartar, often used in place of baking powder.

The floor of the mercantile was lined with barrels. There were two grades of flour: white and middlings, coarse meal, and buckwheat flour. Large barrels of apples from Missouri, sacks of potatoes, turnips, cabbages, pumpkins, and long-neck squashes were in plentiful supply. There was more: salt pork, in a crock under a big stone to keep the pork down in the brine, vinegar, salt, molasses, and three grades of sugar: fine white—twenty pounds for a dollar—light brown, and very dark.

The counters were brimming with baskets of eggs—three dozen for a quarter—big jars of golden butter, selling for twelve and a half to fifteen cents a pound. There was cheese all the way from New York, maple syrup, and dried peaches and apples.

"Do you have any raisins?" Beau prompted.

"Raisins?" Edgar scratched his head thoughtfully. "Afraid not . . . but I could probably get some from over in Hayes."

"How long would it take to get them here?"

"Depends. If the weather cooperates, they should be here in a week or so. They'll be right costly, though."

"I'll take four pounds."

"Four?"

Beau nodded. "Four should do it."

While Edgar wrote the order, Beau looked at the row of watches and rings displayed in a glass case beneath the counter. His attention was immediately drawn to an exquisite emerald brooch that lay nestled on a bed of royal-blue velvet. Something about the brooch reminded Beau of Charity. The stones were elegant and the design most intriguing. Such a delicate piece of jewelry seemed out of place among the large watches and gaudy baubles surrounding it.

"May I see the brooch, please?"

Edgar glanced up and smiled. "Of course. Lovely piece, isn't it?" He moved over to unlock the case. Gently he lifted the box containing the brooch and placed it on the counter for Beau's inspection.

"Just got it in a couple of days ago," Edgar volunteered.

"It's beautiful." Beau lifted the brooch from the velvet box. The green stones caught the light and danced brightly. It suddenly occurred to him why the piece of jewelry reminded him of Charity. The stones were the exact shade of her eyes.

"Yeah, a couple of Indian squaws come waltzing in here day before yesterday and offered the brooch in trade for three bottles of whiskey and a handful of peppermint sticks."

"You don't say." Beau turned the piece over and examined the craftsmanship closely. Indeed, it was worth more than three bottles of whiskey and a handful of peppermint sticks.

"I'll make you a good deal on it," Edgar offered.

"How much?" Beau countered.

The price Edgar set was completely out of line, especially in view of the fact he'd just foolishly revealed to Beau what he'd given for the brooch. However, Beau knew the man would have no trouble finding someone who'd pay the exorbitant price.

"Well, thanks, but I'm afraid that's a little too steep." Regretfully Beau placed the brooch back in the box.

It would be Christmas in three weeks, and he didn't have anything to give his new bride. The brooch would have made a nice gift.

Beau started to walk off as Edgar slid the box back into the case. He suddenly turned and hurried back. "How much did you say those raisins would cost?"

Edgar repeated the price. The brooch would cost four times what the raisins would cost. But Beau had the money to buy the brooch; and he wanted Charity to have it.

"Then cancel the raisins, and I'll take the brooch," Beau said, grinning. He hadn't had a raisin pie in over a year; he guessed he could do without one a little longer.

Edgar smiled. "A gift for your lady?"

"Yeah. I married Charity Burkhouser about an hour ago, and I think she'll enjoy the brooch more than I'd enjoy the raisins."

Beau's grin widened as he watched Edgar's mouth drop open.

Beau noticed Charity was unusually quiet on the way home. It was growing dark, and they still had several miles to go before they reached the soddy.

The baby was sleeping and seemed unaffected by the cold as Beau urged the horse's steps to a faster cadence.

"You cold?"

"A little." The weather was uncomfortable, but Charity found she didn't mind. She was still enjoying such a warm glow from the unexpected turn of events, she barely noticed the discomfort. The baby had been returned to her care, and she and Beau were married. She didn't see how she could complain about a little thing like bad weather.

"I'd hoped to make it back before dark," Beau apologized.

"I don't mind. I'm fine."

"You think the baby's cold?"

"She doesn't appear to be." Charity reached down and adjusted the heavy blanket surrounding Mary Kathleen like a cocoon.

They'd ridden in silence for a few minutes when Charity remembered. "Were you able to get the raisins?"

"No . . . Mr. Miller would've had to order them."

"Oh. How long would it have been before they'd arrived?"

"He said about a week."

Snow began to fall again as the horse briskly trotted down the road, pulling the buggy containing the newly formed family.

Charity let her thoughts wander as the last vestige of twilight faded. The world around her became a fairyland of white as the snow began to sift down in earnest now.

She longed to snuggle closer to her husband's large body, but she didn't dare. He would surely think her forward, and just because they were married now, she couldn't start taking such wifely liberties. After all, it was still to be determined to what extent he intended to participate in their marriage.

Her gaze drifted shyly to him and she found him immersed in his own thoughts. His hands drove the buggy deftly, and she thought how nice it was to have a man perform that task for her.

Would he join her in her bed tonight? The thought jumped unexpectedly into her mind, startling her. It was shameful to be thinking such a thing, but the tantalizing prospect sent goose bumps skittering up and down her spine.

Would she object? The answer came more easily than the question: not at all. She was prepared to be his wife in every aspect he desired her to be. Even if he planned to leave her in the spring, it would not change her feelings. She would seek his comfort, tend his needs, and share his life for as long as he chose to remain with her.

And when the time came for him to leave, she would see him off with a smile and good wishes. She'd made herself that promise, and she intended to keep it.

Charity shifted around on the seat, adjusting the blanket more tightly around her. The darker it became, the colder it was.

"You might be warmer if we moved closer together." Beau's suggestion was spoken so casually that Charity wasn't sure if it was an invitation or not. "Just slide the baby onto your lap. She'll probably be warmer there anyway."

"Oh . . . well, yes. Thank you." Charity carefully repositioned the baby, then edged closer to him until she felt her hip make contact with his solid thigh.

She was so aware of him, not only aware of his masculine build, but close enough now to smell his distinct scent: a combination of soap, leather, wool, and the elements.

"Better?" Beau glanced at her and smiled.

"Yes, thank you."

They were closer than they'd ever been and Charity felt her limbs growing weak.

"Seems like we should be sayin' somethin' a

little more meaningful, doesn't it?" Beau was the first to break the strained silence moments later.

"Meaningful?"

"Yeah, I mean, it is our wedding day. . . ."

"Yes, seems we should have something to say, all right." Charity fondly recalled the day she and Ferrand had married. Birds had been singing, and the grass had been a rich, lush green carpet for her to tread upon. The church had overflowed with well-wishers, and there had been baskets of flowers and a large wedding cake.

"Was the weather nice the day you married Betsy?"

Until now Charity had been able to view and talk about Betsy in a charitable light. But now, just the casual mention of her name sent streaks of jealousy shooting through her as she thought about the intimacy Beau and his first wife must have shared on their wedding night.

"Yes, it was. It was a warm fall day. The leaves on the trees were gold and yellow and brown. . . ." His eyes took on a faraway look, and Charity wished she hadn't brought up the subject.

"What was the date?" It shouldn't matter; yet, for some reason, she had to know.

"Second of October. What about you and Ferrand?"

"June second."

Silently each pondered the coincidence; it was the second of December—their wedding day.

"I—I was quite surprised when you asked Reverend Olson to marry us," Charity confessed. "But very grateful."

"The gossip was bothering you, wasn't it?"

"A little," she admitted. "But I would've seen it through." It hadn't been easy facing the accusing stares from the citizens of Cherry Grove. The few times she'd ridden into town for supplies had been disconcerting, but having Beau remain with her had been worth it.

"No need for either one of us to be the source of malicious gossip. Talk should quiet down now."

"I hope you don't mind, but I—I told several women at the mercantile we were married now."

"I don't mind. I told Mr. Miller myself."

Charity grinned. "You did? Well, thank you."

"It was my pleasure. You should've seen Edgar Miller's mouth drop open."

"Oh, he's the biggest gossip of all."

"That's why I made sure he was the first to know about us gettin' married. Maybe his tongue will have a chance to cool down now."

Charity sighed. "I surely hope so."

"By spring I should have the land in good shape," Beau predicted as he urged the horse across Fire Creek and headed north.

"With the two of us working it shouldn't take long," Charity agreed.

She wanted to ask if he still planned to leave then, but selfishness stopped her. She wanted nothing to interfere with the happiness she was feeling.

"Charity . . . about our marriage . . ." Beau paused, hesitant to approach the touchy subject.

Charity blushed, knowing the conversation was about to take a more personal turn. "Yes?"

"Well, I know you must be wonderin' if I expect to claim my . . ." Beau's voice trailed off uneasily, and she was sure that if she could see his features clearly, he would be blushing!

Her lofty spirits plummeted. She braced herself; next he would inform her that he had no intentions of claiming his husbandly rights because he didn't want to make love to anyone but his Betsy.

Beau started again. "I . . . well, I think we would . . . of course, we both need to . . . Well, hell, we should talk about . . . but then it's not gonna be exactly the same. . . ." He was having a horrible time making his point.

"Are you tryin' to say you don't plan to exercise your husbandly rights?" Charity offered gently, hoping to help ease his painful dilemma.

Beau's gaze flew to meet hers. "Well, no . . . I wasn't tryin' to say that."

"You weren't?" Charity's pulse jumped erratically with his rather adamant denial.

"No . . . I didn't mean that at all. I just meant it might be sort of . . . embarrassing at first. . . . Well, you know. . . . It might take us a while to get used to . . . get to know each other. . . ."

"You mean, you think we should sort of sneak up on it," Charity teased, delighting in the way he promptly scowled at her, clearly shocked by her brazenness.

"A Claxton never sneaks up on a woman," he stated. "Believe me . . . when it's gonna happen, you'll know it."

"I'm sure I will." And she could hardly wait.

She settled deeper into the blanket. A few moments later she scooted closer, pressing herself tightly against his side.

Beau was aware of her movements, and he shifted his leg so it was resting more fully against hers.

He felt desire begin to build, strong and powerful, making him feel almost giddy with the knowledge that once again he felt like a whole man.

"I was just thinking how nice it will be to

get home," Beau remarked as the horse trotted along in the falling snow.

"Yes, it will be nice. The fire will feel exceptionally good this evening."

Her hand reached over to shyly slip into his.

His hand tightened on hers perceptibly. He had no idea what was happening to him, but he was enjoying it. "The bed won't feel all that bad either."

"No, I find I'm rather looking forward to it."

"I was thinking the same thing."

Well, hell, why not, he argued irritably, trying to still the faint twinge of conscience tugging at him. Betsy was gone. And he was still a young man with some very fundamental, long-suppressed needs. It had been over a year since he'd been with a woman . . . and the woman he had in mind now was his wife.

But you haven't given one single thought to whether you'll be stayin' with this woman come spring, his conscience reminded. *You just went off half cocked and jumped into marriage without givin' the future much thought.*

And I don't plan to. At least not tonight, Beau thought stubbornly.

"I hope the baby decides to sleep tonight," Charity said softly.

"If we're . . . busy . . . it won't hurt her to cry a little. I think we're spoiling her," he blurted, his voice coming out louder than he intended.

"If we're . . . busy," she agreed, "it won't hurt to let her fret for a spell." His words, though innocent, excited her. He was sparring with her suggestively, and she loved it.

Charity's head had somehow drifted to his shoulder, and she turned and pressed her face into the warmth of his neck. She no longer cared if she was behaving improperly. "How much farther?" she whispered.

Beau felt his desire leap and tighten almost painfully. "About another mile."

He glanced down and caught his breath when he saw their mouths were only inches apart.

"Don't go to sleep on me," he urged in a voice that had gone husky with desire.

She looked up at him, her heart in her eyes. "I was just thinking how very nice that might be."

Beau's mouth lowered another fraction. "I was thinkin' neither one of us might get much sleep tonight."

"I'm not at all sleepy." Her tongue came out to boldly trace the outline of his mouth.

"Oh, hell, Charity." Beau's voice sounded shaken, raspy, as his lashes drifted closed and he allowed himself to become a willing captive of her sweet seduction.

"I . . . hope you don't mind," she whispered, her mouth moving over his experimentally. She was surprised to see how easily she could take such liberties with him. It felt natural . . . good.

"Mind? Do I look like a fool?" His hand reached to cup the curve of her face, making her mouth more accessible to his.

Their mouths touched, hesitantly at first, their tongues gently tasting and exploring.

"Charity . . ." He whispered her name again before his mouth covered hers hungrily.

Her hands came up to encircle his neck, and they became immersed in firestorm of passion until the horse came to a sudden halt.

Beau opened one eye and groaned when he saw the buggy was stopped in front of the soddy. "We're home."

Charity smiled a little smile, pleased to discover the power she suddenly seemed to wield over him. "Uh-huh," she whispered, her mouth eagerly meeting his again.

"We'd better get in the house," Beau warned, when he was finally able to pull back from her embrace.

"Are you cold?" She gazed at him, her eyes hazy with unconcealed desire.

He placed her hand on the firm proof of his passion, and her breath caught. "No."

"Beau . . ." She wanted him.

"I'll get the baby." His voice held an urgency she'd never detected before.

"All right." She kissed him again, leaving her hand where he'd placed it, gently caressing his ardor. He was her husband. She longed to know every intimate part of him.

Beau's hands shook as he gathered the baby and stepped down from the buggy. "I'll take her inside and come back for you," he promised.

She watched as he started toward the soddy, her heart overflowing with love. She loved him. Maybe not in the exact way she'd loved Ferrand, but it was very, very close.

She began gathering the blanket, eager to become his wife in flesh, not just spirit, when she saw him come to a sudden, abrupt halt. He glanced back over his shoulder and called to her. "Did you leave a lamp burning?"

Charity glanced toward the window of the soddy and frowned when she saw the warm golden ray of light spilling out across the freshly fallen snow. "No."

He groaned. "I hope it isn't those two squaws again!" That was all he needed tonight. He returned to the buggy to grab his gun and hand the baby back to Charity before he turned toward the soddy again.

"You stay here until I see what's goin' on."

"Beau, wait. It may be dangerous!" Charity scrambled out of the buggy as Beau strode back to the soddy and kicked opened the door, gun drawn and positioned.

The young man sitting at the table looked momentarily startled at the hasty entrance. Quickly recovering, he invited in a dry voice. "Well, damn. Do come in."

Charity arrived breathlessly, quickly stepping behind her husband, her eyes widening as she viewed the splendid, dark-headed man in her home.

His boots were off, and his stocking feet were propped casually on the table. He had the tip of a cheroot stuck in his mouth, achingly familiar turquoise-blue eyes, and shamelessly long, thick black eyelashes. His hair was outrageously curly, and he looked as ornery as sin.

The man grinned, flashing a set of brilliant white teeth at her. "About time you and big brother was showing up."

Chapter 19

"Cass!" Beau shot an irritable scowl at his younger brother. "You always did have a way of bein' in the wrong place at the wrong time."

Cass Claxton looked personally affronted by Beau's less than friendly greeting. "Now, what do you mean by that? Here I've ridden for two weeks, through rain and snow and dark of night, just to see how my big brother is gettin' along, and he acts like I was a some varmint come crawling out of the woods."

Cass was being melodramatic, and Beau knew it.

"How'd you find me?" Beau pulled Charity into the room and closed the door. "Don't mind him," he said, nodding toward his younger brother before he hurried across the room to lay Mary Kathleen down in her makeshift bed near the hearth. "He's harmless."

Charity smiled uncertainly as her frozen fingers worked to untie the strings of her bonnet.

Cass grinned and pushed back from the table to get to his feet. A cocky, devil-may-care attitude stood out all over him. "Well, hello, ma'am. You must be the lovely widow Burkhouser." He removed his hat and tipped it politely.

Charity smiled timidly, not at all sure how to take his cavalier attitude. She glanced to Beau for guidance.

"She used to be Mrs. Burkhouser," Beau said easily while busily removing the baby's warm bunting. He seemed to have fully recovered from the shock of finding his brother sitting at the table. "How'd you get here?" He hadn't seen an extra horse when they'd arrived.

"I brought a wagon. It's out back. I wasn't sure where to stable the horses." With undisguised curiosity Cass watched Beau settle the baby.

"And just how did you find me?" Beau turned his full attention to his brother.

"Your letter was pretty clear about where you were. When I reached Cherry Grove, I asked around. An old man gave me directions to the Burkhouser soddy. When it started gettin' dark, and you failed to show up, I began to wonder if I had the wrong place."

"We had business to tend to. Why'd you bring a buckboard?"

"Oh, you know Ma and Willa," Cass complained. "I had to bring half the root cellar, extra blankets, and medicine in case you weren't bein' properly cared for." Cass glanced at Charity and his grin widened. "All that worrying for nothin'. Looks to me like you're bein' taken care of real well."

Beau smiled, thinking how characteristic it was of his mother to think of everything. He left the baby's crib to walk over and clasp his brother's hand warmly. "Good to see you, Cass."

Charity looked from brother to brother and could see not only love but a deep mutual respect shining in their eyes. It was an intangible bond that would be hard for an outsider to penetrate. Loyalty was deep and strong.

Cass held Beau's hand tightly, his face turning somber. "Good to see you, big brother. You're lookin' a whole lot better than I'd expected."

Beau shrugged. "It was close, but, thank God, I'm on the mend."

"We've all been real worried about you," Cass confided.

"I'm sorry I haven't written sooner. I should have done better."

"Oh, we understood."

"The family all okay?"

Cass grinned. "Doin' fine."

"Ma?"

"Strong as an ox."

"Cole?"

"Healthy as a horse."

"And Wynne?"

"Pretty as a picture."

"Did your teachers ever mention anything about enlargin' your sentences?" Beau teased.

"Never said a word about it."

Beau slapped Cass on the back good-naturedly. "Come here. I have someone I want you to meet."

The two men turned their attention to Charity, who was standing by the fire with a smile on her face.

Beau walked over and placed his arm around her waist. "Cass, this is my wife, Charity."

For a moment Cass was clearly stunned by Beau's unexpected announcement, and his face showed it. But to his credit he managed to regain his composure quickly. "Your . . . wife! Well, I'll be damned." He quickly whipped his hat off again, brushed his hand down the side of his tight-fitting denims, and extended it graciously. "Welcome to the family, ma'am. You're sure goin' to be a lovely addition."

"Thank you, Cass. I'm so happy to meet you. Beau has spoken of you often."

"Oh, he exaggerates," Cass objected. "I'm sure once you get to know me, you'll find out I'm not at all like he's painted me to be."

Charity laughed. "I can assure you, it has all been very complimentary."

Charity thought Cass was as adorable and as strikingly handsome as Beau. If Cole, the older brother, was any more handsome, she didn't think her heart could stand the strain.

"Don't tell him that," Beau protested. "It'll only swell his puffed-up head."

"So, you've remarried." Cass's gaze drifted nonchalantly over to Mary Kathleen's crib. "Been . . . married long?"

Realizing what must be running through his mind, Charity spoke up quickly. "Oh, no! Uh . . . the baby . . . she's not Beau's."

Beau looked at her with a stunned expression. "She isn't?" Then he turned to Cass and, to Charity's horror, added, "Isn't that a hell of a thing for a wife to tell her husband?" he said in disgust.

"Beau!"

Beau grinned roguishly as he watched her face flush a bright scarlet. His arm tightened around her affectionately. "The baby's parents are dead, Cass, and Charity and I have been taking care of Mary Kathleen," he explained. "We're hoping Charity will be given permanent custody of the child, once things settle down."

Charity thought she detected Cass's quick sigh of relief. "You don't say? Been taking care of a new baby, huh?" He stepped over and peered down at the sleeping Mary Kathleen. "She's real cute."

"We think so," Beau said proudly.

While Cass filled Beau in on the activities currently taking place in River Run, Charity cut thick slices of pie and made a pot of fresh coffee.

"Wait till you taste her pie," Beau bragged. Charity bustled around the small kitchen, listening to the conversation with growing amusement.

"Good, huh?"

"Best I've ever eaten."

"Better than Ma's?"

"It's almost as good."

The lamp had burned low when it was finally decided that they had more than one night to visit.

"I hope I'm not puttin' you out by stayin' a few days," Cass apologized.

"Not at all!" Charity protested. "I'm thrilled to finally meet a part of Beau's family."

"Well"—Cass began to yank off the boots he had put on earlier— "just tell me where to roll up. I'm so tired I could sleep on a thorn and not know it."

Charity's eyes met Beau's expectantly. In all the excitement it hadn't occurred to either of them that their privacy was going to be drastically affected by Cass's unexpected visit.

With only one room, one bed, and one pallet, any hope of consummating their marriage vows seemed impossible.

"Oh . . . well, I suppose you'll be sleeping . . ." She grappled awkwardly with the problem of where to put him.

"Outside," Beau interjected hurriedly.

Cass's face fell. "In this kind of weather?"

"Beau, he can't sleep outside," Charity reminded.

Cass glanced down and saw the neatly made pallet by the fire, and a relieved smile replaced his worried frown. "Oh, you always did like to pull my leg. I see you've already made my bed. Well, think I'll turn in. I'm plain tuckered out."

Charity smiled lamely. "Yes . . . well . . . good night."

As she turned away, she thought her bed seemed to suddenly dominate the tiny room. She began to edge timidly toward the mattress while Beau banked the fire for the night.

Cass settled himself on the pallet as Charity

proceeded to string a line across the room and hang a brightly patterned blanket over it.

Once she was assured of a modicum of privacy, she began to undress while listening to Beau bid his brother a good-night. A few moments later, he parted the curtain and stepped into the small cubicle.

Once again, the intimate area suddenly seemed stiflingly small.

"I'll get up with the baby for her night feeding," Beau offered. He sat down on the bed and began unbuttoning his shirt. "That way you won't have to . . . dress."

"Thank you." Her voice was so soft he could barely hear her.

"It's so late, I'm surprised she hasn't awakened before now."

"I'd have thought she would, too, but I guess she's real tired."

Charity stepped out of her dress and draped it neatly across a chair. She hurriedly fumbled for her gown hanging on a small hook and glanced at Beau self-consciously. "Would you mind . . . ?"

Beau looked up and saw her holding the gown to her chest protectively. "No . . . of course." He turned his head as she quickly slipped out of her chemise and pantalets, and pulled the gown over her head.

"All right . . . I'm through."

Beau stood up and peeled his shirt off and

unbuttoned his pants. He glanced at her questioningly, wondering if she'd prefer to turn her head while he undressed, but she was busy turning back the blankets, keeping her gaze carefully averted.

A moment later, she scurried beneath the covers. The bed creaked as Beau sat down on his side to remove his socks.

Charity lay stiff with apprehension, awaiting the moment he, too, would be under the blankets. She had no idea where her earlier boldness had fled to, but it had completely deserted her now.

Beau leaned over and blew out the lamp, throwing the room into total darkness as he finished undressing.

Charity lay perfectly still, thinking how much she'd always hated darkness. Fears tended to be amplified, doubts reborn, and small problems inflated to overwhelming obstacles when there was no light.

Many nights she'd slept with a lamp burning, so she wouldn't have to face the emptiness. Now that she was married again, would that horrible loneliness finally be over? she wondered.

And then he was there beside her.

Just as she'd begun to worry about how she would act, he stretched out next to her, his body warm and reassuring—the way it used to be when Ferrand was beside her.

She could still hear the wind howling outside, the tick of the clock on the mantel, the
baby making soft sucking sounds in her sleep,
Cass's soft breathing as he dropped deeper
and deeper into untroubled slumber. But
with Beau beside her it was as if her life had
been miraculously sorted out and put back
into order.

For a moment Beau lay quietly, lost in his
own thoughts.

She wondered if he was thinking of Betsy.

He wondered if she was thinking of Ferrand.

Finally, he rolled to his side and gently
drew her to him. She could feel the outline of
his body: the ridges, the sinewy muscles, the
tuft of springy hair above the opening at the
throat of his longjohns. She could feel the im-
print of his maleness pressed against her side.

His familiar fragrance drifted pleasantly
around her, and her hands trembled as her
arms reached out to encircle his neck. Her
breath caught as he pulled her flush against
him and whispered into her ear. "I'm sorry
about tonight. . . ."

His breath, rasping warmly and stirring her
hair, caused a flood of sensations to seep
through her like warm honey, all breathtaking, all mysterious, all inexplicably exciting.

"I understand. I guess the only thing that's

really important is you're here . . . that
we're together," she returned softly.

It occurred to her that neither she nor Beau
had mentioned to Cass that this was their
wedding night.

To her surprise, Charity felt her gown being moved aside, and she shivered as his hand
found her breast. She hadn't expected him to
touch her this way, but she found the gesture
pleasing. Slowly, Beau began to explore her
body, making slow, gentle forays up and
down her silken flesh. Charity found she
didn't object to his advances but welcomed
the feel of his hands moving warmly against
her flushed skin.

"You're at liberty to discover your husband," he reminded, his voice low and husky
against her ear.

"But your brother . . ."

"Please, Charity . . . just touch me," Beau
whispered. He had denied himself the pleasure of a woman for too long. Tonight, he desperately wanted and needed her touch.

Her hands shakily found the buttons on his
shirt, and she slowly released them. His chest
was broad and hairy just as she remembered.
She pressed her lips into the mat of soft hair
and breathed his name as his lips began to
explore the soft skin down the column of her
neck.

"You smell so good." He groaned and drew

her up even tighter against him. She felt so good, so warm, so alive.

She whimpered and moved against him, their mouths meeting in hungry urgency. It had been so long since she'd been held like this, so long since she'd been made to feel like a whole woman.

His mouth suddenly turned hard and demanding as the dam of his own pent-up emotions finally gave way. A flood of desire came rushing in on them as he crushed her to him, his mouth devouring hers. She moaned as streaks of pleasure darted through her, so intense, so glorious, they left her lightheaded.

He could feel her trembling beneath his touch, and it aroused him more to know her passion was as great as his.

He took her hand and guided it to the undeniable evidence of his desire. "Touch me . . . here . . . and here . . . and . . . here," he urged huskily.

She did, and she heard his sharp intake of breath as his mouth melted back into hers.

Their kisses deepened as the old clock ticked, and the baby searched hungrily for her fist, as Cass began to breathe deeper, and as the wind shook the soddy with periodic gusts.

"He'll only stay a few days," Beau promised, when their mouths would part momentarily. There was an agonizing ache within both of them, one that begged to be fulfilled, yet Beau knew it would be impossible to make love with his brother lying on the other side of the thin, makeshift petition.

Charity sighed as he finally drew her into the shelter of his side, burying his face in her hair, breathing deeply of the fragrant, lemon scent that always surrounded her.

"Just a few days," he whispered again reassuringly.

It was, indeed, a strange wedding night; as the fire began to die down to bright, rosy embers, the bride and groom dispiritedly accepted the unkind twist of fate and began to drift to sleep.

Charity realized that it was almost a perfect night—at least, for her.

It was the first time, in a very long time, she'd fallen asleep with someone holding her in his arms.

Two weeks later, Cass was still there.

When Beau inadvertently told his brother of the large amount of work he had to accomplish by spring, Cass decided to stay for a while, and lend his brother a hand. It seemed to him the only proper thing to do.

Beau was grateful for the help, but his growing frustration at having no time alone with his bride considerably dimmed his enthusiasm.

Each night had become an exercise in self-discipline, one that Beau didn't relish having forced upon him.

And the enforced celibacy hadn't been easy on Charity either. Each accidental touch, each innocent smile, each unexpected brush of hands or coincidental meeting of gazes, only served to revive the deepening ache that screamed for fulfillment.

It was small consolation for her to know that Beau was struggling just as hard as she to remain pleasant until Cass decided to return to Missouri, but their combined attempt at tolerance was wearing noticeably thin.

"It can't be much longer!" Beau whispered fervently, his voice reflecting the anguish Charity felt.

They lay in the dark, closely entwined in their tiny prison behind the curtain. "He'll have to leave before winter sets in for good." The few insignificant storms they'd had would soon give away to howling blizzards, making travel impossible until spring.

The bed creaked, and Charity jumped uneasily. The noise ricocheted across the room like a loud rifle crack as Beau cast prudence aside and rolled her body on top of his. Before she could protest, and remind him that his brother lay only a few feet away, his hands came up to capture the sides of her face, his lips taking hers roughly in an urgent, seemingly insatiable kiss.

"Beau . . . please . . ." Charity tensed as she heard Cass stir on the pallet, and Beau's hands became more aggressive. She was certain Cass had heard the bed squeak. "He'll hear us. . . ." Her warning ran over Beau's lips like warm butter, and she found it hard to think, let alone protest.

"I can't stand this another minute. Let's go out to the lean-to," Beau urged, his hands beginning to take liberties that made her body grow warm and fluid. "I know it's cold, but we can stand it," he promised in a voice that was so suggestive Charity was sorely tempted to do as he asked.

"I'd want to, but Cass will hear us," she murmured as his mouth continued to tantalize and torment, "and the baby will wake up . . . and cry. . . ."

Chances were, they couldn't successfully slip out of the soddy without disturbing both Cass and Mary Kathleen, and both would be made to look foolish. Charity couldn't bear the thought. "Then Cass'll know. . . ." She moaned softly as his hands probed pleasure points that set her body aflame.

"No, he won't," he pleaded. "And even if he does, he's a grown man, he'll understand."

"Beau . . . please . . ."

"Charity . . . please . . ." His mouth slid down to nibble along the column of her neck.

"Beau . . ."

Then farther.

Her breath caught. "Beau . . ."

And farther.

"I'm your husband . . . I want you . . . all of you . . . right now!"

Cass stirred again, and Charity realized this sweet madness must stop before it robbed her of all control. Beau might be able to face his brother tomorrow morning without reservations, but she couldn't!

She cupped Beau's face in her hands and shook it gently. "Soon, my impatient husband, soon."

Beau groaned and flipped over on his back despondently. "I'm gonna die," he announced flatly, his voice holding not the slightest hope he would survive this harsh and unnecessary punishment.

Charity frantically clamped her hand over his mouth to prevent Cass from hearing, but Beau's overblown pessimism brought a reluctant grin to her face.

Beau was right. Cass *had* to leave soon.

The following morning Beau and Cass were sitting at the table finishing breakfast, and Charity was preparing to hang the wash.

While serving Beau's breakfast, she'd playfully heightened his overstimulated senses. She'd pressed intimately against his leg and brushed her hand against his arm when offering him more biscuits. And when refilling his coffee, she'd made sure her breast rested on his shoulder.

The highly provocative gestures had been performed for purely selfish reasons. She loved the feel of him. She loved the deliciously giddy knowledge that at the end of the day, he would once again lie beside her, touch her, whisper tantalizing intimacies that only a man would whisper to the woman he desired. Making love would be wonderful, but she loved this hungry side of him as well.

Beau's eyes had instantly darkened with the knowledge of what she was doing, but she noticed he'd pretended to ignore her. She'd known it was wrong to arouse him when he could do nothing to alleviate his misery, yet the impish side of her had delighted in the way he'd shot her a stern warning before diverting his attention back to his plate.

Even Cass was beginning to notice his brother's unusually sour disposition. Beau had snapped at him twice over something so trivial it had made both his and Charity's brows lift in astonishment.

"Would you mind watching the baby while I hang the wash?" Charity inquired as soon as the last breakfast dish was washed and put away.

Beau was sitting in front of the fire, pulling his boots on.

"How long will that take?" he asked sharply.

Charity glanced up. "Not long. Why?"

"I can't get anything done if I have to stay in the house and baby-sit," he barked.

Charity sighed. Indeed he was in a very foul mood this morning.

"I'll watch Mary Kathleen," Cass offered.

"You can't watch Mary Kathleen and drive nails at the same time!" Beau snapped.

Cass looked at Charity and shrugged good-naturedly. "I can't watch Mary Kathleen and drive nails at the same time. Sorry." He held his forefinger up as an afterthought occurred to him. "But I would, if I could." Charity detected a mischievous twinkle in his eye now as he tried to smooth over Beau's uncharacteristic bad humor.

"I'm perfectly able to watch Mary Kathleen," Beau grumbled. "I merely asked how long it'd be before I'd be able to start on my work." The tone of his voice left no doubt that *his* work was far more important than hers, but she let the thinly veiled implication slide.

"Fifteen minutes at the most," Charity bargained.

"Try to make it ten."

"I'll pin as fast as I can." She shot him an impatient look, picked up the basket of wet clothes, and sailed out the door, letting it bang soundly shut behind her.

Still seething, she marched to the clothes line, flung the basket on the ground, and began haphazardly to pin diapers and washcloths in a long, disorderly row. She knew Beau's long-suppressed libido was the cause of his ill temper, and she could sympathize, but she was getting tired of his nasty disposition. The past two weeks hadn't exactly been a bed of roses for her either.

Submerged deep within her self-pity, she failed to detect the silent steps of a tall, muscular Indian as he moved away from a bush and began to approach her.

The brave's nut-brown hand suddenly snaked out and clasped her arm firmly, making her jump and squeal with fright. She nearly swallowed the clothespin she'd just wedged between her teeth.

"Mhhhhhhhhh?" Her wide eyes peered up at his imposing height helplessly. She prayed Beau was watching from the window, but she knew that was unlikely.

"You White Sister?" His voice was deep and gruff. Had he asked her if she was Mrs. Wahkun-dah, she was so terrified she'd have agreed.

So she nodded wordlessly.

The brave's eyes narrowed. "Why White Sister have stick in mouth?"

"Mhhh . . ." Charity hurriedly reached up and removed the clothes pin. "I—I'm hanging wash."

"Hanging wash?" His black eyes grew confused. How White Sister hang "wash," he wondered. Red Eagle "wash" in water, and water cannot be hung up with funny-looking sticks.

Charity's heart was pounding, and her knees had turned to pulp as she looked at the exceptionally tall brave. He wasn't Kaw, she was sure of it.

Cheyenne, perhaps. He was breathtakingly handsome, with high cheekbones, a proud aristocratic nose, and long black hair that whipped freely about in the blustery wind.

He was wearing buckskins, moccasins, and a massive buffalo robe draped over his broad shoulders to ward off the chilly morning air.

"Did . . . can I do something for you?" she squeaked, wondering if he'd come here to harm her. Maybe he'd been hunting and when he happened to notice her hanging the wash, he'd become curious. She hoped that was the case.

"No can find Laughing Waters."

"Oh?"

"Laughing Waters say to Red Eagle, 'White Sister make good medicine.' "

"Oh . . . she said that, did she?"

The brave crossed his arms and stared back at her authoritatively. "Squaw heap big sick. White Sister make good medicine."

Charity decided he must be trying to tell her that his wife was sick and Laughing Waters was not available to tend her.

"Well, I'm not very good. . . . Laughing Waters and Little Fawn are much better at this sort of thing," Charity hedged.

"No can find cuckoo sisters," he announced flatly.

"Oh, dear. Well, I . . ." Charity searched for a reasonable excuse to deny his request but failed to think of one. "What's wrong with your . . . squaw?"

He rubbed his stomach. "Big hurt."

"Oh. Well, come with me, then." She had no idea what the problem could be, but she figured a good dose of castor oil couldn't harm and might cure his under-the-weather squaw.

As Charity traipsed into the soddy with the brave following close behind, Beau and Cass caught sight of the pair and their mouths dropped open.

Beau scrambled for his gun, while Cass sprang to his feet, every muscle tensed and ready for combat.

Without a word of explanation Charity hurried to the cabinet and extracted a large bottle, then poured a small portion of the contents into a fruit jar. Screwing the lid on tightly, she handed the jar to the Indian. "Make squaw drink."

The brave held the jar up to closely examine the thick, gummy substance. He scowled. "Make squaw drink?" He wasn't sure he'd heard her right. This did not look like something someone should drink.

"Yes, I know. It looks awful, but it might help."

The brave, taking her at her word, nodded. He looked sourly toward Beau and Cass, their bodies posed for immediate confrontation. Then he turned his gaze back to Charity. "Red Eagle no forget White Sister."

If the castor oil didn't do the trick, Charity sincerely hoped that, at least in this particular instance, his memory *would* fail him.

"Who in the hell was that?" Beau demanded after the brave made a quick exit out the door.

Charity shrugged. "I have no idea. I was busy hanging the wash, and he came up and said his squaw was sick and needed medicine."

Beau hadn't failed to notice how handsome the young brave was, and he found himself annoyed when he realized he was jealous of his wife's attentions toward another man. Just how well did she know that strapping, blatantly potent young buck?

"You mean, just out of the clear blue sky, he waltzed up and asked you for medicine?"

"He did, but that isn't unusual," she pointed out. "The Indians around here are rather straightforward when it comes to getting what they want."

"You've never met him before today?" Beau challenged again.

"If you mean, do I have any of his papooses running wild around here, the answer is no." Though she didn't understand or appreciate the insulting insinuation in his voice, she couldn't help but add, "But he was quite a striking man, don't you think?"

She was pushing her luck, and she knew it.

Beau looked back at her coolly. "I hope you mentioned you were under a man's protection now—just so he doesn't get the idea of comin' around when I'm not here," he countered tersely.

Cass watched the growing fracas with barely concealed amusement. Beau was jealous as hell, but didn't want to admit it, even to himself.

Charity's chin lifted with unmistakable defiance. "I don't believe we got around to that subject."

Their eyes locked stubbornly.

"Well, well." Cass awkwardly reached for his coat. "Guess we best be gettin' to those chores, Beau. We're burnin' daylight."

"I was thinkin' the same thing." Beau swiped his coat from the peg and opened the front door. "I suppose you're through hangin' wash?" He glared at Charity.

"It certainly looks that way, doesn't it!"

The door snapped shut briskly.

The next morning, bright and early, a brisk rap sounded at the door.

Both Charity and Beau went to answer it.

"I'll get it."

"I'll get it," Beau corrected.

"I'm perfectly capable of answerin' my own door."

Their gazes locked obstinately.

Beau gave in first and Charity opened the door.

The handsome brave who'd caused all the trouble the day before stood before them, his face wreathed with an ecstatic grin.

"White Sister make good medicine." He held up three fingers. "Many papooses!"

Chapter 20

The following morning, the bell hanging over the door to Miller's Mercantile tinkled melodiously as Beau and Cass stepped inside. The store was empty, except for Edgar, who was busy putting turnips in a large barrel.

"Mornin', Mr. Claxton." Edgar wiped his hands on his apron and stepped behind the counter. "What can I get for you today?"

"I'm gonna need nails, wire, and a few more fence posts."

"Sure thing. Just got a new load of posts in yesterday. Who's that you got there with you?" Edgar eyed the tall, blue-eyed man with Beau, already deciding the two must be kin; there was a strong family resemblance.

Beau introduced Cass to the friendly little proprietor.

Edgar reached out and shook Cass's hand cordially. "Thought you two must be brothers. Where you from, Mr. Claxton?"

"Missouri."

"Missouri, huh? Never been there. Always wanted to, just never got the opportunity."

Beau told Edgar the amounts he needed, and Edgar wrote it all down on a large, thick pad.

"Got those raisins in," Edgar mentioned.

Beau gazed longingly at the large glass jar of raisins sitting on the shelf. He could buy the raisins, and Charity could make a pie . . . or he could save the money and apply it toward a new plow this spring. He quickly tossed the temptation aside. Charity needed a plow worse than he needed raisins. "Thanks, but I'll be passin' up the raisins today, Edgar."

"Just thought I'd mention it," Edgar replied easily.

"Appreciate it."

While Beau and Cass browsed, Edgar went about filling the order.

The door opened again, and a small, rather harried-looking man entered the store, accompanied by a girl who looked as if she must be his daughter.

She was a beauty with an exquisite figure and lovely, amethyst-colored eyes. Her golden blond hair, scooped up into a mass of ringlets, trickled down the back of her head beneath the brim of the latest fashion in Paris.

She had a wide, innocent-looking gaze, but her full lips formed a petulant look as if she'd just finished sucking a lemon.

Cass glanced up and took note of the new arrivals. Upon seeing the man and his daughter, he promptly returned his attention to the shirts he was examining.

The bell tinkled again, and Reverend Olson entered the mercantile. Catching a glimpse of Beau, he immediately came over and struck up a conversation.

"How's Mary Kathleen?"

"Growing like a weed."

"And your new bride?"

"She's just fine."

The reverend chuckled. "I hope the baby is allowing the newlyweds some privacy by sleeping longer periods at a time."

Beau flashed a tolerant grin. "She's not botherin' us."

And Mary Kathleen wasn't.

"Well, I haven't been able to locate any of Ansel or Letty's kin. I've sent letters, but as yet, I haven't received an answer," Reverend Olson admitted. "Now, the Farrises have offered to look after the baby, if you and Charity want, but with nine in the family and another on the way . . ."

"Mary Kathleen's doin' just fine with us,"

Beau dismissed abruptly. "Charity would be lost without her."

Reverend Olson gazed back at Beau kindly. "And what about you?"

Cass approached the two before Beau could answer. "I don't believe you've met my brother, Reverend. Cass, I'd like you to meet Reverend Olson."

Cass extended his hand, and Reverend Olson grasped it firmly.

The Reverend's smile was as pleasant as always. "Will you be staying in Kansas long, Cass?"

Funny. That was the question uppermost in Beau's mind too.

"I will *not* have that *filthy, disgusting,* piece of slime on my back!"

The men pivoted at the sound of a woman's shrill voice raised in self-righteous anger.

"Now, Patience, dear . . ." Leviticus McCord ducked hurriedly as a bolt of material came sailing over his head and landed with a thud at the feet of the three men, who stood watching the enveloping ruckus with growing curiosity.

"I am *sick* and *tired* of having to look like a —a common *peasant* all the time!" With one fell swoop Patience McCord angrily cleared the table of calico, cotton, and muslin. The floor of the mercantile suddenly looked as if it had been hit by a cyclone.

Cass watched as the girl turned tail and flounced over to rifle through the display of ribbons and fine laces.

Cass, Reverend Olson, and Beau haltingly resumed their conversation as Leviticus began to gather up the bolts of material, mumbling something softly under his breath about having only suggested the material might look nice on her—nothing to get all that upset about.

"I'm planning on headin' back to Missouri while the weather holds," Cass said, answering Reverend Olson's interrupted inquiry.

"Well, I'm sure Beau has appreciated having another set of hands to help with the work."

Reverend Olson cautiously eyed Patience, who, having moved to the rack of cooking utensils, was plainly trying to eavesdrop on the men's conversation.

"Patience McCord is a high-spirited girl," Reverend Olson whispered. "Extremely high spirited."

"Acts like a spoiled brat," Cass observed curtly. He was shocked by such an unladylike display of temper. "The woman has the manners of a goat."

Patience heard his remark, and her perfectly arched brows lifted with disdain. When Cass shot her an imperious look that not only matched hers but topped it, she quickly moved on.

"Oh, dear. Well, remember, *I* didn't say that," Reverend Olson insisted nervously. "The McCords are new in town. Leviticus is a retired circuit judge. He and his daughter came from back East, and it seems the girl hasn't quite made the adjustment her father had hoped she would."

The men began to drift apart, trying to remain nonchalant in the wake of a wildcat being turned loose in their midst.

A few minutes later, Cass was forced to duck again when he heard Patience scream and a bottle of perfume came sailing over his head to smash noisily against the west wall.

His head shot up, and his hands moved defiantly to his hips, but the girl had diverted her full attention to bullying poor Edgar Miller.

"Why don't you have something as simple as a spool of red thread? You have every other color," she accused. *"Why* don't you have red?"

"I did have red," Edgar said, eager to console her, "but Ethel Bluewaters came in yesterday and bought the last—"

"Incompetent fool! Sheer incompetence!" Her eyes narrowed threateningly. "It's a lucky thing you have the only mercantile in town, Mr. Miller, or I would certainly take my business elsewhere!"

Edgar prayed daily that such colossal good fortune would befall him. "Miss McCord, I have a new shipment of thread coming in next week, and I'm sure there will be plenty of red—"

Edgar's sincere apology was interrupted as she bombarded him with a barrage of spools. "I wouldn't buy your stupid thread even if you had it!"

He cringed and ducked, throwing his arms over his head protectively as the spools continued to bounce off the counter . . . and his balding head.

"Patience, dear! You must stop this!" Leviticus sucked in his breath and drew up his slight five-foot-two frame to boldly confront his daughter. Since the day his wife Althela had died, he'd had a terrible time controlling this unruly child. "Mr. Miller can't help it if Ethel Bluewaters bought his last spool of red thread!"

"The service here is *wretched*!"

Edgar was tempted to blurt that he was just thinking the same thing about her, but he valued his life.

"Now, dear"—Leviticus balled his fists up tight—"now, dear, we just can't have this! You'll just have to go back home until you can get yourself under control."

Cass leaned against the doorway, lit a cheroot, and watched the way the girl had managed to tree two grown men without firing a single shot.

It was amazing, he thought.

"That's perfectly all right with me." Turning her nose up haughtily, Patience lifted the hem of her skirt and swept past her father with the regal air of a queen holding court.

She paused momentarily when she came face to face with Cass, who by now had stepped over to deliberately challenge her path through the door.

"Get out of my way, cowboy." She spat the words out contemptuously, her violet eyes flashing with renewed anger.

Cass slowly placed the cheroot between his teeth, his dark eyes glittering combatively. Lazily, he reached up and pushed his hat back on his head. "And if I don't?" He grinned insolently. He'd put a stop to this real quick. No way would she push him around.

After a tense pause Patience hauled off and hit him squarely in the groin with her purse.

The blow was so unexpected, so explosive, that he saw stars. Staggering, he groped blindly for support as Beau stepped over and prevented him from falling down, face first.

Patience slammed out of the mercantile, rattling windowpanes and sending jars dancing merrily about on the shelves.

As Cass slid to the floor limply, Beau looked at his brother and shook his head sadly. "I don't suppose you've ever heard: 'Hell hath no fury like a woman scorned'?"

Cass shook his head lamely, not at all sure what had just hit him.

"Well," Beau sighed, offering him a hand, "you have now."

Charity opened the door to the soddy and scanned the flawless expanse of blue sky. It was an extraordinarily beautiful day.

She sighed. Christmas would be here next week, and she still didn't have a gift for Beau.

She'd finished knitting Cass a warm pair of socks, and Mary Kathleen a lovely new bonnet, but she wanted something special for Beau.

She wished now she'd ridden into town with the two brothers when they'd asked her to this morning. Instead she'd remained behind to do her weekly baking. By late morning she'd prepared six loaves of bread, and three sweet potato pies were cooling on the windowsill.

The pies reminded her of Beau's penchant for raisins, and the idea suddenly came to her that that's what she'd give him for Christmas: two large, plump raisin pies. By now Mr. Miller should have received the shipment of raisins.

Beau would be overjoyed when he woke up

Christmas morning to the smell of his favorite pies bubbling in the oven.

First thing tomorrow morning she'd bundle up Mary Kathleen and make the hour's ride into Cherry Grove.

"You feelin' any better?" Beau noticed Cass wasn't quite as pale as he'd been earlier. He was still trying to ride easy in the saddle and having a hard time of it.

"That woman's meaner than a two-headed snake," Cass grumbled.

"You shouldn't have provoked her," Beau reminded him. "Women like Patience Mc-Cord you need to leave alone."

"You don't need to worry about that. I hope I never have the misfortune of meeting up with that hellcat again."

They rode on for a few moments in silence, enjoying the unseasonably warm afternoon. "You know, you've been as testy as an old cow standing on her bag," Cass accused, reminding Beau of his own display of bad temper of late.

"I know," Beau said simply.

"Well?"

"Well, what?"

"Well, what in the hell's gotten into you? You never used to be so short fused. I don't know how Charity puts up with you."

Beau shrugged.

"Just exactly how long have you two been married, anyway?"

"How long you been here?"

Cass glanced at him confused. "What's that got to do with anything?"

"Because we'd just gotten married the afternoon you arrived," Beau said curtly.

Cass was flabbergasted. "Are you . . . you've got to be pullin' my leg," he accused.

Beau shook his head.

"You mean to tell me . . . you and she . . ." Cass frowned. It was beginning to dawn on him what his brother's problem might be.

Beau nodded sagely as he watched Cass figure out the extent of his intrusion into their honeymoon.

"Well, I'll be damned." Cass absently withdrew a cheroot from his shirt pocket, mulling over this surprising bit of news. No wonder Beau had been on edge. He'd slept in the same bed with his bride for two weeks, and unless Cass missed his guess, Charity was too shy to let her new husband make love to her while his younger brother was sleeping not twenty feet away. "Why didn't you say something?"

"I don't know. Maybe I wasn't exactly sure if I would be doin' the right thing by her if we had consummated our vows," Beau confessed.

"Now what's that supposed to mean? She's your wife, isn't she?"

"Yes, but the marriage isn't what you think."

As the two men rode along through the bright sunshine, Beau began to fill Cass in on the past year of his life. At times his voice filled with emotion as he relayed how miserable he'd been until that fateful day the wolf attacked him in the stream.

He spoke of how Charity, along with two Indian squaws, had worked to save his life. Cass could hear gratitude and deep appreciation in his brother's voice.

Beau told him of how Charity's husband had been killed in the war, leaving his young widow to struggle through the hardships of pioneering a homestead.

He talked about Mary Kathleen and how Charity had been left to carry on when both baby's parents had died untimely deaths.

Beau said he felt sorry for Charity. He said he'd married her because there had been ugly talk about their living together and because he wanted to make repairs to her land that would enable her to have a clear title come spring.

Never once did he say he loved her.

Never once did he say he intended to make their marriage permanent.

The strange omission bothered Cass.

"Are you sayin' you plan to leave, once Charity has the title to her land?"

Beau fixed his gaze on the winding road. Cass could see a muscle twitch in his brother's jaw, and he knew he'd hit a sore spot.

"I'm sayin' I'm not sure what I'm gonna do."

"Well, hell, Beau. If you're not gonna stay with her, do you think it's fair to . . . to . . . bed her?"

"I don't know."

"Do you love her?"

Did he love her? It had been such a long time since Beau had felt love, he wasn't sure he would even recognize the feeling again.

"I don't know . . . I still think of Bets. . . ."

"She's gone, Beau," Cass reminded him gently. "We all loved Betsy, but you have to go on. She'd want it that way."

"I know. It's just been real hard for me, Cass."

"Well, I think Betsy would approve of Charity," Cass pointed out, trying to ease his brother's conscience. "She seems like a fine woman. And she's beautiful. You have noticed that, haven't you?"

"Of course I have. And I can't deny that I desire her," Beau admitted. "Living together all winter . . . well, it would be impossible not to want her."

Cass recalled how jealous Beau had become over the Indian brave the day before, and he wondered if Beau even realized he loved the woman. Apparently he didn't.

"So you're not sure you love her enough to make a lifetime commitment?" Cass prompted.

Beau laughed mirthlessly. "Hell, who knows how long a lifetime is gonna be?"

"Well"—Cass sighed—"you'll have to decide what to do about Charity, but I'll make it a little harder on you." He flashed his brother an enlightened grin. "The weather's real nice, and it looks like there's gonna be a full moon tonight. I'll just saddle up and ride out to do a little huntin'." He winked knowingly. "Been meaning to do that, anyway."

Beau shook his head, but he couldn't deny the thrill of expectation that shot through him at the thought of being alone with his wife. "Leaving me and Charity all alone," he concluded dryly.

"You'll still have the baby—unless Mary Kathleen wants to go huntin' with me."

"I doubt she will. She's out of bullets."

Cass grinned and spurred his horse into a faster gait. "Well, let's get going, big brother." His grin widened. "We're burnin' daylight."

Chapter 21

When Beau and Cass arrived at the soddy, Beau asked Charity to prepare hot water for a bath.

Charity was surprised by his strange request, especially since it was the middle of the week; but she quickly set about filling kettles and putting them on the stove to heat.

After supper Beau dragged in the old washtub, laid out a bar of soap and a fresh towel, and requested complete privacy.

He bathed, shaved, combed, and brushed. By six o'clock he was immaculate, though he wasn't sure what for.

Throughout his preparations he'd weighed the dangers of embarking upon the course he had in mind.

Was it wise to consummate their marriage vows?

At first there had been no question in his mind. He would. He was a man who'd been without the company of a woman for over a year. And although his emotions had lain dormant during that time, his natural desires had not.

Charity was a beautiful woman who, like himself, had missed the pleasures of the marriage bed. So would it be so wrong if they took refuge in each other this long winter?

Neither he nor Charity had false expectations concerning their marriage. He'd been honest with her all along, and he understood she needed a man to gain the title to her land.

Yes, they desired each other. The past two weeks had proven that, but would desire be enough to see them through a lifetime, if he chose to remain with her come spring?

And for that matter, although it'd sometimes seemed like ten years, it had only been a little over a year since Bets had died. Fifteen months, sixty weeks, four hundred and fifty days . . . it seemed like a lifetime, yet it had been like only yesterday. Would it be a mockery of his vows to Betsy to bring another woman to his bed this soon?

He wrestled back and forth with the weighty questions until he grew short tempered again.

"I thought you were going hunting!" he snapped. Cass was contentedly sitting in the rocker, playing with Mary Kathleen, when Beau's accusation ricocheted across the room.

Charity glanced up from the sampler she was working on and frowned. "My goodness, Beau. Why would he be goin' huntin' to-night?"

"How should I know? But he said he was going." Beau focused a pointed look in Cass's direction.

"Oh, yeah. Well, listen, I am. I'm going," Cass promised. He sprang to his feet and carried Mary Kathleen back to her crib. After nuzzling her fat cheeks affectionately, he kissed the baby good-night, then reached for his coat.

"Don't look for me to be back till late," he warned. "I may even do a little fishin' while I'm out."

"Don't rush on our account," Beau told him in the most congenial voice he could summon.

Charity found Cass's odd behavior almost as puzzling as Beau's. "Fishing? Tonight?"

"Yeah, thought I'd take advantage of the mild weather. Won't be many more days like this one," Cass predicted as he pushed the brim of his hat high on his forehead. "Well, you two have a nice . . . evenin'."

"Cass!" Charity glanced at Beau worriedly.

Beau shrugged. "A man's got a right to go fishin' if he wants."

Cass jerked the door open before Charity could question him further.

And came face to face with Patience Mc-Cord.

He drew back defensively, a sharp pain shooting through his still tender groin as he recalled his earlier encounter with her. "What are you doing here?" he demanded.

"Mr. Claxton?"

"Yes!"

"Mr. *Cass* Claxton?"

He frowned at her. "That's right."

Patience recognized him as the man she'd tangled with at Miller's Mercantile that morning. She'd thought all along that the blond-headed man accompanying him was Cass Claxton, not this arrogant mule. Apparently she'd been mistaken. "Oh . . . I didn't realize who you were," she murmured.

Cass's eyes met hers coolly.

Patience took a deep breath and drew her shoulders up primly. It didn't really matter which Claxton he was. She was here to speak to him on a purely business matter. "I wonder if I might have a word with you, Mr. Claxton?"

"Me?" Cass couldn't imagine what she would have to speak to him about.

"Yes, if I may."

Charity and Beau had come up behind Cass, catching part of the conversation.

"Won't you come in, Miss . . ." Charity smiled and looked to Cass to provide the girl's name.

His stubborn look indicated he wasn't going to.

"Why, yes, thank you. I will." Patience quickly stepped into the soddy before Cass could protest.

She nodded pleasantly at Beau as her skirts brushed past him, and he nodded back.

Quickly closing the door behind her, Beau wondered what Patience McCord wanted with his brother. He surmised that she must have come to apologize for her outrageous behavior that morning.

"May I get you something warm to drink, Miss . . . ?" Charity glanced helplessly to Cass again. Now that the sun had set, the air had turned frosty. She was sure the young lady would greatly appreciate a cup of tea or coffee to ward off the chill.

"Miss McCord won't be staying long enough to socialize," Cass stated firmly.

Charity was stunned by his lack of hospitality. She had no idea who this woman was, but it was clear that Cass did not like her.

Patience returned Cass's fixed gaze, her nose lifting a notch higher. "Why thank you, Miss . . . ?"

"Mrs.," Charity supplied warmly. "Mrs. Claxton."

"Oh . . ." Patience's eyes turned coolly back to Cass. She was surprised anyone would have the man. "I hadn't assumed you were married."

"Charity is my wife, Miss McCord." Beau stepped over to place his arm around Charity's waist.

"Oh . . . well, as I was about to say, I don't care for anything to drink, Mrs. Claxton. I'm just here to speak with Cass."

"Then Beau and I will take a short walk and let you speak with him in private," Charity offered.

"You don't have to do that," Cass objected. He had no idea what Patience McCord wanted, but he wasn't going to make her visit any easier.

"Thank you. I would like to speak to Mr. Claxton alone," Patience acknowledged stiffly.

Charity checked on the baby, then smiled encouragingly at Patience as she reached for her shawl. "Take all the time you need. We'll enjoy the outing."

"Thank you ever so much." Patience moved closer to the warmth of the fire as Beau and Charity closed the door behind them.

"Who is she?" Charity asked as they stepped off the porch and began walking.

"Patience McCord. She and her father

were in Miller's Mercantile this morning where she made quite a scene." The recollection of Cass's unfortunate encounter with the highly temperamental Miss McCord brought a smile to Beau's face.

"Oh? She seems like a lovely young thing."

Beau wrapped his arm around his wife's waist and drew her ear up close to his mouth. "You think so? Well, let me tell you what that 'lovely young thing' did to *my* little brother."

Inside the soddy Cass squared off to meet his unwelcome adversary. "Now, what is it you wish to speak to me about, Miss McCord?" His gaze traveled impersonally over her petite figure, elegantly sheathed in an outfit he'd bet had set poor Leviticus McCord back a pretty penny.

Patience cleared her throat. "I understand you're from Missouri?"

"That's right."

"And you plan to return there soon?"

"I might."

He wasn't being the least bit cooperative, Patience realized, but then it really didn't matter. Her violet eyes were staunchly confident as she met his. "When you leave, I want you to take me with you."

Her pronouncement could have knocked Cass over with a feather. His forehead puckered, he shifted his weight to one foot, and stared at her as if he hadn't heard correctly. "You want *what?*"

"I want you to take me back to Missouri with you," she repeated.

"The hell I will." He turned and irritably jerked the buttons of his coat open and fumbled in his shirt pocket for a cheroot. The woman must be mad, he seethed.

"I'm prepared to offer you five hundred dollars if you'll escort me to my aunt's home in St. Louis."

Cass glanced up from lighting the cigar, and his eyes narrowed.

"Where would you get that kind of money?"

"That's none of your business," Patience informed him. "But I assure you I have it, Mr. Claxton. You see, it's imperative that I leave this little gopher hole they call a town and leave it immediately!"

"Imperative for what?"

"Imperative for my sanity," she snapped. "I simply cannot stand the thought of living in Cherry Grove, Kansas, another moment."

She eased forward, her eyes revealing her desperation as she reached out to clutch the sleeve of his coat imploringly. "You *must* help me. You are the only sane person in this hellhole who is wise enough to think of leaving. From what I can tell, the entire population of Cherry Grove is blissfully happy." She spat the words as if they left a bad taste in her mouth.

"When I overheard Reverend Olson telling Edgar Miller that you were planning to return to Missouri, I knew this was my chance to escape." Her eyes lit up like two Christmas trees at the exquisite thought of returning to civilization.

Coldly, Cass eyed the hand clutching his coat sleeve, and the hand dropped away. Patience began pacing the floor of the soddy. "You see, Mr. Claxton, if you'll get me safely back to St. Louis, I will pay you handsomely. Once I'm there, Daddy will understand how unhappy I've been in this—this rat's nest, and he'll let me stay. Oh! There will be parties and balls and lovely gowns once I'm under my Aunt Merriweather's excellent supervision." She gaily whirled around the floor, caught up in her fantasy.

Patience tactfully omitted that Aunt Merriweather tipped the bottle a wee bit more than she should, and that that was the reason Leviticus McCord had not left his daughter in St. Louis before. But it didn't really matter, Patience concluded. Mr. Claxton would never even have to meet Aunt Merriweather.

"Why, my daddy will surely be overjoyed to let me remain there once he comes to his senses and moves back there himself!" She paused, her face flushed prettily from the heat in the soddy. "Well?" She tipped her head flirtatiously. "Are you interested, Mr. Claxton?"

She didn't see how he could refuse. There was no way on earth for him to make such a vast amount of money by doing so little.

Cass stared at her while he slowly lifted his foot and struck a match across the bottom of his boot. "Not in the least."

Patience's brows shot up with surprise. "You're not?"

"Not on your life, sweetheart."

"What if I increase my offer to six hundred dollars?" It was a fortune, but she had part of her mother's inheritance left. She would gladly give every cent she owned to get out of Kansas.

Cass shook his head skeptically. "You don't have six hundred dollars."

Her eyes darted away momentarily, but seconds later they snapped back to meet his defiantly. "I do have that amount . . . and I'll give it all to you if you'll only take me with you."

Cass sighed. "Miss McCord. Not only will I not escort you to Missouri for six hundred dollars, but you could sweeten the deal with a herd of longhorns, a ranch in Texas, a chest of gold, and a lady of the night, and I *still* wouldn't take one step anywhere with you."

Her eyes turned icy. "You're despicable."

He shrugged and took a long draw on the cheroot. "So are you."

"Why won't you take me?" she demanded.

"Because"—he smiled, showing a row of even, perfectly white teeth—"I don't *like* you, Miss McCord." If she wanted him to be frank, he could.

She cocked her chin rebelliously. "I don't *like* you, either, Mr. Claxton, but I see no reason why that should interfere with your escorting me to St. Louis. If it would help to persuade you to take me along, I'll promise not to even *speak* to you during the journey."

Cass drew on his cigar and walked over to stare thoughtfully out the window. "Does your daddy know you're running around asking men you don't even know to take you to Missouri?"

"No."

That didn't surprise Cass. "What would he do if he found out?"

"He'd be very upset, naturally. But he isn't going to find out, Mr. Claxton—unless you tell him." Patience doubted he would. He didn't seem the sort who'd want to involve himself in other people's lives.

"I'm not gonna tell him." Cass turned and walked back to the fire. "Your leaving would probably be the best thing that ever happened to him."

She shot him another scathing look. "Exactly why don't you like me? As you pointed out, we don't even know each other."

"I know you about as well as I plan to."

"Why?" she persisted.

"I don't like little girls with nasty tempers."

She sighed. "You're upset about what happened at the mercantile this morning. Well, it was your own fault. You should never have blocked my way."

"You're damn lucky you're still breathin'," he shot back irritably. "What kind of woman goes around hittin' a man in his—"

Patience blushed and tried to change the subject before he graphically described to her where she'd struck him. "Then you refuse to escort me at all?"

"That's about the size of it."

"You won't change your mind?"

He pitched the cheroot into the fire. "No, ma'am."

"Then I suppose I've said all I came to say."

Cass tipped his hat politely. "It's been a real pleasure, ma'am."

Patience brushed by him frigidly as she walked to the front door. She paused with her hand on the latch, refusing to look at him again. "If you should change your mind—"

"I won't."

Oh! The man was just damned hard nosed! She yanked the door open. "I'd appreciate it if you'd check my horse before I return to town."

"What's the matter with it?"

"He developed a slight limp just before we got here."

Cass grumbled something uncomplimentary under his breath, but she noticed he began to follow her out to the buggy.

After a hurried check he discovered the horse had thrown a shoe.

"What does that mean?" Patience inquired hesitantly.

"It means, you're gonna have to have it replaced before you go anywhere."

Her eyes met his expectantly. "Can you fix it?"

She saw him bristle again. "Lady—"

"I'll pay for your services, sir!" she snapped.

"Oh, brother." He took a deep breath. "All right. Wait a minute. I'll see what I can find to shoe your damn horse." Cass stalked away while Patience slumped wearily onto a bale of hay to wait. It was pitch dark, and she began to wonder if she could find her way back to town. Leviticus had moved her to this godawful Cherry Grove three months earlier, and she'd rarely ventured out on her own.

Beau and Charity returned from their walk and paused to chat with Patience for a few minutes. Informed of the problem, they moved on to the soddy to check on the baby.

Thirty minutes later Cass had the horse reshod and ready to travel.

"Which direction is Cherry Grove?"

Cass glanced up from a last check of the hoof. "What?"

"What direction is Cherry Grove?"

His expression turned incredulous. "You honestly don't know?"

She shook her head meekly.

"To the west," he said curtly, and returned his attention to the horse. "Okay," he said a minute later. "You shouldn't have any trouble."

He glanced up to confront two large, violet pools of tears.

"Now what's wrong?"

"I'm afraid. I don't think I can find my way back to town," she sniffed.

"Why not? Just follow the road."

"I—I have a terrible sense of direction," she confessed. "And this is the first time I've ever traveled . . . alone."

"You'll make it fine." Cass wasn't about to get stuck with her till morning. "Just give the horse his head. He'll find the way."

He noticed her hands were trembling as she reluctantly took the reins he was offering. He felt a tug of conscience and tried his best to dismiss it, but he found he couldn't.

"Well . . . look . . . what do you want me to do about it?"

"I—I don't know."

Cass glanced down the darkened road, then back to her. "You'll be all right. You have a gun, don't you?"

"A gun?" She shook her head. She'd never thought of bringing a gun. Besides, she wouldn't know how to use one.

Cass sighed and reached in his pocket for a cheroot, trying to buy some time to study the situation.

He could drive her back to Cherry Grove, but it was getting bone cold. Or he could let her stay here tonight, and she could drive herself back in the morning.

Neither solution suited him.

"You want to stay here tonight?" he finally asked when her sniffling grew more pronounced.

"I . . . whatever you think . . . but I have a horrible headache and I'm beginning to feel faint."

Cass groaned. Lord. He couldn't send her on her way in the dark if she was gonna faint.

"What about your pa?"

"Well . . ." She sniffed and blew her nose daintily into a lace handkerchief. "He'll be beside himself tonight, but I'm sure he'd be even more upset if I started out alone, got lost on the way, and was never found again."

Cass was annoyed by her simple-minded logic.

"Well, come on. It's cold out here." He helped her out of the buggy, and they walked toward the soddy.

"Will Mr. and Mrs. Claxton mind having an unexpected houseguest?"

Cass didn't even want to think about it. Beau was expecting a romantic evening alone with his bride, and now he was going to have not only his brother underfoot but Patience McCord as well.

"They won't mind," he lied.

As Cass and Patience burst into the room, Charity and Beau guiltily broke apart from their heated embrace.

On their walk Beau had explained to Charity why Cass was going hunting, and they were eagerly counting the minutes until they could finally be alone.

"Oh, you haven't left yet?" Charity blushed and made an attempt to straighten her mussed hair as Cass stalked over to the fire.

"Miss McCord's horse threw a shoe."

"We know."

"But you fixed it," Beau prompted.

"Yeah, but now it's dark, and . . . she's afraid she can't find her way back to Cherry Grove." Cass glanced at Beau apologetically. "She's gonna have to stay here tonight."

"You take her into town when you go huntin'!" Beau thundered, so loudly that the other three jumped with the impact of his sudden explosion.

Cass took a deep breath. "I can't. She has a headache and feels faint."

"You do?" Charity immediately forgot her own disappointment and moved to assist her guest. "May I do something for you?"

"If I could just rest for a moment," Patience said softly, her voice sounding very weak.

Beau looked at Cass helplessly as Charity moved Patience to the bed. "Now, now. You just lie down here, and I'll get you a bite to eat. Maybe you're just tired and hungry," she soothed.

"You're ever so kind." Patience shot Cass a smug look as Charity untied her leather kid shoes and removed them.

"Can't you do somethin'?" Beau demanded under his breath as the two women chatted.

"Well, what do you want me to do? Let her wander around on the prairie in the dark, threatening to faint?" Not that Cass would necessarily have objected, especially after the self-satisfied smirk she'd just sent him.

But he'd sure hate to face Leviticus McCord's ire if anything happened to his daughter because of Cass Claxton's negligence.

"I suppose this means the huntin' trip is off." Beau scowled at him sourly.

"I could go, but it wouldn't really do any good . . . would it?"

"Well, it's gonna be another damn miserable night," Beau predicted, in a voice that had turned as bleak as his face.

Cass felt bad about getting Beau's hopes up, then having to dash them this way, but what else could he do?

He wished he'd never heard of Patience McCord.

Beau watched as Charity turned the blankets back and tucked Patience in like a small child. "There, now. You just rest. You're not puttin' us out at all," she assured over Patience's constant fretting that she was. "You can sleep with me tonight. Beau and Cass can sleep on the pallet."

Beau glanced at Cass accusingly.

Cass shrugged and grinned back at him lamely. What could he say? He'd tried his best, and it just hadn't worked out.

Chapter 22

Breakfast the next morning was a subdued affair. Charity and Patience were left to carry on the brunt of the conversation, while Beau and Cass silently ate their meal.

Beau had slept little the night before. He'd missed the warmth of Charity's body snuggled intimately against his. And more, he'd missed the smell of lemons, the clean fragrance of her hair, the feel of her hands caressing him gently during the night.

The moment breakfast was over, Patience announced she was leaving. Beau and Cass prepared to leave, too, saying they planned to spend the morning building fences on the north section.

When Beau found a rare moment alone with his wife, he drew her into his arms and kissed her soundly. "My, my." Charity was breathless when he finally relinquished his overly zealous embrace. "What was that all about?"

Beau sighed and blissfully nuzzled her hair, breathing its familiar fragrance. "I think I missed you last night."

She smiled, closing her eyes with ecstasy as his mouth played along the outline of her throat. "You think?"

He growled suggestively as he pulled her back for another long kiss that was disappointingly interrupted by Cass, who'd returned to the soddy to search for his forgotten gloves.

When Beau regretfully released her, affection was shining deeply in his eyes. "I wish Ferrand had built you a bigger soddy," he teased.

"I'm sure he would have if he'd known I'd need one so badly," she bantered back.

His good humor restored, Beau winked and swatted her fanny as he reached for his coat. "I'll see you at dinner. Looks like it's gonna be another fine day. Cass and I should be able to finish up the fence before dark."

"Mary Kathleen and I will be waiting for you."

Beau paused, realizing how good that sounded. He had someone waiting for him. It had been a long time since he'd had that warm, comfortable knowledge. "Good. I'll see you tonight."

When the house had settled down again, Charity quickly finished her chores and dressed Mary Kathleen. If she hurried, she could make the trip into Cherry Grove to purchase raisins and be back before Beau discovered she'd even gone.

The morning was unusually warm and balmy for December. The sun was shining brightly amid a scattering of fleecy clouds. It would be a perfect day to make the trip.

She selected a lightweight jacket—which she wouldn't need, but wanted to take along just in case. After harnessing the horse, she carried Mary Kathleen to the waiting wagon.

"Easy, now, Jack." She spoke to the horse reassuringly as she settled the baby, then climbed up on the seat beside her. Suddenly she thought to take a shovel along, in case she came across a few sassafras roots along the way. After she retrieved the shovel, the small party got under way.

Charity couldn't remember when she'd felt so good; it had been a long time. She hummed the hauntingly sweet melody "Aura Lee" to the baby as the horse trotted briskly down the road.

The wheels of the buckboard rolled effortlessly through Fire Creek and picked up

speed as Charity urged the horse into a faster
trot.

If she didn't dawdle at the mercantile,
she'd have plenty of time. Beau wouldn't return to the soddy before noon. An hour into
Cherry Grove, and an hour back, and she'd
have the raisins safely tucked away and dinner on the table. Beau would never suspect
she'd made a trip to town.

A small, puffy cloud passed over the sun,
but Charity didn't notice. She was busy wondering if Beau would have a Christmas present for her. Quickly she reminded herself that
all the work he was doing to the land was a
gift in itself. It wouldn't hurt for her to surprise him Christmas morning with two delicious raisin pies even if he had nothing for
her. Though she had to admit, a small, insignificant token would be nice. . . .

A second cloud skimmed over the sun and
was quickly joined by two, then three. Charity glanced up as an unexpected chill crept
into the air. Strange, the day had been perfectly clear a few minutes ago. Now it was
becoming rather cloudy.

Deciding she'd better stop long enough to
readjust Mary Kathleen's blankets and slip
into her light jacket, she guided Jack to the
side of the road. It took only a minute to perform the simple tasks, and she was ready to
move on.

Glancing up again, she uneasily recalled how fast a Kansas blizzard could move in. But after careful study of the innocent-looking clouds, she concluded they were nothing to be concerned about. She clucked her tongue, and Jack's big hooves clopped noisily back onto the road.

Thirty minutes later, the first minuscule flakes of snow began to drift lazily down, melting as soon as they touched the ground.

Charity still wasn't worried about the abrupt change in weather. It would be about as far to turn back as it was to go on, and the snow appeared to be nothing more than a flurry. But she noticed it was getting noticeably colder, so she urged the horse to a brisker gait.

The snow continued to fall, but in the same gentle manner. The pristine beauty had always fascinated her, and Charity watched the pea-sized flakes float peacefully from the heavy, leaden sky, marveling at yet another one of God's wondrous creations. She hoped they weren't in for a big snow this time, but with Christmas only a few days away, it might be nice.

The wind suddenly shifted directions, and the snow began to fall more heavily. Periodic wind gusts whipped the wagon about on the road as Charity gripped the reins tighter and urged Jack to move faster.

The wind, steadily picking up in intensity, began to swirl snow back into her face, taking her breath away with its growing ferocity. It was becoming evident that once she reached Cherry Grove, she'd be forced to wait out the storm there.

She was a mile from the town when she began to panic. By now, Mary Kathleen was cold and crying, and Jack was becoming increasingly spooked by the freakish nature of the storm.

Drifts began to build beside the road so quickly that Charity found herself losing her perception. If it weren't for the aid of familiar posts and fences, she knew she'd soon be completely lost.

She reached over to try and soothe Mary Kathleen's frightened screams, finally admitting to herself that the trip had been a foolish mistake. At the first sign of snow she should have turned around and headed back to the soddy.

From all indications this was going to be a full-blown blizzard, and she and the baby would never survive the storm if she didn't find shelter—and soon.

Above all she must keep her head, she cautioned. She'd find proper shelter and wait for Beau to find her.

But Beau has no idea where you are, her mind shouted as stinging sleet turned her face a tomato red. She hadn't left a note or even the slightest hint of where she was going.

She pulled Jack to a halt in the middle of the road and gazed helplessly at the chilly alabaster prison she found herself locked into. She realized with sinking despair that Beau wouldn't have a clue where to begin to looking for her.

Not the vaguest idea.

The blizzard hit full force as Beau and Cass finished setting the fourth fence post.

"Looks like it's gonna be a real bitch!" Cass shouted over the rising wind.

"Yeah, we'd better be headin' in!"

The two men quickly gathered their supplies, loaded up, and kicked their horses into a full gallop.

The snow swirled around the riders, and by the time they reached the soddy, the horses were having difficulty plowing through the deepening drifts.

"I've never seen a storm move in so fast," Cass remarked as they rubbed down the horses.

Unexpectedly the image of Patience McCord's snippy little face crept into Cass's mind, and he wondered if the little twit had made it home before the storm hit.

"I've heard of such things happenin', but this is the first one I've ever been in." Beau glanced over and noticed Jack's stall was empty. "Where's Jack?"

"I don't know. Maybe Charity turned him out to pasture before the storm."

The men hurried toward the soddy, their heads bent low against the gale-force wind. Beau shoved the door open, puzzled that Charity hadn't opened it for him.

They stepped inside, and Beau paused when he saw the room was empty. The fire was flickering low, the soddy was chilly, and there was no sign of Charity or the baby.

Beau felt his insides knot with apprehension as he turned to Cass. "Where the hell is Charity?"

"I don't know. Maybe she's out trying to help the stock?"

"No, she wouldn't have taken the baby with her to do that." Beau jerked the door open and scanned the swirling mass of white. Encountering nothing but endless drifts of mounting snow, he felt the knot in his stomach grow tighter. Where was she?

Bounding out of the house, he made his way back to the barn, ignoring the howling storm. There wasn't a sign of the stock, except for the two oxen, Myrtle and Nell. They were in their stalls, contentedly munching on hay.

He stepped behind the lean-to, and his heart sank when he discovered the buckboard was missing too.

Cass followed Beau. As he watched his older brother resaddle his horse, Cass automatically reached for his saddle, too, trying all the while to calmly reason out the more positive possibilities.

"She's probably fine, Beau. She may be caught at one of the neighbors—"

"Charity wouldn't be socializin' on a day like this," Beau said shortly. "Besides, if she'd planned to go visitin' she would have said somethin' about it this morning."

The men remounted, and Cass handed Beau one of the two wool scarves he'd brought along. He tied one around his neck and pulled it up to cover his mouth. "Where do we start?"

Beau shook his head and remained silent as the full implication of Charity's unexplained absence closed in on him.

"Well, I say we try the neighbors first, then head toward Cherry Grove," Cass suggested.

"Cherry Grove? She wouldn't be going to town!"

"You don't know that."

"And you do?"

"No," Cass admitted, "but I figure that's where I'd be goin' if I had a husband and a small baby, and it was three days before Christmas."

"In a damn blizzard?" The horses shied

nervously as a violent gust of wind threatened to collapse the drafty lean-to.

"Well, hell, Beau! It looked like a spring day just two hours ago!"

"Okay, okay, let's get movin'." Beau wasn't going to waste time arguing. Cass's reasoning might seem insane, but it was bound to be better than his own right now.

"We'd better stay together," Cass warned, the tone of his voice reminding Beau that they weren't embarking on a Sunday picnic. They were well aware how crazy it was to ride off in a storm this severe. Their lives would be at risk.

"Let's go." Beau viewed the worsening storm again, and a fresh feeling of despair threatened to engulf him. "Where are you, Charity?" he whispered brokenly. "Where are you . . . sweetheart?"

Charity was growing numb with cold. She'd searched for over thirty minutes, but had found nothing in the form of shelter. In the process she'd managed to get the buckboard off the road and into a steep ditch. One wheel had sunk into a deep drift, and the back end was gradually tilting grotesquely to one side. She crawled to the back of the wagon and placed Mary Kathleen on the floor, then lay down beside her. Huddled together in the warmth of the baby's blankets, she began to pray.

The day wore on, and the snow continued to come down in heavy wet sheets. Charity managed to stop the baby's periodic crying by letting her nurse from the bottle she'd brought along. The milk was icy cold, and Mary Kathleen spit the bottle out angrily several times, but Charity forced her to drink enough to pacify her hunger momentarily. She wondered what would happen when the bottle was empty. She'd only brought one.

An hour later Mary Kathleen had settled peacefully inside her blankets, her large eyes watching the snow with fascination. Charity knew the child was getting colder, and she had no idea how much longer an infant could survive in the falling temperatures.

By afternoon both Charity and the baby had begun to doze.

Charity lay next to Mary Kathleen, vacantly watching the snow slowly begin to bury the wagon. She tried to make herself stir, vividly recalling how Ferrand had once described a man who'd frozen to death. The man had succumbed to the temptation of sleep, an irreversible mistake, Ferrand had lamented.

Charity forced her eyes open, but her lashes were becoming frozen, and they soon drifted back to lie stiffly on her snow-covered cheek. Beau . . . don't let me die . . . don't let me die. . . .

Beau and Cass methodically made their way through the snow to the closest neighbors. Beau's despair increased with each worried shake of head, and the distressing news that virtually no one had seen Charity that day.

The two brothers had been persuaded to warm themselves and drink hot coffee at Jacob Petersen's dugout before starting out again. Ten minutes later, they were back in the saddle. "I think we'd better split up!" Beau had to shout to make himself heard above the shrieking wind. "Charity and the baby are out there somewhere . . . I know it, Cass. We'll have a better chance finding them if we ride in different directions."

Cass knew it was risky to separate, but he also knew they were running out of time. "I'll veer east; you take the road to town!"

Beau nodded as he reached across his saddle horn and clasped his brother's hand tightly. "Be careful, Cass."

"I will. You do the same." Their eyes locked silently.

"If we don't find them before nightfall, go back to the soddy. I'll meet you there." It made Beau sick to his stomach to consider the possibility, but he knew if they didn't find

Charity and the baby by dark, it would be futile to continue the search.

Cass nodded. "Don't worry. We'll find them."

Beau acknowledged the statement with a brief nod, then reined his horse away and disappeared into the swirling mist of snow.

Cass proceeded in the opposite direction.

Charity woke with a start. She was in some sort of cave . . . a white one. And it was warmer.

Outside she could hear the wind screeching, but the sound seemed muted, softer somehow.

She carefully moved her hand to see if it was frozen, and, to her surprise, she discovered it wasn't. Though it was bright red and stiff, she could still wiggle her fingers, though it was painful to do so.

Her eyes moved slowly, and she found that she and the baby were completely buried under snow.

A scream escaped her, and she frantically began to dig her way out. But after a few futile attempts she sank back down beside the baby. It was hopeless. She didn't have the strength to break through the heavy drifts. Her gaze searched Mary Kathleen's face. The baby's eyes were closed, and she was very still.

Tears formed in Charity's eyes, and she felt a tremendous sadness overtake her as she laid her head beside the baby's, lovingly patting the small mound.

If Mary Kathleen died, she would be responsible. Once before she had risked the baby's life because of her foolishness, but mercifully, the child had survived. She supposed the good Lord could be getting tired of her blunders.

Charity knew she couldn't withstand the storm's fury for long, and she, too, might die. She lay limply across the foot of the blanket, peacefully awaiting the moment.

She thought of Beau, and how she'd come to love him. She wished now that she'd told him how much she cared. She'd started to, many times, but she'd always stopped herself because she was afraid he'd think she was pressuring him to make a similar declaration. She'd convinced herself he wouldn't want to hear her foolish prattle.

Betsy still lived so deeply within his heart, no other woman would ever be able to exorcise her ghost. Oh, Beau . . . oh, God . . . I love you. . . . Please find me so I can tell you. . . .

She thought of Ferrand. Would he be there, waiting to meet her when she passed from this life into the next? She heard herself chuckling, her voice sounding hollow against the walls of snow. Would she remember what her first husband looked like? she wondered.

Would Beau be saddened by her death? Had he made it back to the soddy before the storm hit? If she survived, would she ever be able to win his love? Her mind turned from tormenting her with questions to playing tricks on her. Strange tricks.

She saw Beau coming to her. A warm smile creased his face. She could see the way the corners of his eyes crinkled endearingly, and a small sigh escaped her as she eagerly reached out to touch him.

He caught her hand and brought it to his mouth. His eyes, his beautiful blue eyes, probed deeply into hers. They were in a room . . . alone . . . a lovely, quiet room with candles burning low in crystal holders . . . and flowers, lots of beautiful flowers filling the room with their perfumed fragrance. . . .

Her breathing became shallow as his mouth caressed the fullness of hers. He reached out to slip the straps of her chemise off her shoulders, his mouth eagerly acquainting itself with every inch of her silky skin.

She could see a bed, a large, comfortable bed draped in a rich, scarlet-red comforter . . . beckoning to them . . . beckoning. . . .

Charity could feel herself growing warm.

Her strength slowly ebbed as the illusion wove its way in and out of her numbed mind.

She could feel Beau's mouth searching for hers as his hands slid down her back, cupping her buttocks tighter, pulling her against him, letting her feel his need. He was whispering his love for her. Her body ached, sensing that, through some merciful gift, she was to experience his love before she died, even if it was a hoax.

The wanting in his face made her tremble as he drew her across the bed, his gaze telling her more clearly than spoken words that he adored her. She came to him, raining kisses over his eyes, his cheekbones, the thick column of his neck.

And then the terrible waiting was over.

She felt his power encompassing her, drawing her into him, boldly claiming her as his wife . . . flesh of his flesh. . . .

She sighed, giving herself fully to him, joyously, wildly. . . .

Beau rode through the storm, stopping his mare frequently to cup his hands around his mouth to shout, "Chari–ty! Char–i–ty!" Time after time, the wind blocked his words and flung them mercilessly back in his face.

He nudged his horse forward, his shoulders hunched against the howling wind. "Please God, don't let me lose her."

* * *

Sometime during the fantasy it occurred to Charity that even if Beau was looking for her, he wouldn't be able to see the wagon. It was completely buried in the snow.

Feeling as if she were suspended from somewhere far above the wagon and looking down at it, she saw herself struggle out of her petticoat. She watched, spellbound, as she saw herself sit up and begin to feel around in the wagon for something to slide the petticoat onto.

Her hand found the shovel she'd brought along to dig sassafras roots, and with stiff fingers she tied the piece of fabric around the handle and hoisted the shovel into an upright position.

In the smooth, unbroken surface of snow, a lone makeshift flag began to flap at half mask.

She watched as she laid her head back down beside Mary Kathleen's, and closed her eyes once more.

Surely she'd still recognize Ferrand . . . he had blue eyes . . . no, green. . . .

Darkness was falling rapidly.

Beau's horse made her way laboriously through the tall drifts, moving noticeably slower. Beau knew the animal was close to dropping from exhaustion, and yet he couldn't make himself turn back and ride to the shelter of the soddy.

He knew he was running out of time, and he cursed himself for having listened to Cass. He should be searching south or west, not north. Charity had had no reason to go to town. Why had he let Cass talk him into riding to Cherry Grove when he knew better?

The horse squealed, her eyes widening in fright as she stumbled and suddenly went down, her heavy weight dropping wearily into the folds of the deep snow. Beau swore under his breath and waited until the horse struggled clumsily back to her feet.

This was insane. He was going to kill both the horse and himself if he didn't turn around soon, and yet how could he go back without Charity . . . and the baby?

God, he suddenly realized he loved that baby as if she were his own.

No, he wasn't going home till he found both of them. If the storm took his life, so be it. He'd already lost one wife and child; he wasn't strong enough to lose another.

He steeled himself against the bitter wind and rode on. His gloves had frozen to the reins, but he was past feeling the cold. He was aware of nothing except the pitch and sway of his horse as she labored through the drifts. He tried to ignore the deep ache growing in his heart.

* * *

Charity wondered if there would be a way she could leave Beau a letter. She knew it was impossible.

She wished she could, though. It would be a simple note. *I love you, Beau. Forgive me for never telling you so.*

She should have told him.

Beau had nearly given up hope when he saw the flag.

The horse slowed, and he squinted through the blowing snow at the piece of cloth flapping wildly in the wind. Leaning forward in the saddle, he tried to make out the strange signal but couldn't.

He clucked to his horse, and she eased forward. He held the lantern in front of him, watching its mellow beams spill out on the crusty snow. As he moved closer, he could see the flag was a woman's petticoat.

His pulse jumped erratically as he quickly slid off his horse and began to run toward the peculiar flagpole. When he reached the petticoat, he dropped down on his knees and began digging his way through the snowdrift with his hands.

"Charity! Charity! Are you in there?" He hastily pulled off his gloves so he could dig faster.

From somewhere far away Charity could

hear Beau's voice calling to her, and she wondered why he was shouting so. Her head lifted weakly from the blanket. "Yes, darling?"

Beau's hands dug frantically through the drifts, tears blinding him as gut-wrenching fear turned to searing, white-hot anger and frustration. She had to be in there. She had to be!

"Charity, dammit! Answer me!" Snow flew in a furious white cloud as heartbroken sobs began to rack his large frame.

"I'm right here, Beau . . . there's no need to shout. . . ."

The wind continued to howl, and Beau continued to dig. She was there, beneath the snow. He felt it.

"Daddy's coming," Charity crooned, patting Mary Kathleen. "See, I told you he'd be here."

When his hand hit the side of the wagon, Beau was stunned for a moment. He glanced down and saw large red stains on the snow. His hands were raw and bleeding.

"Beau?" Charity called weakly.

Suddenly, he heard her.

His pulse jumped, and his sobs turned to hysterical laughter. He began digging again, ignoring the cuts on his hands, scooping the snow up in large armfuls and flinging it wildly into the wind as he shouted her name.

He saw her hand first, then part of her

dress. He was alternately laughing and crying as he uncovered her and the baby and caught them both up tightly against his chest.

"Oh, God . . . oh, God . . . thank you . . . thank you. . . ." he cried.

He had the baby in one arm, and he was covering Charity's face with kisses, clasping her close against his chest, then releasing her long enough to claim her mouth again and again.

"I didn't think I was gonna find you . . . I was afraid. . . ." He cupped her face with one hand and continued to shower her with loving kisses everywhere. "Are you all right? Are you all right?"

"I'm . . . co-co-ld, B-B-B-ea-u."

"Oh, sweetheart, I'll get you warm," he promised.

"Th-th-the ba-b-by?"

Beau gently uncovered the thick layers of blankets to encounter a tiny pug nose which suddenly began to wrinkle in disgust at being awakened so abruptly. Mary Kathleen let out a wail that threatened to impair their hearing permanently.

The familiar bellow was music to Beau's ears.

His face broke into a radiant smile. "She's fine!"

He pulled Charity and Mary Kathleen back to his chest once more and squeezed his eyes shut in pure joy as he held them tightly in the shelter of his arms.

"Both my girls are just fine, Lord." His voice broke before he finished raggedly, "And I'm not gonna be forgettin' your mercy."

Chapter 23

Reverend Olson was surprised to find Beau, Charity, and the baby waiting when he opened his door. He quickly called to Rebecca, and they warmly welcomed the small, half-frozen family in from the fury of the storm.

Hasty explanations were made, and Rebecca promptly put Charity and the baby to bed.

Dr. Paulson was rooted out early from his bed to make the cold trek to the parsonage to examine the weary travelers.

"I think they were both mighty lucky," he told a worried Beau as he entered the parlor an hour later and set his worn leather bag down. A fire blazed high in the hearth, and the smell of fresh coffee permeated the air.

Beau stood, his blue eyes penetrating the doctor's hopefully. "Will they be all right?"

The doctor could see Charity's husband was worse for wear than she was. His eyes grew kind. "They're doing fine, son. With a little bit of care, they'll both be able to go home for Christmas."

Beau visibly slumped with relief. "Thank you . . . thank you, doctor."

"I happen to have an extra piece of chocolate cake, Harlow." Rebecca had just returned from settling the baby. "I couldn't interest you in it, could I?"

"You know I'd come out in any weather for a piece of your chocolate cake, Rebecca. Thank you, I'd love some."

"How about you, Beau—won't you join us for cake?"

"No, thank you, Mrs. Olson. I'm waiting to see Charity."

Dr. Paulson followed Rebecca to the kitchen as Beau walked to the window and stared out thoughtfully. The storm still raged, but he felt an inner peace that he hadn't known in a very long time.

"You say your brother's still out there?" Reverend Olson inquired.

"No, I expect when it got dark, he went back to the soddy." Beau knew Cass was a reasonable man and that he'd have given up the search at dark as they'd agreed.

"By the way, Beau, I received news from Ansel and Letty's families."

Beau turned slowly from the window. "And?"

"It turns out that Ansel's father passed away two months ago. Phedra Latimer is finding it hard to cope with her husband's death. Coupled with poor health, I'm afraid she'll be unable to take care of Mary Kathleen at this time."

"And Letty's family?"

Reverend Olson sighed. "Letty's parents are willing to take the child and place it with proper relatives because they, too, are in their mid-seventies, and physically . . ." Reverend Olson shrugged apologetically, "Children are for the young, Beau. When a person reaches his seventies, his body gives out, and he simply doesn't have the stamina to raise children."

Beau turned pensively back to the window, his eyes deeply troubled. "Place Mary Kathleen with strangers?"

"They wouldn't be strangers. They'd be Letty's kin. Of course, Mary Kathleen would have to grow to love them. And then there'd be the problem of sending the child back East. But these are decisions that don't have to be made tonight. You sure I can't have Rebecca fix you a bite to eat?"

"No, thank you. Maybe I'll get something later, but right now, I'd like to see my wife."

"Then you run along. Rebecca and I will see to the baby tonight. Mary Kathleen's sleeping soundly, and the doctor says she shouldn't have any lasting effects from her adventure." A tender light came into his faded gray eyes. "You know, son, it was the Lord's hand that allowed that wagon to be buried in the snow," he offered. "It surrounded your wife and the baby and conserved their body heat. It virtually saved their lives."

Beau's gaze met the reverend's solidly. "I know where the credit belongs, sir."

"Just wanted to make sure you did." Reverend Olson smiled. "See you in church Sunday morning?"

"Yes, sir, you will."

"Now, I believe you have a wife you want to see?"

Beau smiled. "Yes, sir."

"Then why are you hanging around here talking to an old codger like me? Go to her, son."

It was dark when Beau stepped into Charity's room to say good-night. She recognized his footsteps as he cautiously approached the bed.

"Hi."

"Hi. I thought you might be asleep."

"No, just resting."

The bed creaked as he sat down beside her. "The baby all right?"

"She's sleeping. Reverend Olson said he and Rebecca would see to her tonight. You need your rest. Are you warm enough?"

She nodded.

"Good."

Charity reached out and took his hand. "Come to bed with me."

Beau's pulse jumped. "I—I thought I'd best sleep over by the fire and let you rest. . . ."

He couldn't see her face in the dark, but the plea in her voice drew him like a moth to a flame. "I want you beside me, Beau."

He stood and stripped out of his clothes, then crawled between the sheets beside her. He wrapped his arms around her small body and drew her close.

She sighed, burying her face in the warmth of his chest. "I love you, Beau."

"I love you, too, Charity."

She felt tears spring to her eyes. Her happiness was complete now.

His mouth searched and found hers, and he kissed her with a tenderness that overflowed with his love. They needed no words. They had nothing left to prove. Today had proven it all.

They fell asleep in each other's arms contentedly.

* * *

"We go home tomorrow." It was Christmas Eve, and as Beau sat on Charity's bed, an air of excitement dominated his voice.

"I know. I can hardly wait." She had weathered the close call amazingly well, and tonight the doctor had pronounced her well enough to travel.

Beau leaned over to steal a kiss, his eyes sparkling like a small boy's. "Cass was afraid you wouldn't make it home before Christmas, so he brought your and Mary Kathleen's presents by this afternoon."

"Wonderful! Where are they?"

"Not so fast." Beau drew back from her defensively. "I'd like to give you *my* present before you open his."

Her eyes widened at his sudden show of immaturity. "Why?"

"Because . . . mine's better than his."

"Beau!" She had to laugh. "How do you know?"

He shrugged. "I asked him what he got you; he told me, so I know mine's the best."

"You're terrible."

"Yeah, I know." He grinned and stretched out beside her, devilishly dangling a small, gaily wrapped box before her eyes.

She started to reach for the box, and he quickly withdrew it. "Not so fast."

"I thought you wanted me to open it."

"I do, but I want you to beg for it first," he teased.

"Beg for it?" Casually, she rolled over and slid on top of him, and his eyes widened as her mouth came down to meet his hungrily.

"What are you doing?" he sputtered.

She broke the kiss and traced a lazy finger across his cheek and over the outline of his lips. "What do you want me to do?"

"Well, that wouldn't take much thought," he admitted with a guilty grin. "I want to warn you, Mrs. Claxton—when we get home tomorrow, I have plans." His hands began to take liberties she adored.

"Tomorrow. Why wait so long to implement them?" Her tongue came out to tease his, and she felt him tense.

"Charity . . . remember, we're in Reverend Olson's house. . . ." His words trailed off weakly as she began to unbutton his shirt.

"You talk too much, Beau Claxton."

His hands came up to tangle in her hair, pulling her face closer to his. Their mouths were inches apart, his breath softly mingling with hers. "You think so?"

"I know so."

"What about the reverend?"

"I can't think of where you'd find a house more filled with love."

"You really think it'd be safe?" Beau

groaned as she brought his mouth back to nibble at his lower lip.

"I think so, but we could always put a chair in front of the door . . . if you're worried."

"I'm not worried." Beau nuzzled her neck, drinking in her fragrance. "I was only thinking of your less-than-sterling reputation, Mrs. Claxton."

"Well, I would hate to have the reverend or Rebecca drop in unexpectedly," Charity retracted hesitantly. They slid off the bed together, and Beau walked her to the door, still kissing her.

He quietly moved the old chair against the door.

"Okay, now what?"

"Now"—she snuggled against him, her tongue teasing his ear suggestively—"I want you to make me your wife."

Beau caught his breath sharply. "My pleasure, Mrs. Claxton."

He felt her tremble as he slipped her gown over her shoulders and let the delicate material float to the floor. Their gazes met as he reached out and slid his hand down her hip, feeling the silken texture of her skin. Then his fingers skimmed up to her breasts and lingered.

He smiled, his eyes growing dark with passion. "You are so beautiful."

Her fingertips touched his lips. "You make me feel beautiful."

Her breasts filled his hands, and he dipped his head to kiss each one tenderly. It had been so long since her body had experienced such pleasure. She sighed as she buried her fingers in the thick texture of his hair. Slowly, she cupped his face in her hands and lifted his mouth back to hers.

His heart pounded as he began to kiss her, mindless kisses, filled with hungry urgency. He was aroused, magnificently so, and she could feel his need pressing against her bare skin, eager to claim her.

"Love me," she whispered.

"I do," he whispered back, "Oh, God, Charity, I do. When I thought I'd lost you and the baby . . . I didn't know what I would do. . . ." His voice broke with raw emotion as she drew his head against her breast to comfort him.

"Oh, my darling. I love you so very much. That's all I could think of as I waited for you to find me and the baby. I wished that I had told you of my love, long before now."

He guided her back to the bed, and they lay down.

With surprising efficiency he rid himself of his clothing. Then, with agonizing slowness, he began to take his pleasure discovering her body. His masterful touch made her grow weak with anticipation. The blue of his eyes darkened deeper with passion as his mouth caressed her silken flesh lovingly.

The feel of his lips moving against her bare skin made her catch her breath. She stared up at him helplessly, feeling as if she were drowning in his exquisite torture.

Silken arms twined around his neck; silken legs lay softly against his hair-roughened ones as their mouths met again and again.

A moment later she sighed, her breath softly stirring the hair on his chest. "Oh, Beau." She could not find the words to tell him of her joy.

"I know, I know. . . ." His mouth captured hers again, drinking in its sweetness as he levered his large frame above her small body. No longer could he think. He could only experience the essence of her, the sweetness flooding his body, crying for release.

"I love you . . . I love you. . . ." His whispers were muffled against her throat as he entered her. Fire flashed through them, searing, burning, driving all else from their minds.

The long wait had made their loving all the sweeter, Charity realized. And now the wait was over.

Beau was her love.

He was her gift.

* * *

Though it seemed improbable that either of them could have forgotten how wonderful lovemaking could be, they lay in each other's arms afterward, marveling at what had happened between them. They had been good together. Unbelievably good. Sated and lazy, they continued to share long, languorous kisses.

"You know, I'm kind of glad it happened this way," Beau admitted. He toyed absently with a strand of her hair, intrigued by its softness.

"What way?"

"This . . . way."

She sensed he was trying to tell her something, so she waited.

"At first . . . well, I would have gladly taken my rights and not thought much about it," he began hesitantly.

"But?"

"But"—he sighed and rolled over to cup her face in his hands—"it wouldn't have been right. I still had Betsy in my heart."

She gazed at him lovingly. "And now?"

"Now"—he sighed—"I've let her go. Though I suppose she'll be with me from time to time." He paused, trying to sort out his feelings.

"Beau, I don't resent your feelings for Betsy. Betsy and Ferrand were our first loves, and they'll always hold a special place in our hearts."

Charity wasn't afraid to voice what he apparently couldn't. "But we're older now. We share a different kind of love. I'm content with that."

"I love you, Charity." Beau wanted that clear. "Maybe not in the same way I loved Bets, but what I feel for you is just as deep, just as right, as what I felt for her."

Charity's love shone brightly through her eyes. "I know. You don't have to explain."

"And Ferrand?"

"I will forever hold him in my heart." Her hand reached out to gently caress her husband's face. "Ferrand was my first love; you are my last."

Their mouths touched and lingered sweetly.

Beau reached for the small box he'd been about to give her before they'd made love. "I bought this for you several weeks ago."

She took the box and slowly slipped off the ribbon. "I'm afraid I have nothing to give you," she confessed. "I was going into town to buy raisins to make you a pie, when the storm came up."

"You were?" His eyes shone brightly with admiration. "You almost got yourself killed over raisins?" The realization only made him love her more.

"I wanted to do something special for your Christmas present." She thought about the raisins and wished she had the pies to offer him. She had nothing to show her gratitude, even now, after he'd risked his life to save her and Mary Kathleen during the storm.

"You saved my life . . . and I have nothing. . . ." She looked at him sadly.

He winked at her. "You've given me back my life. I think that's enough."

Smiling, she removed the paper and opened the box. Her breath caught. Nestled in the paper was her emerald brooch. Ferrand's grandmother's brooch.

"Oh, Beau." She was speechless.

"I hope you like it. I bought it one day at the mercantile. It seems two Indians had traded it." He reached out and gently caught the tears spilling from the corners of her eyes. "The color of the stones reminded me of your eyes."

Charity took the brooch in her hands and pressed it to her heart. She wouldn't dream of telling him that long ago another man had once given her the same gift with love. Beau's gift meant just as much, and she would cherish it as deeply as she'd treasured Ferrand's.

"My beloved husband, have I told you how very much I love you?"

He pulled her mouth back to his. "Yes, but

I'd have no objections if you'd show me again."

"I still say you should wait till all the snow's melted." With a frown Charity passed the sack of ham sandwiches up to Cass. "It's almost January. There could be another storm any day!"

Cass glanced at Beau and shook his head. "Your wife frets too much."

Beau grinned. "I know, but I love her anyway."

"I need to be gettin' home before another blizzard hits," Cass explained patiently. "You two don't want me underfoot all winter, now do you?"

Beau and Charity looked at each other and grinned.

"That's what I thought." Cass climbed into the buckboard and tapped his hat back cockily on his head. "I'll probably be seein' you again one of these days. Ma'll have me draggin' another wagonload of them damn pickles and preserves out to you, thinking you all will be starvin' to death."

Charity pulled the blanket up closer around Mary Kathleen to shield her from the sharp wind. "You do that, Cass. We'll always be happy to see you."

Beau leaned over and kissed his wife. "I'm gonna ride out a ways with Cass. I'll be back."

Charity smiled. "Take your time. I'll be waiting."

He winked at her lovingly and swung into the saddle. "Let's go, little brother. We're burnin' daylight."

The wagon and rider moved out of the yard down the snowy pathway. For several miles the brothers traveled in compatible silence. Then as they crested a small rise, they reined their horses to a stop. Beau swung out of his saddle, and Cass got down off the wagon.

"Well, looks like I'll be goin' it alone from here on."

"Yeah, I best be gettin' back to Charity and the baby."

The two brothers shook hands. Beau remounted his horse, and Cass got back in the wagon.

"Oh, by the way, tell Ma I won't be comin' home this spring."

Cass grinned as he picked up the reins. "Didn't figure you would be."

"Yeah." Beau stared contentedly at the snow-covered countryside. "Sorta feels like I am home."

"Well, Charity's a fine woman," Cass acknowledged. "You going to adopt Mary Kathleen?"

"Figurin' on it."

"That's good. Ma likes bein' a grandmother."

"Yeah, can't wait till she sees my baby."
Beau looked at his brother solemnly. "Mary
Kathleen's about the cutest little baby you've
ever seen . . . isn't she?"

"She's cute, all right."

"Yeah." Beau's grin widened, "I think so
too. One of these days you'll settle down and
have one almost as cute," he predicted.

Cass hooted merrily. "Don't count on it. No
woman's gonna rope and hog-tie me till I'm
good and ready."

Beau shook his head skeptically. "Don't be
too sure. A thing like that can slip up on a man
before he knows it."

"Not on me, it won't." Cass released the
brake on the wagon. "Well, best be movin' on.
I'm burnin' daylight."

"You take care. Tell Cole and Wynne we'll
write. Maybe they can make the trip out to
see us someday."

"Sure thing. You behave yourself, big
brother."

"You do the same."

Cass grinned arrogantly. "Not a chance."

Beau threw his head back and laughed, his
merriment rumbling deep in his chest as
Cass's wagon rolled jauntily away.

Cocky kid, he thought affectionately. Some
woman will come along someday and tie his
tail in a bow knot.

He took a deep breath and held it, tipping his face up to drink in the bright sunshine. It felt good to be alive.

Damn good!

In October Dell introduces a writer of exceptional talent, Elaine Coffman, and a book that will capture your heart, MY ENEMY, MY LOVE. Enjoy the following excerpt.

April, 1860
Memphis Tennessee

"This *is* the Ragsdale Plantation?" The dark-haired stranger asked.

"Yes," she answered.

"Do you live here?"

"Yes."

"Where's your master?"

She blinked at him. "My master?"

"Your master, my sweet simpleton, would be the person who owns this plantation and pays your salary."

She blinked again in confusion. "My salary?" Had the blow she'd dealt to his head addled his wits?

"Hellfire! This conversation is going nowhere fast. One round of questions with you goes in more damn circles than a spinning top." He scowled at her, his head still feeling as if it were making a few revolutions. "You do know what a top is, don't you —that cute conical device that spins on a steel-shod point?"

He was staring at her with an intensity that made her feel a few points below stupid. She hesitated, then her irritation, as it usually did, got the best of common sense. "I am familiar with the *toy* you speak of. Have you lost yours?"

She had an inkling that restraint did not come easy to this man, for his entire body screamed irritation; his hands clenching in a manner suggestive of a powerful desire to be placed around her neck. Having acquired a pretty fair grasp of the somewhat monstrous, if not twisted complexity of his mind, she decided to jump before she was pushed. "I don't work here," she said, her throat closing with the involuntary gulp that comes after being force-fed castor oil.

She wasn't convinced he wasn't a thief, but she knew one thing—he unequivocally was a breed of man she was unaccustomed to. There was no decorous behavior, no soft and lilting speech, no glorious and dignified respect for her gender. Not one drop of the milk of human kindness flowed through his veins. He was everything a well-bred man was not: a resolute barbarian, wholly uncivilized, offensive, and basely crude. His language was atrocious and unfit for a lady's ears, his manners despicable—belonging in a barnyard, and his bearing bordered on debauchery. Any woman would be a fool to give him a second glance. She looked at him again.

His eyes traveled across her face, not with cold indifference, but lingering on each detail with the heated devotion of a man with an appreciative eye for feminine flesh. The hot weight of his eyes on her mouth . . . *Lord! Is this what it's like to be kissed? Only better?* She watched him across the short space that separated them, feeling her senses peppered by diversions, as if she could still feel the gentle caress of his breath stirring more than the soft blond curls that had fallen on her face. It was frightening, this new realm of perception, these new emotions not guided by reason. The onslaught left her uncertain and beguiled, unable to respond normally.

"You may not work here, but it's apparent you're not the lady of the house. Who are you?" he said. "Some poor orphaned relative?"

"Poor orphaned relative?" she repeated, her brow creasing in puzzlement.

"Damn! My brains have been addled by a half-wit! I'll see if I can phrase it simply enough for even your inadequate mind. If you don't work here . . . and it's obvious you aren't the lady of the house . . . what the hell are you doing patrolling the premises like some three-headed dragon?" Immediately his face illuminated with understanding. "Of course," he said with new insight, "you're here for the amusement and companionship of one Francis Ragsdale. You're his mistress, is that it?"

It was the last straw, an insult past tolerating. He had thrown her to the hay, crushed the life out of her, cursed like a field hand and now had the unmitigated gall to call her a mistress. Eyes shimmering with tears, she stammered, "What kind of monster are you to even suggest such a thing? I would never . . ."

He saw the horrified expression in her green eyes and interpreted it correctly. "Spare me your incessant chatter expounding your virtue," he said. She started to speak, but he cut her off. "I know, I know, I've shredded your reputation and defiled your honorable name. Tell me, angel, have you ever bedded a man?"

She spoke with that puzzled softness compounded of confusion and distraction. "Not by myself, but I helped my aunt once."

"Hellfire and damnation . . . I didn't know it could be a family undertaking." He smiled then, looking at her with an expression that wavered between tolerance and disbelief. "I have a very lurid imagination, but the vast possibilities of what you've just suggested escapes even my creative powers." He considered her a moment, humor playing about the corners of his mouth. "So . . . you helped your aunt bed a man, did you?" He gave her a lazy smile of admiration—considerably warmer than its predecessor. "Tell me, sweet . . . how, exactly, did you manage to do that?"

She looked at him as if she were convinced fools grew without watering. "It was quite simple," she said in that breathless little way she had, thinking surely no one could be this dense. "My aunt's cousin, who happens to be a man, was kicked by a horse and I helped her put him to bed."

His entire body relaxed and one corner of his mouth tilted up in a rather charming, lopsided manner. Then a smile that would've knocked the most celebrated beauty in Memphis flat on her bustle split his face. "You," he said honestly, "are either functioning with half a brain or you're undeniably innocent. Tell me, angel, which is it?"

Seeing her blank face, he added, "What I want to know is . . . have you ever done anything with a man that could make you pregnant? You do know where babies come from, don't you?"

She felt sick. Her usual headlong lack of caution had once again put her in a vulnerable position. "I didn't just get off the boat," she said, glaring at him. *Please, dear God, don't let him ask me that again.*

"Well? Have you ever been on a belly ride?"

She tried her best to form a mental picture of that, her eyes almost crossing from the effort. But it was no use. Mental pictures didn't seem to be forming. She directed an angry glare toward heaven. *Thanks,* she mumbled under her breath. *What fool said, if God doesn't give what we want He gives what we need? I need this?* For the first time in her eighteen years she questioned the workings of divinity.

"Don't answer," he said. "I have other ways of finding out."

They say the heart's letter is read in the eyes . . . and he was sending her a billet-doux that would scorch the paper it was written on. She was green as gourds, as far as men were concerned, but a plastered wall could read the intent in those hot eyes.

"You have the morals of a jar of slop," she said. "I'd rather die than have you touch me." She rose to her knees, forgetting his threat, the consequences if she moved.

It happened so fast, she had no time to react. A hand shot out, clamping around her wrist, yanking her around and jerking her into his arms. It was at this point that she realized, for the second time that day, that a body was pressing her back against the hay.

Feeling the sting of tears she moved her hands to push against his chest. Beneath her fingers she could feel the restraining wall of muscle that surrounded a heart beating with irritation.

"Dammit! Hold still!"

Scorched but not defeated, she was gaining momentum like a rolling snowball. What had transpired between them, instead of making her submit, made her more stalwart in revolt. Every intolerable insult she had suffered made her anger more instant and furious. Like her prideful South, convinced she was right, she was determined to the last drop of her blood to defend her honorable person, despite the opposition. She was one angry, defiant woman.

She bucked again, hoping she jarred his arrogant brains. She did, and the face before her loomed, ominous and dark. "I'm warning you . . ."

Apparently unaware a woman and glass are ever in danger, she replied, "What else can you do besides curse and make threats? You better guess again if you think your words are going to frighten me." Spitefully, she wiggled again.

He contemplated showing her just what other things he could do. His head pounding, his patience tried, he looked down for a moment at the snarled ball of yellow fluff with the sizzling green eyes that were shooting daggers through him. For some perverse reason he found what he saw enchanting, and that irritated him. Then he made another startling discovery: The man who desires a woman that irritates the living hell out of him is supremely frustrated. And that made him speak with more anger than he actually felt. "For your benefit," he said succinctly, "I will repeat myself once, and only once." He paused, and then phrased the words with great care. "Keep . . . your . . . lily . . . white . . . ass . . . still!"

Her mouth dropped faster than ripened fruit. They eyed each other, each one looking for a place to drive the fatal shot. His head was splitting and he wanted answers to some questions. Her nerves were frazzled and she wished she'd hit him harder. They were like two cats thrown over a fence with their tails tied together. Every time one moved it caused the other discomfort. Lamentable though it was, she was too angry to see the flash of compassionate admiration in his eyes for what it was. Honest.

A disturbing smile curled across his lips. "What's the matter, sweetheart? You afraid I'm going to toss your skirts?"

The heart that had been pounding furiously crashed to her feet. She was too nervous, too frightened, and too inexperienced to artfully evade the bluntness of this brute with any finesse. "Toss my skirts?" she repeated, thinking surely he didn't mean it literally.

"Rape," he said, feeling as deranged as she was from the thrill he received in scaring the overstarched drawers off her.

She gave him a sour look. "It crossed my mind."

"A short trip, obviously."

Her flayed skin burned under the prick of his amusement, while her bewildered constitution considered another alternative. Feeling the stinging swell of tears behind her eyes, she discovered what a hopelessly embarrassing situation it is to be bested by a man.

The stranger studied the delicate heart-shaped face, the tightly held mouth that tried in vain to quell its own trembling. The thought that he could have pushed her too far lingered like the after-burn of a slap. Intuition told him that overriding her fear was a spirit that would push her to fight to the finish. Any other time he would've given her a run for her money, but right now his head was hurting like a sonofabitch. "Don't worry," he said, "I'm not going to rape you . . . at least I don't think I am."

The darkening shadows within the barn lent sharp outline to the beauty of her face, but it was her hair that held his attention. He had never seen hair that fair, nor that curly. This woman's hair had not been crimped; it crinkled and curled as tight as the wool on a newborn lamb, and of its own accord. He lifted his hand to rub the back of his knuckles across the fresh texture of her cheek. Her eyes, as they watched him, held the soft impatience of a little creature nuzzling for its milk. *Little mouse, if that look was meant to distract me, it's doing the trick, but I'm not too sure you want my thoughts headed in the direction they seem to be taking.* He closed his eyes, sorry that he was putting her through this cat-and-mouse routine— ready to wring her neck one minute, wanting to feel her body respond with passion the next. He opened his eyes slowly, making no attempt to hide the sleepy, heavy-lidded look. "No," he said, his words gently spoken against fragrant curls, "I'm not going to rape you . . . Perhaps I'd settle for a kiss."

"Either way I lose."

His face darkened with annoyance, but his voice still maintained that tone of mocking sarcasm that made her want to slap his arrogant face. "You sound like a woman lacking experience in either."

The look she gave him declared her innocence, but she was too beautiful to be that. "Innocence or guile?" he said, then paused. "I wonder if it's possible?" He closed his eyes, unable to distinguish if it was because of the dull throb in his head or his overriding impulses. When he opened them, he focused on her face, as if considering something for a moment, then he answered his own question. "No," he said, "not innocence. Not with a face like that." A tapered finger trailed from the point of her temple to follow the curve of her lips. "Poor buttercup. It doesn't matter anyway." He laughed a low, husky chuckle. "No, don't look like a skinned rabbit. You're safe for now. Thanks to this rumbling in my head."

The heat of his body was burning a hole through her and she squirmed beneath him. A blue flame flared in his eyes. "Have a care, girl, I'm no eunuch."

She endured his dissecting gaze because she was afraid if she said anything he would put her in a more uncomfortable position than the one she was already in—an absurd idea, really, for as far as uncomfortable positions went, this one was in a league all by itself. She cast an eye up at him, and what she saw made her draw in a sharp breath. A fool could see what he was thinking, what he intended to do. He was going to kiss her!

It wasn't the idea of a kiss that worried her. She had been kissed before—sloppy youthful pecks on the mouth, chaste kisses on her cheek, even a fairly long, inexperienced kiss from a childhood beau who pressed his tight dry lips against hers until they both collapsed with laughter. But this was no laughing matter. This was no callow youth experimenting behind the smokehouse. This was Adam *after* the apple, all full of knowledge and information. And that frightened her. *Apples . . . temptation . . . sin . . .* She knew what happened to Eve, skipping around Eden buck naked.

"You don't have to look like a scalded cat. It's been years since I throttled my last woman," he said with a deepening smile.

"Why are you doing this?" The words croaked from her dry throat as she pushed against unsympathetic chest muscles. What little energy she possessed was spent on that tiny protest. Not a thimbleful of resistance remained. "I'm sorry I hit you. It was an honest mistake. If you had any feelings at all you'd let me up."

"Oh, I have feelings," he said, his gaze following the velvet line of throat to the rise and fall of generous breasts, "and they are functioning perfectly."

He did something quite delicious with his hips as he spoke and that was the spark that revived her. Suddenly finding the spunk she was famous for, she said hotly, "If you value that homespun hide of yours, you'll let me up."

Showing no surprise, he said, "My, my, now we're cutting our teeth on threats. Should I consider that an advancement in stupidity, or a retreat in logic?" He had planned to say more, but the tempting little filly beneath him bucked like her first saddling, sending fragmented shards of glassy pain shooting through the top of his skull. "Damn your eyes! Be still!"

She stared up at him, wide-eyed. His furious grimace struck fearful defiance to her very soul. He spoke under his breath, saying what he'd like to do to her. Thankfully she was unable to understand that indistinct garble of words. He cursed again, and roughly jerked both of her hands above her head, locking them in one clenched fist as he clamped his other hand upon her overproductive mouth. It tasted like sweat, leather, and horse. She squirmed and mumbled against his hand, trying to expel it along with a few salty words.

The flecked green eyes glaring at him were dilated with anger. "Hellfire, you stupid woman. Don't you know what I could do to you?"

It really mattered little if she knew or not. What mattered here was whether *he* knew. The immediate press of her panic button came from lying prostrate beneath a body that not only knew, but knew plenty. That made her squirm again and repeat salty, muffled words against his hand.

"Holding you," he said, shifting his weight to immobilize her, "is about as easy as tying a bell around a wildcat's neck. Don't you have any fear? I'm going to move my hand, but you open that mouth of yours again and so help me God, I'll clamp it shut . . . permanently." He read defiance in her eyes as he lifted his hand. "Don't you dare say another word. You're in no position to argue."

"That's pretty obvious," she said. "Naturally, you're the strongest."

He gave her a look that could boil water with the leftover heat. "I also happen," he said softly, "to be on top." The slow movement of hipbone against hipbone, although commonly flagrant, was a pretty lame trick. But quite effective.

She felt the first stirrings of a sweet response that she was unprepared for—a slow awakening of sleepy innocence, a naked awareness of intimacy that beckoned like curled fingers calling her to follow—then leaving her trembling at the precipice of a whole new world that yawned before her like a smoldering abyss. Out of the blur, a face took form above her. She had been right to think him the old serpent, the tempter; for surely he dangled before her like Eve's apple. One bite . . . just one succulent bite. *No! No!* . . . her mind was screaming, fearing the loss of Eden, the regions of sorrow and torture without end. She was frightened, bold, shy, reckless—afraid of him now for softer reasons—and that made her harsh. "Get off me, you oaf! Why don't you go blow up a train or something?"

He had the audacity to look amused. "Tough little baggage . . . I'll hand you that. Are you always this entertaining?"

"Do you always take this kind of pleasure with helpless women?"

A smile seemed to loiter about his erotic mouth. "I take extreme pleasure," he said, lowering his head and brushing his lips across hers, "with helpless women. I also give it."

Another surge of breathless desire ran through her with such suddenness she accepted, as the absolute gospel, every word he spoke.

Unable to think of anything clever to say, and some primeval female instinct telling her that resistance would only serve to . . . She snapped her eyes together, but it was no use. Even with her eyes closed, her cheeks continued to burn beneath the gentle pressure of his kiss.

Warm and dry, his hands moved across the wisps of hair along her nape to rest on each side of her face. Talented fingers traced the outline of her ear, stroking the sensitive lobe, and then slipping around to the back of her head while his thumbs stroked the pulsing softness of her throat.

She gave a tiny, strangled whimper, and he kissed her forehead reassuringly. "Don't be afraid, little buttercup," he whispered, then lowered his mouth to press against the black silk of her lashes. "I won't hurt you." His tone was strangely gentle, soothing. He was beginning to draw her into his powerful control with the innocent reassurance of his kiss and the gentle stroke of warm, strong hands.

By kissing her, he had taken the upper hand, dissolving her defiant anger. Suddenly she was in way over her head.

This man had outgeneraled and outfought her at every turn. And now they were on his home ground, grappling in an area he possessed an inordinate amount of experience in—and, she'd be willing to bet, even more creative inventiveness. Muscle, maleness, and magnetism shrieked his expertise with a thousand tongues. Every movement of his lithe-limbed body declared promise, delight, and delivery. As that distressing fact glared like a red flag, her body weakened. It collapsed completely when she saw through a tear-shimmering blur that the monster was laughing. Laughing! He obviously knew the knowledge she possessed about sensual pleasure could be expressed in one word: Nothing.

Shaking, she was filled with remorse. Nothing in her gentle Southern breeding or education had prepared her for this. It was humiliating enough to find herself two blinks away from crying, and now her self-reproach was sharpened by one glaring fact: She was at his mercy and she knew it. To make matters worse, he knew it.

She listened to the soft tapping of rain on the roof; the sound of a bird nesting in the rafters making her wish she could sprout wings and fly away. It just wasn't her day. Everything from hairdo to resolve was collapsing around her. With a sickening sense of dread, she dared wonder what was next.

She didn't have to wait long. Once again, his mouth came hungering, but instead of a deep, satisfying kiss, he brushed his lips across hers: once, twice. Three times he faintly touched his warm mouth to hers, saturating her with unfulfilled promise. Something about this was immensely frustrating. If she had possessed any strength at all she would have pushed him away. As it was, every ounce of strength was used to clamp her mouth shut while something deep within her said *don't*.

He lifted his dark head, the gray eyes giving her a puzzled look. As if finding what he sought, he lowered his mouth to hers once more. The man-smell of him was terrifying, yet his touch carried reassurance. His lips were warm, dry and smooth —pressed against hers softly, as if giving her time to adjust to the strange feeling, like a new colt being broke to bridle. Her fear receded and the pressure increased, bringing with it the subtle touch of his tongue.

Without breaking the kiss he brought his practiced fingers to her lips and with subdued pressure parted them. His hands moved across her, one following the line of her throat, the other nestled in the downy soft hair just below her ear. She never thought a kiss between a man and a woman would be like this. It was addictive, carrying both promise and fulfillment, settling around her like a sweet, drugging cloud of opium smoke.

A head swimming with emotion is mindless with lack of control. Thoughts, as soon as they entered her head, rolled right out her mouth, with no regard for consequence. Confusion permeated every limb, leaving her weak-kneed and out of focus. It was the effect of this dreamlike state that prompted her to whisper, her mouth moving against his, like a seduction. "I feel as limp as a dishrag . . . a scarecrow with no stuffings."

He laughed, of half a mind to tell her she didn't have a thing to be concerned about. The soft feminine swell of flesh beneath him said she was stuffed with something that felt mighty damn good. He smiled down at the angelic honesty lying prone beneath him. "I'd be happy to fill you," he said in husky tones, "but not with straw." His mouth came seeking, driving all thought of meaning from her mind, while his was filled with images of what it would be like to bury himself within this whimsical creature with the apple-green eyes.

He raised his head. "I haven't had a kiss like that since I learned to dress myself," he said. A smile spread in teasing mockery. "That was a kiss, wasn't it?"

Her eyes flashed. "You tell me. You're the one with all the experience. What would you call it?"

He raised a brow, a wicked smile curved his mouth. "Well, if I was blindfolded, my first guess would be I'd had too much to drink and woke up with my tongue stuck to the pillow."

What kind of satyr was she up against? The man had a face that belonged on a gold coin, the body of a Roman gladiator, the discernment of a wizard and the disposition of a jackass. Blushing violently, she said, "Do you know what you are? Disgusting." She had a few more choice selections to deliver to him but he placed two fingers over her lips to silence her.

"That," he said gently, "is one of your problems, angel. You talk too much. Now be quiet, and let's try again."

"Again? Why I'd sooner . . ."

Rude though it was, he had a way of interrupting that was really quite pleasant. It was a few minutes before she found the necessary air to say, "Instead of ravishing me, why don't you just steal what you came for and leave?"

He studied her, allowing his curiosity to move over her exquisite face. "I hate to disappoint you, buttercup, but this is *not* ravishment, and I didn't come here to steal anything. This will probably chaff you all the way down to those little pink toes, but I'm an invited guest."

The perfectly shaped mouth he had been admiring dropped open like a dew-filled tulip. "Oh." She looked at him with disbelief. Then her eyes narrowed suspiciously. "I've never seen you around here before."

"I have the perfect explanation for that," he

said. "I've never been here before." Then, with a soft muttered oath, he released her wrists and sat up, propping himself against the wall. Gingerly, he touched the back of his head with a handkerchief removed from his pocket.

She scrambled to a sitting position, rubbing her wrists as she watched him dip the bloody handkerchief in a water bucket. "You're bleeding," she said.

He cocked a brow at her. "That's what generally follows a head-cleaving. Don't tell me drawing blood wasn't your idea. It sure as hell wasn't mine."

With a groan he closed his eyes and dropped his head, his wrists resting over his knees, which were bent before him. She glanced in the direction of the barn door, rattling gently against the force of wind-driven rain.

"Don't even think about it," he said. "Do you think you could outrun me? I wouldn't advise you to try. Even with my head busted, it would be a miserable match. You'd never make it."

Her frustrated gaze flicked back to his face. There wasn't a sliver of emotion in those cool eyes regarding her. He settled himself more comfortably against the stall, lanky legs crossed, his arms folded across his chest.

"Where is everyone?" he asked.

"They've gone to a Church Basket Meeting . . . a picnic," she answered, and then thought that wasn't too clever of her to reveal that. "But they're due back soon . . . any minute now . . . before dark."

Gray eyes glanced toward the barn door, passing over long shadows of late evening creeping across the floor. "They better get a move on. It's almost dark," he observed. "Is it their habit to take everyone with them and leave you here alone . . . *unprotected*?"

That last word went across her like a rasp. "I'm not completely helpless."

Touching his head, he curved his mouth into a smile that left her a witless lump, boneless as a jellyfish.

"No, you're not helpless. I've proof of that," he said rather good-humoredly.

Fighting back a smile she said, "We've had an outbreak of fever in the slave quarters so the household help is down there. Today was my day to oversee. That's why I'm not at the picnic. I was just coming back to the house for more quinine when I saw you."

"So . . . we're all alone?"

The humor drained, like blood, from her face. She shifted, feeling the strain all of this was placing on her nerves. She said in a desperate voice, "I've already told you they will be returning shortly."

Amused, he watched her. "Smooth recovery. You know, you're a very clever girl. Beautiful. Intelligent. Clever. You even cover your mistakes with finesse. I like that. You don't often see that quality in a girl as young as you."

"I'm not that young," she said with irritation. "You make me sound like a . . ." She immediately conjured up all kinds of fun he could have with the rest of that and snapped her mouth shut.

"Child . . . innocent child . . . inexperienced child" he offered before another one of those gut-twisting smiles spread across his face. Then he said, "No," and giving her the once-over, added, "you're no child, innocent or otherwise."

The rain passed, leaving as quickly as it had come, taking with it the welcome chill. The air was heavy now, saturated with moisture, the stillness interrupted by the steady drip of rain off the eaves and the croaking chords of bullfrogs in the distance. Everything was so still—she could almost to hear the evening mist as it rolled up from the river.

"How old are you?" he asked.

The sound of his voice after a moment's lapse startled her, and her voice was like a bark. "Eighteen." Then speaking more softly, she said, "How old are you?"

"Twenty-eight."

So many conflicting emotions were doing flip-flops within her, she was beginning to feel deranged. Her insides were playing leapfrog, jumping from fear to anger. Next came anxiety, and embarrassment followed by humor, and now she was on the verge of liking the man.

He was still watching her silently. She looked at him, met his stare, and looked quickly away, as though he might be able to learn something about her, some secret she was hiding. She was an interesting combination, mouse and tiger. Two opposites he would have never expected to see living in harmony within a body that should, by all rights, be captured on canvas and hung over a gentlemen's bar. There was a tenseness in her tightly drawn mouth with its perfect shape and rose-petal blush.

"Who are you?" he asked.

"No one you'd be interested in knowing."

Oh, but he would, he would. It was unlike him, but he checked himself, keeping his badgering thoughts to himself. "Do you know Mourning Howard?"

She looked at him as if he had insulted her. "I might. Why?" She made a move to get up, but discovered her skirts were pinned beneath the sharp points of the rowels on his spurs.

"Would you move your feet? My skirts are caught." She tugged at the fabric, but he made no move to lift his feet. He was certainly different from the men she was accustomed to. He did not treat a lady like a lady. Of course, she didn't exactly look like a lady; wearing her oldest dress, her skirts rumpled, her hair going in more directions than a road map.

"I asked if you knew Mourning Howard. Do you want to answer my question, or does this stubborn streak mean you'd rather kiss?"

If the devil can't come, he will send someone, and she was convinced this man was the replacement. "I *know* Mourning Howard but I don't know you or why you want her."

"Just tell me where I can find her."

"Not until I know why."

"You're a daring little saucebox, aren't you?" His look was direct. "It's perfectly honorable, I assure you. She's the reason I'm here."

Her head flew up, her eyes widened. Her heart threatened to fly right out of her chest. Panic. Alarm. A swiftly spreading sense of dread. Emotions crowded along nerve passages all at once, not one of them getting through, leaving her blank. "What—" It came out as a croak. She tried again. "What are you going to do with her?"

Amusement glittered in his eyes. "Do? Why nothing. Not in the sense you mean, anyway." She was even more alluring when she blushed. "Her mother is married to my father. I've come to take her back to Texas with me."

All the color he had admired in her lovely face vanished. Instantly. *"You've* come?" she managed to squeak. "You've come to take her with *you?"* It was obvious he wasn't going to help her make a fool of herself, merely giving her a look that said she was giving a gilt-edged exhibition all by herself.

The grooves on either side of his mouth deepened. "As an escort, nothing more. I've just come from St. Louis, so it wasn't out of my way to stop here in Memphis." Seeing the shocked look on her face, he added, "At her mother's request."

She was deathly pale. "You can't be," she said. "There must be some mistake. All the way to Texas with you? But you're . . ."

As if reading her thoughts, he said, "Listen, my little paragon, I don't seduce family members if that's what you're thinking. Even I had a mother. And, believe it or not, unlike you, I have a name."

"I know who you are, Clint Kincaid."

He stared at her with an expression that was startled, but difficult to read. "Who the hell are you?" he asked.

"Mourning Howard."

"Oh, shit."

It was her turn to smile. He eyed her with amused astonishment and then threw back his head in laughter, but only momentarily. As soon as the skull-splitting pain ricocheted from temple to temple, Clint groaned. "I guess I deserved that," he said.

"Yes . . . you did." The look he was giving her made her uneasy. Mourning bristled, then changed the subject. "You're early. We didn't expect you until next week."

"Finished my business in St. Louis a little ahead of schedule," he said. Eyes gray as goosedown considered her. So this was Caroline's daughter. Too bad. She was a real eyeful, but she was family. That made a difference. A *big* difference.

"Why in God's name didn't you tell me who you were?"

"I just did."

"I mean earlier."

"You didn't ask."

"Christ! Now we've regressed to platitudes. I don't think I deserve that," he said flatly.

Mourning smiled, thinking he deserved anything she decided to throw at him, including the cast-iron skillet and the rolling pin.

Clint's face darkened. "Are you packed and ready to go?"

A flash of irritation came and went. "I'm packed and ready . . . but I'm not sure I want to go . . . at least not all the way to Texas with you."

"Why is that?" he asked in a blandly curious tone.

"Because I have decided I don't like you."

"Don't tempt me," he said, "or I might take the time to find out just how true that statement is."

"You lay one hand on my person again and I'll . . ." Mourning couldn't think of a warning foul enough to threaten him with. Any fool knew the devil wasn't afraid of anything—except God—

and He had been avoiding her a lot lately. She looked around for something to throw.

Clint laughed.

And that made Mourning furious. She jerked her skirt, which gave with a loud rip, and scrambled to her feet.

For an injured man he moved surprisingly fast as he grabbed her wrist. "Don't be in such a hurry," he said softly. "I know you hate to leave such a romantic setting, but do you suppose you could see to my head? I think I'm in need of a stitch or two."

"Come into the kitchen," she said sharply, then yanked her arm free. She turned and hurried from the barn. She stepped lightly across the barnyard to avoid soaking her slippers in the mud. She did not wait for him, the *ching, ching, ching,* of his spurs telling her that Clint Kincaid followed close behind.